CRAZY Wicked LOVE

THE WICKEDS: DARK KNIGHTS AT BAYSIDE

MELISSA FOSTER

ISBN-13: 978-1948868761

Cover Design: Elizabeth Mackey Designs
Cover Photography: Michelle Lancaster

WORLD LITERARY PRESS
PRINTED IN THE UNITED STATES OF AMERICA

A Note to Readers

Friends-to-lovers stories are some of my favorites to write because the characters know all the nitty-gritty about each other's lives. I had so much fun letting Sidney Carver take control of her feelings and watching the pieces fall into place for Dwayne "Gunner" Wicked until he finally opened his eyes to what had been right in front of him the whole time. I hope you love them as much as I do.

The Wickeds are set on the sandy shores of Cape Cod Bay and feature fiercely protective heroes, strong heroines, and unbreakable family bonds. All Wicked novels may be enjoyed as standalone romances or as part of the larger series. On the next page you will find a character map of the Wicked world. You can also download a free copy here:
www.MelissaFoster.com/Wicked-World-Character-Map.html

The Wickeds are the cousins of the Whiskeys, each of whom has already been given their own story. You can download the first book in the Whiskey series, TRU BLUE, and a Whiskey/Wicked family tree here:

TRU BLUE
www.MelissaFoster.com/TheWhiskeys

WHISKEY/WICKED Family Tree
www.MelissaFoster.com/Wicked-Whiskey-Family-Tree

Remember to sign up for my newsletter to make sure you don't miss out on future Wicked releases:
www.MelissaFoster.com/News

For information about more of my sexy romances, all of which can be read as stand-alone novels or as part of the larger series, visit my website:
www.MelissaFoster.com

If you prefer sweet romance with no explicit scenes or graphic language, please try the Sweet with Heat series written under my pen name, Addison Cole. You'll find the same great love stories with toned-down heat levels.

Happy reading!
~ Melissa

THE WICKED WORLD

DARK KNIGHTS AT BAYSIDE

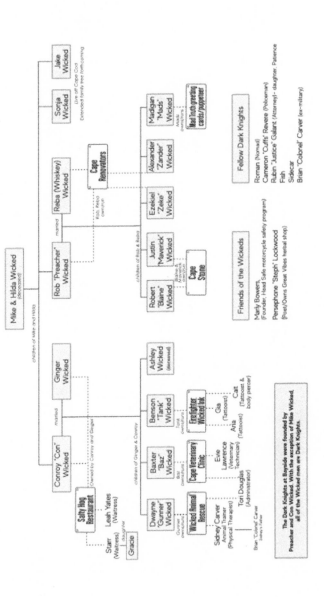

Chapter One

SIDNEY CARVER HAD a big problem.

She sat at the kitchen table in her underwear and T-shirt early Sunday morning, pondering her situation. It wasn't like she'd planned on falling in love with her best friend, who also happened to be her roommate *and* her boss for the last three years. She swirled a waffle finger in the pool of chocolate syrup on her plate, staring absently, as if a solution might magically appear there.

If only...

Short of leaving Cape Cod and the dog rescue she adored, her father and friends, and the only man she'd ever loved, she saw no reasonable way out of the situation. It was too bad holding a gun to his head and forcing him to love her back would land her in jail, because that sounded easier than walking away. She had been attracted to Gunner since they'd first met, but her feelings had deepened over the years, and lately those feelings had gotten too big to deny.

This was one of the few times in her life that she wished she had a mother to talk to. She'd been raised by an amazing father who had been only twenty when she was born, and he had taught her all about life, loyalty, and bravery. She could face a battlefield head-on, shoot a gun with expert precision, train dogs to save people's lives, and nurture them back to health when they were injured. But winning her bestie's heart was foreign territory, and she'd never been schooled in flirting or using her feminine wiles. She was more of a *love me as I am or leave me* girl, and she knew Gunner loved her as a friend just as she was, but way deep down, she also knew they could be so much more if he'd only let himself see her in that light.

She heard a door open upstairs and froze, her pulse quickening as said *problem's* heavy footsteps sounded above her, followed by the scampering of his rescue dogs, Granger, Belleau, and Opha Mae. The farmhouse stairs creaked beneath his weight, reminding her of the woman Sidney had heard leaving his room around two in the morning and causing a resurgence of the jealousy that had been driving her nuts lately. She needed to either figure out how to win him over without risking their friendship or get over him altogether, because watching a trail of women do the walk of shame from his bedroom wasn't on her to-do list.

Why did she have to fall for a player?

Maybe a better question was why she'd had to fall for her best friend, Dwayne "Gunner" Wicked, but that answer was easy. They'd served in the military together, and the stocky ex-marine/badass biker was the funniest, most thoughtful, and most generous man she'd ever known. Like Sidney, he loved every animal he'd ever come in contact with, and except for her father, he was the *only* man she could really be herself with, including laughing so hard she snorted like a donkey. Gunner was also a great boss and a fantastic workout partner who pushed her to be the best she could be. Beneath his player facade was a big, breakable heart that she wished he'd allow to love *one* woman—*her*—the way he loved his animals. But several years ago, the death of his younger sister, Ashley, had changed him. He acted like he didn't give a damn about much of anything outside of family and animals, but Sidney knew better, even if the guy who had once let her into his heart and his head now kept conversations superficial at best. As an ex-marine and a member of the Dark Knights motorcycle club, which his father and uncle had founded years ago, Gunner was all about unbreakable bonds. That was another reason the way he was with women made no sense to her.

Sidney knew in her heart that *she* was the person Gunner needed, the one who could help him rediscover those parts of himself that he'd buried along with his sister. The trouble was, while she was totally his type on the inside, she was a twenty-nine-year-old, nearly-flat-chested woman who could pass for nineteen, and she preferred T-shirts, jeans, and sneakers to short skirts, provocative tops, and heels, while the women he gravitated toward were bodacious beauties who liked to show off their bodies and knew how to flirt a man into submission.

Sidney could coerce *dogs* into submission, but *guys?* Not so much.

She liked her body, and she didn't long for big boobs and a plump booty, even if those curves might help Gunner see her differently. She was simply aware of the challenges she faced. Besides, when Gunner Wicked wanted a woman, nothing held him back, and he'd never once made a move toward being anything more than friends with her. *That* was the issue. She knew where she stood, and she didn't want to risk their friendship to try to change it. But she had to do something before she lost her mind.

She heard Gunner open the front door to let the dogs out.

"Go on, make your rounds."

His deep voice floated into the kitchen. Sidney's German shepherd, Rosco, popped to his three paws beside her, awakening Blizzard, Gunner's old, gray rescue cat who hated everyone except *him*, who was lying on the chair beside Sidney. The cat hissed as Rosco limped past, excited to greet his second-favorite human. Blizzard settled back onto the chair, giving Sid a snide look.

"Hey, Rosco. How's my boy?" Gunner's voice floated into the kitchen.

Sidney didn't have to see them to know Gunner was crouched in front of Rosco, probably wearing nothing but his underwear, as her pooch slobbered all over his face. Sidney had been Rosco's handler in the military, and she had adopted him almost four years ago, after they'd both been injured when she'd sent Rosco in to clear a tunnel that Gunner's unit was set to infiltrate and found a suicide bomber waiting for him. She and Rosco had suffered shrapnel wounds and broken bones. But while Sidney had gotten away with a mild traumatic brain injury, Rosco had lost his left back leg near his hip, his hearing in one ear, and much of his fur to burns. He was lucky to have survived.

She heard the front door open again, and Gunner said, "Go on out there and find your buddies."

Sidney's heart raced as his footsteps neared the kitchen. *Do not look. Do not look. Do not look.* She trained her eyes on her plate and not on her thickly muscled bestie as he sauntered into the room. His hand dipped over the chair where Blizzard was sleeping, and he set Snowflake, another rescue kitty, next to Blizzard. The hisser rubbed her head against Gunner's arm, purring loudly.

Sidney could relate to the two-faced cat who had loved Gunner since he'd found her in a snowstorm two years ago and had claimed her as his own. Sidney wasn't sure why she'd gone from crushing on him to fantasizing about a future with him full of love and lust and a house full of animals. Maybe it was because his cousin Maverick had recently fallen in love and married their friend Chloe. Or maybe Sidney's hormones were just going bonkers because Gunner's oldest brother, Tank, had fallen desperately in love with Leah, a waitress at the Salty Hog, their parents' restaurant, and her two adorable little girls. Leah was pregnant, and their wedding was only two and a half months away. Sidney didn't know if those happy couples were messing with her brain or *why* her feelings for Gunner had climbed to the forefront of her mind, but they had, and seeing him in his underwear would *not* help that situation.

Gunner walked over to her, standing so close it was impossible not to see the black boxer briefs stretched tightly over his beefy thighs, his tattoos snaking out from under them. She fought the urge to steal a glance at the *other* beefy package he paraded around her like she was just one of the guys.

"Mornin', MOS." He'd called her MOS, which was short for Military Occupational Specialist, since they'd first met.

"Good morning." *Don't look. Don't look.* She stared at the table.

He plucked a waffle finger off her plate.

"There's more by the stove." She knew it wouldn't matter. She used to make plates for both of them, but he always ate from hers, so now she piled enough food for both of them onto one plate. It worked out well. She made breakfast and he did the laundry.

He ran his fingers through the ends of her hair. "But they're not as good as yours." He grabbed ahold of her hair and tugged her head back.

Her gaze swept up his tatted torso and neck until she had no choice but to look at the dimpled face she knew by heart. Was that a flash of heat in his eyes? Her pulse quickened as she drank in his closely shorn blond hair. It was spiky on top but matted here and there from sleeping on it. She wanted to run her fingers through it, to rise off the chair and kiss his lips, to feel the scratch of his scruff on her cheeks and all the way down her body as he—

"Hope I didn't keep you up last night."

Fantasy shattered, she narrowed her eyes. "You mean for the seventeen seconds you lasted with your flavor of the night?"

He leaned down so close she could smell his minty toothpaste as he brushed his calloused hand tenderly over her forehead, gazing deeply into her eyes. If she didn't know better, she'd think he was about to kiss her or say something sweet. But *three, two, one*...

An arrogant grin curved his lips. "So you *were* listening."

She rolled her eyes. "Hardly. I heard your plaything bitching to someone on her phone as she snuck out." The bitching part was a lie, but this was how they rolled, giving each other crap.

He laughed and went to the refrigerator, and she couldn't resist stealing a glance. He was tatted from neck to waist and shoulders to wrists. His muscles flexed as he grabbed a jug of orange juice and guzzled it from the container. She'd long ago stopped trying to get him to use a glass. He put the jug back in the fridge and closed the door, looking thoughtfully at the pictures hanging on it. Gunner was big on pictures. He was always taking shots of her at the most inopportune moments.

Like those on the fridge, one of which he'd taken the morning after they'd stayed out late at the Salty Hog. Her hair was a tangled mess, and she was sitting at the kitchen table in her underwear and a T-shirt with her knees pulled up to her chest, making a face at the camera from behind her splayed hand. And the picture where she was windblown and rain soaked, looking like a drowned rat with her hair in her face during a storm last fall. There were a few pictures of them in fatigues when they were in the military. In one picture, Gunner had his arm slung over her shoulder, and Rosco was by her side. In another, she was in full military garb from helmet to boots, carrying Rosco on her shoulders, the pooch's tongue hanging happily out of his mouth, while she held a peace sign up in front of her face.

"This one's still my favorite." He tapped a picture of Sidney sitting on the couch in her favorite jeans with a hole in the knee, one leg extended, the sole of her white high-top aimed at the camera in an effort to get him to stop taking pictures. He'd taken that picture two years ago and had caught her taking off the white sweater with a heart on it that he'd given her. Her shoulders were bare, save for the straps from her tank top, and the sweater was bunched up on her arms, blocking her body. Her hair was in her face, but her smile was visible, and she was holding up a peace sign with her fingers, peering out from between them and her hair.

Gunner didn't turn around to see her rolling her eyes as he poured himself a cup of coffee. He picked a favorite picture at least three times a week, and it was usually that one. Sidney's favorite picture was of him with Granger, Belleau, and Opha Mae on the first birthday she'd celebrated at the farmhouse. The dogs were lined up in the living room with signs around their necks, each with one word on it, spelling out HAPPY BIRTHDAY

MOS. Gunner was standing beside them, holding a bouquet of balloons and a chocolate cake he'd made for her.

Sidney tucked those memories away, letting her gaze travel down his back to his butt. He had a great butt. Who was she kidding? He had a great *everything*.

Frustrated with herself for ogling him, especially after he'd had some girl over last night, she turned around and swirled the rest of her waffle finger in the chocolate syrup. "Don't you ever get tired of one-night stands?"

"Does Santa get tired of giving out presents?" He set his mug on the table as he lowered his big body to the chair beside her, flashing the cocky grin she knew so well.

She couldn't help but laugh. "Don't you want *more?*"

"You know I get plenty." He snagged another waffle finger and took a bite, his blue eyes glittering devilishly.

She'd seen those eyes cry more tears than she'd thought possible when he'd lost his sister, and she'd seen them change in the years since as he'd walled off that corner of his heart that was once so open. But they still resonated magnetic energy, underscoring how much bigger than life he'd been before losing Ashley.

"I haven't seen *perfect Mark* in a while," he said, bringing her mind back to the moment.

"Why do you always make fun of him?" Mark was a failed attempt to trick her brain into liking someone other than Gunner. She'd met him at the gym last fall and had seen him on and off for a couple of months, which was longer than she'd gone out with anyone else. Not that there had been that many, but there had been enough for her to know her feelings for Gunner were real.

She hadn't dated when she and Gunner had first lived together. There wasn't time. They were always working, and they hung out together all the time, often with his brothers and cousins at the Salty Hog, Dark Knights events, or community functions. Then there was the little tidbit about liking him as more than a friend. But he never made a move, and after a while he began hooking up with other girls, so she'd dated sporadically. She'd made it a point *not* to bring guys back to the house, and when she'd brought Mark home, she hadn't known *why* she was doing it. Now she wondered if it was to gauge Gunner's reaction to the tall, dark, and athletically built computer specialist.

Gunner finished the waffle finger and said, "You can't trust a guy who's that pretty."

"The same thing could be said about the women you bring home."

He smirked. "Why do you think they're once and done? So why hasn't Pretty Boy been around lately?"

Mark had wanted more of a relationship, but her heart was tied up in *this* waffle-finger-stealing goofball. But she wasn't about to tell him that. She shrugged. "I got bored."

"I know how that is." He ate another waffle finger. "But it's been a while for you, MOS. Why haven't you brought any other guys home?" He sipped his coffee and lifted Snowflake into his lap.

"Because I don't need you knowing all of my personal business." *Or lack thereof, thanks to thoughts of you messing with my head.*

"Then there *is* hooking up going on?"

"What did I just say? It's *none* of your business."

"You're right. I don't want to know. But for the record, you're my best bud. I might meet the guy at the door and give him a good shakedown, but I'd never judge you for hooking up."

Like you did to Mark? That was fun. "Would that shakedown happen *before* or *after* your seventeen seconds with your booty call?"

His brows slanted in concentration.

"Don't answer that. I'm not bringing a guy home just to have him interrogated by my big-ass roommate who walks around in his underwear. I do *not* want to answer the questions that'd come from that scenario again." She shook her head, remembering how long it had taken her to convince Mark that nothing was going on between her and Gunner.

"Hey, if he can't handle another guy in your life, then he isn't the right guy for you anyway." He ate another waffle finger. He was like a human vacuum.

"Does that mean I get to start meeting your lady friends by the door and giving them a little shakedown?"

"Why not? We're usually together at the Hog or Undercover when I meet them anyway." Undercover was a club they frequented in Truro, a nearby town. "Fuck 'em if they don't like it. You're my roomie and best bud, and that's not going to change."

He held up his fist for a fist bump, but there was no way she was going to do that to her remaining as just his *best bud*. She rolled her eyes as she ate another waffle finger and pushed the plate in front of him.

"Thanks, babe."

Babe was another endearment he called her, along with *beautiful*, *sugar*, and *sweetheart*, all of which in his mind were probably equivalent to *dude*.

He motioned to the Wicked Animal Rescue events notebook on the table. "How's the list for the calendar shoot coming along? Do we have enough guys signed up?"

To raise money for the rescue, they published a June-to-June calendar each year of guys holding adoptable animals and sold it at the annual fundraising ride and event held by the Dark Knights in early June. The photo shoot for this year's calendar was taking place a week from Saturday. Sidney was in charge of finding people to model, creating the schedule, matching the dogs to the models, and coming up with layout ideas, while their office administrator, Tori Douglas, was coordinating with a photographer for the calendar shoot and fundraiser. Gunner's mother and his aunt Reba handled the fundraiser each year.

"There's never a shortage of guys willing to pose half-naked. Your brothers and cousins have signed up again, but as we agreed, we're adding girls this year to widen the audience. So don't get overprotective when Mads has her picture taken. She's excited to do it." Madigan was in her midtwenties and was the youngest of Gunner's five cousins who lived in the area. "I hope to wrangle a few more girls into signing up today." Later this morning, she and a few other friends were helping Gunner's mother and aunt get ready for the annual Dark Knights Easter egg hunt, which was two weeks away.

"How many more people do we need? We've got you, me, Tank, and Baz, plus my cousins? So we need three more?"

"*Four.* I'm not doing it. But I can ask Justice and Cuffs. I know they'll do it." Attorney Rubin "Justice" Galant and police officer Cameron "Cuffs" Revere were Dark Knights and always up for anything.

"What do you mean you're not doing it?" His brows slanted. "We agreed you'd be in the calendar."

"No, *you* agreed. You know I hate that stuff. But don't

worry. I'll get some cute girls to do it."

His jaw tightened. "You helped me *build* this rescue. It was our idea, remember?"

How could she ever forget? They'd both planned to remain in the military until they were too old to keep up, and they'd spent countless hours trying to figure out what they'd do when they retired. They'd come up with the animal rescue idea together, but she hadn't expected to get injured and need a second career so soon. She'd been at a loss after her medical discharge, missing the life she'd loved and her friendship with Gunner. He'd kept in close contact throughout her recovery, and when his tour had ended a few months later, he'd come to see her before even going home to see his family. She'd just started an internship as a canine physical therapist, but as much as she'd enjoyed working with the animals, she'd missed being with him even more. He'd shocked the hell out of her when he'd told her that he hadn't reenlisted and was going to open an animal rescue. He'd offered her a job and a place to stay. The rescue wasn't even open yet, but he'd given her a Wicked Animal Rescue T-shirt, and she'd almost cried when she'd seen the logo. He'd made a silhouette of a picture he'd taken of her and Rosco a few months before they were injured. They were sitting on a hill watching the sunset. Their backs were to the camera, and she had one arm around Rosco. His head was tilted toward her, his pointy ears alert as always. Gunner had used that picture as the background on his phone since the day he'd taken it.

To say she'd been blown away, overwhelmed, and grateful wouldn't even skim the surface of how she'd felt. But she'd also felt guilty that her best friend was giving up the career he'd always wanted to help her, and she'd told him as much. She'd never forget the way he'd put her at ease without hesitation when he'd slung his arm over her shoulder, and with the most earnest look in his eyes, he'd said, *Did you really think I'd leave you hanging? You're my girl, MOS. I told you I'd always have your back, and you can count on that.* He was the only person she'd ever really talked to about her mother abandoning her and her father when she was just a little girl, and Gunner's conviction to stand by her meant more than anything else in the world. Only now the rescue meant just as much to her, because they were helping animals together.

"I remember," she said softly, caught up in the memory of a few months after that visit, when she'd come to the Cape and moved in with Gunner. She'd secretly hoped that they might become more than friends, and even though she'd been able to tuck those feelings away for a long time, now she wondered if she'd been falling in love with him all along.

"You're just as big a part of this rescue as I am. I let you skip being in the previous calendars because you're stubborn and I didn't want to argue. But you're an important part of this team, and I want to see your face on that calendar. There's no way you won't be in it this year."

"Sure there is." She sipped her coffee. "I'm making the schedule, remember?"

His eyes narrowed, and he sat back, crossing his arms. "If you don't do it, I'm not doing it."

"Don't be ridiculous. You love this stuff."

"Yeah, because it's *fun.* And you'll love it, too. You're doing it with me, Sid, and that's *that.*"

"Dream on, Gunny." She downed her coffee.

"We're holding that slot on the calendar for you, or there won't be a calendar to sell."

She glowered at him, but she knew he wouldn't cancel the calendar. The rescue needed the money, and he'd never let the animals down. "I don't have time to argue. I'm going to shower and feed the animals before I head over to your mom's."

"Hey, if Steph makes those caramel brownies, snag some for me, will ya?"

Sidney smiled to herself. It had always been this easy between them. They could argue one minute and move on to something else the next without any awkward feelings or grudges. "If you ask her, she'll make you a dozen and deliver them herself." Steph Lockwood was another of his close friends. Her sister, Bethany, had been Ashley's best friend. After Ashley died, Bethany had gotten involved with drugs, and she'd come and gone from Steph's life ever since. The Dark Knights had been trying to track her down for a while, but it seemed every time they got a lead, she'd disappear again.

"Why would I do that when you're seeing her this morning at my mom's?"

"In case she doesn't bring enough. There's going to be lots of girls there, and you know how we love her brownies." She got up to wash her cup.

"Hey, MOS, you got a new tank and undies. I *like* 'em."

A little thrill scampered through her. She'd hoped he'd notice. The black tank had IF YOU DON'T LIKE DOGS, I DON'T LIKE YOU written in white across the back, and the black boy shorts underwear had NOW THAT YOU'VE PASSED THE TEST, GET BUSY above her butt, IT AIN'T GONNA KISS ITSELF on one butt cheek, and red lips on the other.

"Did you buy them just for me?" he asked coyly.

As a matter of fact, yes, I did, you oblivious brat. As much as she'd like to tell him the truth and toy with fantasies of him sweeping her into his arms and proclaiming his love for her, she wasn't that naive. She put her cup in the dish drainer and turned around to give him shit, but he spoke before she had a chance.

"Because we both know no one else is looking at your undies." He chuckled and went back to eating.

Ugh! He was infuriating, even if he was only teasing, but two could play at that game. She smirked and stole a waffle finger, pointing it at him. "You don't know squat about who's looking at my undies."

"Maybe not. But I know what's beneath 'em." He puckered up, making kissing sounds.

She narrowed her eyes, trying not to laugh. When they were in the military, she'd gotten tipsy one night with Gunner and the guys, and they'd dared her to get a tattoo on her ass. Her catchphrase back then was *Kiss my ass*, so she'd gotten lips on her butt cheek. The next morning she'd thought it was silly and had regretted it. Two days later, Gunner came to see her when she was working with Rosco, and he'd dropped his drawers, showing her a matching lip tattoo on his ass, and had said, *Now it's not silly. It's our little secret.*

"Yes, but you don't know how many other guys also know." She bit half of the waffle finger, tossed the rest on his plate, and sauntered out of the kitchen with an extra sway in her hips to show him what he was missing. But she had a feeling she could walk around naked and he still wouldn't see her as more than one of his *best buds*.

A LITTLE WHILE later, Sidney sat in Gunner's childhood kitchen with his mother, Ginger, his aunt Reba, and the other girls, surrounded by the scents of freshly baked cookies, family, and friendship. Sidney had never known family or friendship had scents, but from the moment she'd met the Wickeds, it had enveloped her like a warm hug.

Ginger and Reba had made a variety of cookies and sand-wiches, which now littered the counters alongside Steph's famous brownies. Sidney hadn't been surprised that Steph had brought an extra half-dozen brownies for her to take home to Gunner or that Steph had said, *Don't worry, if only three make it home, I'll tell him that's all I gave you.* Steph was one of the coolest friends Sidney had, and her relationship with Gunner ran deep. Steph's parents had given up on her sister years ago, and because of that, Steph rarely saw them. Gunner was her go-to person when she was upset about her sister or just needed a friend, and she'd spent many holidays with his family. Sidney knew their friends had wondered if there was more going on between Gunner and the curvy brunette with red streaks in her hair, but if there were, Sidney hadn't seen any signs of it.

Sidney hummed along to a country song playing on an old-fashioned radio, listening to the others talking about everything from fashion to men as they put together goody bags and filled plastic eggs with candy and toys from the bowls in the middle of the table. Sometimes it was hard to believe she had all these wonderful women in her life. Before moving to the Cape to work with Gunner, she hadn't had many female friends. She and her father had moved a lot when she was growing up, and she was ultracompetitive and more likely to be found running track, volunteering at a local veterinarian's office, or doing homework than worrying about hooking up with boys or the latest fashion, hair, or makeup trends. She'd worked hard to graduate from high school at sixteen and had finished college in only three years, so she could follow in her father's footsteps and join the marines.

Her father had been an officer, but she'd wanted to be a dog handler for as long as she could remember. She'd never had her own dog, but when her father was deployed, she'd stayed with his parents on their farm in Ohio. They'd worked from sunup until sundown, and she was expected to do the same before and after her schoolwork was done. But they'd also fostered dogs from time to time, and when she was there, it was her job to care for them. She'd always felt a kinship to those dogs, having been left behind by her mother, and she was pretty sure her grandfather had known that, because he'd taken the time to teach her how to train them and had even allowed the dogs to sleep in her room.

That seemed like a lifetime ago.

Her father had retired to be close to her when she'd been injured, and he'd moved to the Cape shortly after she had. Gunner had introduced him to the Dark Knights, and as a lifetime motorcycle aficionado, he'd become a member and was given the road name Colonel. For two people whose lives had revolved around military missions, she and her father had really gotten lucky when they'd come to the Cape. Not only had they finally put down roots, but they'd also found more friends who had become like family than they could have ever hoped for, and for the first time in Sidney's life, she had a close-knit group of female friends. She'd never be a fashionista, and she wasn't all that comfortable talking about her personal life, but she liked and trusted these women and felt lucky to be among them.

Ginger put her hand on Sidney's arm, her kind eyes smiling

behind tortoiseshell glasses, exuding the warm demeanor that drew people in. "Are you okay, honey? You're kind of quiet this morning."

Even though Sidney's grandmother had been good to her, she'd never acted like her mother. It wasn't until she'd met Ginger and Reba that she'd felt what she'd missed out on by not having a mother in her life, and she was grateful for their love. "Mm-hm. I'm just listening."

"There's always a lot to hear around this table, especially this time of year, when there's so much going on." Ginger reached for another plastic egg.

"Is there anything I can do to help with the fundraiser?"

"No thanks, sweetheart," Ginger said. "Reba and I have been doing fundraisers for so long, we're like a well-oiled machine."

Sidney put a toy into a goody bag. "You've obviously got it down to a science. Pulling all of this together for Easter and coordinating the fundraiser is no small feat, and you never seem stressed out." Ginger and Reba were also hosting Easter dinner for both families, and they'd invited Sidney and her father every year since they'd moved to the Cape.

"It's hard to be stressed when you're doing something you enjoy." Ginger pushed her strawberry-blond hair over her shoulder. "And we have a lot of support. Just look around the table."

Sidney did just that, and even after three years, she was still surprised by how eagerly the Dark Knights families and friends came together in times of crisis, celebration, and community outreach. They'd been there for Leah and her girls last year when she'd lost her younger brother, River, in a tragic car accident, and they'd always supported the rescue. The women around the table helped with the fundraiser every year. This year Chloe had made pink bows and blue bow ties for the adoptable animals, and everyone was donating items to raffle off. Leah was making animal-themed quilts, and Steph was donating a basket of goods from her herbal shop. Gunner's older brother Baz was a veterinarian, and he was donating three free veterinary visits. Maverick was even making a small sculpture to raffle off. Reba and her husband, Preacher, were donating renovation work through their family business, and Ginger and her husband, Conroy, were raffling off a month of dinners from the Salty Hog. Those proceeds would go a long way toward the care of the animals at the rescue, and that was just from close friends and family. The Dark Knights had dozens of members, and their support was endless.

"Sid, did you and Gunner like the new animal boards I dropped off for your meet and greets next weekend?" Chloe asked. She and Maverick had adopted two dogs from the shelter last year, and she'd been making cute, informative posters for each of the animals that were up for adoption ever since. She included pictures of the animals enjoying different activities, along with all their pertinent details, which helped to showcase their personalities when Sidney and Gunner took them to adoption events, which they called meet and greets.

"Yes, we loved them. Especially your clever descriptions, like saying Boon likes to *sing* and that Chino is not to be judged by his *cover*, that he's a couch cuddler and a *happily ever after* waiting to happen." Boon was a hound dog who howled *all* the time, and Chino was a chow/bulldog mix who always looked grumpy.

"It was fun coming up with them. I was thinking about making different color bows and bow ties for the calendar shoot, like red for February because of Valentine's Day and green for March for Saint Patrick's Day. What do you think?"

"I *love* that idea," Evie exclaimed, tossing her long dark hair over her shoulder. She was Baz's firecracker of a veterinary technician and best friend. "You should make them for the guys, too."

"That would be hilarious," Sidney agreed.

"Yeah, but you know if you do that, they'll call themselves Magic Mike or Bayside Thunder or something even more ridiculous," Steph said.

"Tank would *never* wear a bow tie," Leah said quietly, her wild mane of brownish-red corkscrew curls framed her heavily freckled face. "But I'd pay to see it. He's so cute." She might be soft-spoken, but she was stronger than most women. She'd lost her father as a teenager and had raised River on her own. She'd also raised River's two adorable daughters, Junie and Rosie, since they were infants. Losing River had devastated all of them, but Leah and the girls were doing better, in no small part due to Tank's love and the support of the rest of their family and friends.

Ginger raised her brows. "I love my son, but I haven't heard anyone call him cute since he was a little boy." At six feet four, burly, bearded, and as heavily tattooed as Gunner, Tank was the biggest and most intimidating of Gunner's siblings.

"I think Tanky is cute," Madigan said. She was as sweet and petite as her brothers—Blaine, Justin aka Maverick, Zeke, and Zander—were tough and brawny, and she shared her mother's beautiful auburn hair.

Reba set her wise eyes—that could see through just about anything—on her daughter. "You also think that scary fake smile he used to flash was cute. But I would pay a pretty penny to see any of our boys in bow ties. That would soften all their hard edges. Sid, how's the calendar shoot coming along? Do you need Preacher and Con this year, or did you fill all the months?"

Before Sid could respond, Madigan's arm shot up, and she shouted, "I'm doing it!"

"You *are?*" Reba arched a finely manicured brow. "Do your brothers know?"

"Yes, they do, and they've already given me crap about it." Madigan wiggled her shoulders. "I'm doing it anyway."

Reba winked. "That's my girl."

"I'm hoping Chloe, Steph, and Evie might agree to do it, too," Sidney said hopefully. "I'd ask you, Leah, but Tank would kill me and you're pregnant, so I didn't think you'd want to do it."

"You're right about both," Leah said. "But I appreciate the thought."

"Sorry, Sid, but I'm out, too. With my position at LOCAL, I don't think I should have something like that out there." Chloe was the director of the Lower Cape Assisted Living Facility, where Gunner's grandfather Mike lived.

"I totally understand." Sidney looked at Steph and Evie. Steph volunteered at the rescue, and the veterinary clinic was on the same property as the shelter. Evie and Baz treated many of their rescue animals. "How about you guys? You're part of our team, and it's a great way to show the guys that they're not the only ones who can sell calendars."

"I'll do it," Steph said excitedly. "Anything to help the rescue. But I'm not wearing a bathing suit."

"Awesome." *One down, only a few more to go.*

Chloe closed the plastic egg she was holding and said, "Baz won't like Evie doing it."

"All the more reason that I'm definitely *in*." Evie grinned. "I might even go for a bathing suit, because I *love* pissing off my bestie."

"We have that in common." Sidney high-fived her across the table and grabbed another goody bag.

"Speaking of my overprotective boys." Ginger put a bag of jelly beans into a plastic egg. "I bet they're itching to get back to Sunday rides after Easter." A number of the Dark Knights went for long rides off the Cape when the weather allowed, which was usually from Easter until early November.

"Gunner always gets a little edgy when he's gone too long without riding," Sidney said. "He and Baz hit the road last weekend, and Gunner was a different guy when he got back."

"I think men need to ride more than they need sex," Madigan said.

"Are you dating a biker we don't know about?" Steph asked.

"*Please.* A possessive man telling me what to do is the last thing I need. Not that I'm opposed to taking one for a *ride*, but I'm not looking for permanence." Madigan grabbed a handful of toys from the middle of the table. "I've just noticed how cranky they get. It's like they've got their periods, but all they have to do is jump on their bike or have sex, and *voila*, they're happy again."

Reba nodded. "It's true. I love Preacher, but my husband does not do well being cooped up. By the end of winter, I'm about ready to wring his neck."

"I feel like winter went quick this year," Sidney said. Despite Gunner getting edgy about not riding, she loved the homey feeling of winter because they spent more time cuddled on the couch, watching movies or sitting by the fire, and they always decorated the shelter and the farmhouse for the holidays, which was fun.

"Me too," Chloe said. "I can't believe Leah and Tank's wedding is almost here."

"Neither can I." Leah grinned. "I cannot wait to make that man my husband."

The girls exchanged knowing glances. Ginger was planning a surprise bridal shower for Leah, but they weren't about to spill the beans.

Evie got up and snagged a cookie, waving it at them. "What I can't believe is how romantic Leah's badass man is. Who knew that Tank had it in him to hire *the* Jax Braden to make her wedding gown? It doesn't get more romantic than that." Jax Braden was a sought-after designer who made wedding gowns for many Hollywood starlets. He lived in Peaceful Harbor, Maryland, and he was friends with the Wickeds' cousins, the Whiskeys.

"Tank is *very* romantic. He rubs my feet and takes the girls on special dates. They *love* gettin' all dolled up for their Papa Tank." Leah's Southern drawl gave her softly spoken words a special flair.

"I bet the girls could get him to wear a bow tie," Sidney said.

"They could get that man to do anything. He's so good to us. He knew I was worried about finding a dress that would allow for my expandin' belly." Leah ran her hand over her little baby bump. "So he talked with Jax about it, and Jax created the most gorgeous lace-up back. It's just perfect."

"Your gown is stunning, and we're all looking forward to your big day," Ginger said.

"You're going to be a beautiful bride." Sidney had never dreamed of weddings and picket fences like other girls did.

She'd dreamed about a lifetime of fighting for her country, and after she was injured, her dreams were made up of the rescue and Gunner. But as her feelings for Gunner had grown, she'd toyed with how wonderful it would be to marry into this family, and she was a little envious that Leah was getting to.

"Thank you," Leah said. "Tank is dead set on givin' me a fairy-tale wedding. I told him I don't need anything special, but that's his romantic side coming out."

As Evie sat down, she said, "I wonder if the other Wicked boys have hidden romantic sides."

"Oh, *please*." Steph rolled her eyes. "Zander's and Gunner's ideas of romance is probably saying thank you after sex."

Sidney felt a pang of jealousy. She always felt a little protective of him. "Gunner just saves his sweetness for Snowflake."

"And doles out sexual innuendos like Ginger and Reba dole out hugs," Steph said.

"My Gunny *does* have a mouth on him," Ginger said.

Evie leaned forward, lowering her voice like she was sharing a secret. "And from what I hear, he knows how to use it."

Those claws of jealousy dug a little deeper.

"I think dirty talk is a biker thing, and it's *hot*," Madigan said.

Reba eyed her daughter curiously. "Are you *sure* you're not seeing someone?"

"I think I'd know if I was," Madigan said exasperatedly.

"She just *wishes* she was with a dirty-talking scrumpdil-lyiscious man," Evie said.

"And I hope she finds one." Reba put her hand over Madigan's, looking at her in the motherly way that caused a little pang in Sidney but at the moment was making Madigan blush.

Evie waved. "Hey, I could use a little of that hope over

here."

"Me too!" Steph chimed in.

"I'm spreading hope like confetti over you girls. Not that any of you need it," Reba said. "You're all smart, beautiful, and determined. I have no doubt that when you find your soul mates, you won't let them slip through your fingers."

I'm trying to get him to notice me, but he's a slippery one.

"I love that you and Ginger aren't weird about sexy stuff," Evie said.

"That's because we *get* it." Ginger fluffed her hair. "We might not be twenty-five anymore, but we've still got it *all* going on."

"Darn right we do," Reba agreed. "You girls listen to me. Every woman deserves romance, but we also deserve to be loved down and dirty."

"Mom." Madigan glowered, while everyone else laughed. "Can we please change the subject?"

"Oh, honey," Reba said. "It's just sex."

"But we were talking about *romance*, not sex," Madigan reminded her.

Reba looked amused. "Yes, sweetie. They go hand in hand."

"Based on the dates I've had, I'm pretty sure romance is dead for those of us who don't have or want a Wicked man." Evie smirked. "Actually, I *would* like a wicked man, just not with a capital *W*."

"Wouldn't we all?" Steph agreed.

I'd like mine with a capital W, please. Sid shoved candy into an egg and snapped it closed.

"Romance doesn't die, girls." Ginger looked around the table. "Some guys just don't discover their inner romantic until they find their forever love, but then they can't hold back."

Sidney liked the *idea* of romance, but it wasn't something she'd sell her soul for. Her relationship with Gunner wasn't romantic, but it was the realest thing she'd ever known, and it was everything she wanted except for the intimacy. But she hoped getting him to see her differently might fix that.

"Romance dies in *some* relationships," Steph pointed out. "Otherwise the divorce rate wouldn't be so high."

"I don't believe it dies. I think it's just forgotten," Ginger explained. "Life gets busy—babies come along, work is stressful. There are dozens of reasons people put romance on the shelf. The key is remembering to dust it off and give it a whirl once in a while. But romance isn't one-sided. It's not the man's job to romance us. We have to keep it alive, too."

"I agree with that," Chloe said. "I do romantic things for Justin. Little things, like leaving notes in his jacket pocket and sending him sexy texts."

"Attagirl," Reba said. "Keep those sparks alive."

"First you have to *find* the sparks," Evie said. "It seems like guys only want the women they can't have. I swear I draw the interest of the most men when I'm out with Baz."

Sidney definitely felt sparks when Gunner was around, even if it was only one-sided and in fleeting moments, like when he'd pulled her head back at breakfast, she'd thought she'd seen heat in his eyes, too.

"You know what? You hit the nail on the head," Madigan said. "The best way to get a man's attention is to pretend to be interested in someone else."

That piqued Sidney's interest. "You think so?"

"Absolutely," Madigan said. "And it helps if you don't have brothers to scare them off, or in your case, guys who act like brothers."

Sidney was dying to get their advice about Gunner, but she worried they'd try to talk her out of it because of his revolving bedroom door, so she played along. "Well, that's not a problem for me. This morning Gunner was basically telling me to bring guys home for one-night stands. Not that I'd ever do that."

"That does *not* sound like my Gunny," Ginger said. "I'm sure he was kidding. He's very protective of you."

"In some ways he is. But I'm pretty sure he thinks of me as one of the guys," Sidney said.

"Join the club." Steph said it like it was a good place to be.

"You girls are too beautiful for anyone to think of you as one of the guys," Reba added.

"Has that ever bothered you, Steph?" Leah asked. "I know you said you and Gunner have always just been friends, but did you ever want it to be more?"

Sidney held her breath, waiting for Steph to answer.

Steph looked amused. "Ohmygod, *no*. We're too close. It would seriously be like making out with my brother. *Blech.* Right, Sid?"

"Yeah. *Yuck.*" She hated keeping the truth from them, but if she tried to get Gunner's attention and failed, she'd be mortified.

They laughed and continued stuffing eggs and putting together goody bags.

"Steph, you and Gunny have always been like siblings," Ginger agreed. "But make no mistake, he's protective of both you and Sid. When you go out with guys, he always has Cuffs check them out."

"Seriously?" Sidney was shocked. "I'll be sure to give him hell for that."

"Me too," Steph said. "This conversation has been *very* helpful. I'm seriously considering finding a wingman to pretend to be my date."

"There is something to be said about playing hard to get and sparking a little jealousy in a man's heart," Ginger agreed.

"Look at Maverick and Chloe," Reba said. "He tried to get her attention for months before she finally gave in to what he'd known was there all along."

The girls murmured their agreement, and an idea began forming in Sidney's mind.

"Trust me, Justin had my attention from the get-go." Chloe smiled. "I wasn't trying to make him jealous. I was just leery of bad boys. But he's only bad in the very best ways."

"That's a Wicked thing, too. Maybe I should borrow Baz and see how good of a wingman he is." Steph sat back, brows knitted, like she was seriously contemplating the idea.

Sidney needed a wingman, too, but using Baz for that would be far too awkward since they worked together often. But maybe a little jealousy would do the trick with Gunner. Could it be that simple? He hadn't seemed jealous of Mark, although he *had* made snide comments about him. Was that jealousy? Was she too close to the situation to see it clearly? Maybe she needed to take a step back to reassess, as she'd been taught in the marines.

"You know, as much as I talk about wanting a guy in my life, I have to wonder if Mads is right, and we're better off without one," Evie tossed out.

"For the record, I'm always right." Madigan grinned.

"I'm serious," Evie said. "It's nice to come and go as we please and not have to compromise on the shows we watch and what we have for dinner."

"I love our family dinners," Leah said.

As the girls debated the woes and glories of being single and taken, Sidney thought about her and Gunner's interactions and tried to figure out if she'd imagined things that weren't there. But she quickly gave up, because it was too easy to convince herself that everything meant something and, in the next second, that none of it meant anything. She needed to start from scratch and go all in, putting their relationship to the test so she could figure it out once and for all. She didn't want to go out with anyone else, but she could *pretend* to have an interest in someone who didn't exist. There was no harm in that.

Excitement prickled her limbs. But if she was going to do this, she was going to do it right. She needed to come out knowing *exactly* where Gunner stood, and she had a feeling being interested in just any guy wouldn't be enough. To get Gunner's attention, she needed to pretend the guy was exactly like him.

Like a beacon in the night, the answer came to her.

She'd ask Gunner to be her wingman to get her fake love interest's—his fictional twin's—attention.

It was the perfect plan.

Gunner would be her wingman *and* her prey. But what if he wouldn't help her? What if her plan backfired and she opened his eyes to see her in that way, but he still wasn't interested? Could she handle the rejection?

Her stomach knotted, and she debated forgoing the plan altogether, but that wouldn't change her feelings, and every day it got harder to ignore them.

She *needed* to do this. Even if it led to her realizing he'd never like her as more than a friend, she had to know for sure, and she had to give it her all, because in her heart, he—*they*—were worth it. Her nerves caught fire as she committed to Operation Now or Never.

Come hell or high water, by summertime she'd either be on Gunner's arm or on her way out of his house.

Chapter Two

"YOUR HOUSE IS clean, Master Chewy." Gunner petted the old black-and-gray Alpine goat he'd rescued from a hoarder. She'd had him tied up out back and had kept seven dogs, eight cats, and two guinea pigs in a two-bedroom shack. Gunner had adopted out all the animals except Chewbacca. When he'd found the poor boy, he'd been skinny as a rail, and his hooves had been in rough shape, having been cut with improper tools. Baz had checked him out, and Gunner and Sidney had nursed him back to health. They'd brought him into the house and had spent nearly every night camped out with him in the living room for the first few weeks. If Sidney had gotten her way, they'd have moved Chewbacca into the house for good.

Sidney...

Something was up with her. She'd been acting weird since she'd gotten back from his mother's house yesterday afternoon. She'd barely said two words when they'd had dinner last night or this morning when they'd gone to the gym. They worked out together three times a week, fitting in morning runs in between. They pushed each other hard, and they usually talked and joked around. But this morning she hadn't given him a hard time even once, and he hadn't seen her for more than a few minutes since they'd gotten home. If he was in one of the two shelters, she headed into the other, or she'd take a dog out for some exercise, and when he'd tried to talk with her while she was working with one of the injured animals, she'd said she needed to concentrate and would catch up with him later. It was almost six thirty, and usually by this time they'd not only had breakfast and lunch together, but they'd batted around ideas for dinner or headed out to grab something. But he'd eaten lunch alone and had made her a sandwich and left it on her desk, along with a Kit Kat bar, a bag of Fritos, and an orange Gatorade, all of her favorites. She must have eaten them, because they weren't there when he'd gone into the office a while later, but he still had no frigging idea where she was.

"I think she's avoiding me, Chewy." He'd wondered if he'd pissed her off somehow, but if he had, she'd have given him hell. She never avoided issues, and if someone else had pissed her off, she'd bitch to *him* about it. The same way he unloaded to her when he was upset.

He heard a car and waved as Tori drove by on her way out for the day. He looked out over the property he'd sunk blood, sweat, and tears into, remembering the day that had changed the course of his life. He'd never forget that terrifying moment when he'd thought he'd lost Sidney. He'd never run so hard and fast as he had when he'd seen her thrown through the air, landing on the ground with such force, he'd feared the worst. He could still feel the hammering of his heart, the prickling of fear in every iota of his being as his best friend lay lifeless with a body full of shrapnel, surrounded by medics. It had nearly killed him to be stuck on a mission and unable to be with her when she was taken back to the States. He'd called to check on her every chance he'd had, but he hadn't breathed right again until a few months later, when he was stateside and had her in his arms.

The day after that explosion, he'd called his father to let him know his plans to leave the military and open a rescue. He'd called Baz to see if he'd be interested in partnering with him, and finally, with most of his ducks in a row, he'd called Sidney's father, who had been beside himself with worry. Gunner had told him that he would make sure Sidney had the opportunity to continue doing the work she loved, no matter how her recovery went. A few months later, when his tour ended, he'd put his plan into action and opened the rescue he and Sidney had spent years dreaming up. He and Baz owned several gated and secure acres in Harwich, their small hometown. His farmhouse sat on the west side of the property, and Baz lived above the veterinary clinic, which was set far back from the road on the east side, along with two animal shelters. There were a few pens with smaller shelters like Chewbacca's for the farm animals they occasionally rescued and several exercise areas for the dogs. Gunner had never regretted his decision. He couldn't ask for a better business partner than Baz, a better friend and copilot for the rescue than Sidney, or a business he cared more about.

His phone rang, startling him from his thoughts. He pulled it out of his pocket and saw Zander's name was on the screen. "Hey, Zan. What's up?"

"Not your dick, that's for sure." Zander had always been a jokester. When he was a kid, he'd used his mischievous ways to distract others from his dyslexia. Needless to say, as the class clown, he'd gotten in a lot of trouble. If not for his older brother Zeke, who took it upon himself to try to keep Zander out of trouble, he might have gotten himself kicked out of school.

"I should hope not, since I'm with Chewy."

"Don't get me started on you and that goat. How're you doing, man?"

"I'm having a shit day, but it's all good." Gunner patted his leg and whistled as he walked out of the goat pen, and Belleau, a nine-year-old chocolate Lab mix, ambled out behind him. Belleau was a big boy at about eighty pounds, with white around his eyes and snout, which gave him a ghostly look. He'd also been in rough shape when he was rescued, having been passed from one bad situation to another. He and Gunner had bonded so deeply, Gunner couldn't let him go. "What's going on with you, Zan?"

"Not much. We're working in Brewster, renovating an old house that three chicks inherited. They're hot as *fuck*, and they're going out with me and Blaine tonight. You want to be our third?"

Gunner spotted Sidney walking up from the lower field toward the shelter with one of the dogs. "Maybe. Let me call you right back. I've got to take care of something." He ended the call and pocketed his phone as she disappeared into the shelter. "Belleau, *porch*." The old dog headed up to the farmhouse to join Rosco, Granger, and Opha Mae, and Gunner went to see what the hell was going on with his buddy.

He found Sidney loving up Chappy in his kennel. The young beagle had been found on the side of the road with a torn ACL, most likely from a hit-and-run accident. Now he was six weeks post-surgery and madly in love with Sidney. Gunner didn't blame the little guy. She was the best canine physical therapist around. She gave more love to the animals that came through the rescue than they'd probably gotten their whole lives, and she was the toughest, coolest chick he knew. If she ever put the same amount of energy into a guy that she put into the animals, the dude would be a lucky bastard.

"Hey, MOS."

She kissed Chappy's head and pushed to her feet in her T-shirt, jeans, black high-tops, and the black leather jacket she wore regardless of whether or not she was working with the animals. She was five feet five of lean muscle, with narrow hips, small breasts, and a well-controlled attitude that could take down a man twice her size if the situation called for it. She never wore much makeup, but she didn't need it. She was naturally gorgeous, in a badass elfin way. Her hair was a mix of light and dark browns, parted on the side and cut just above her shoulders in long choppy layers. She liked to hide behind it, the way she was now as she fiddled with one of her necklaces.

"Hey." She walked out of the kennel and turned to lock it.

"How'd he do?"

"Great. We did some figure eights and a few sit-to-stand exercises. He'll be ready to go off leash in another couple of weeks."

She didn't look at him as she walked down the hall toward the exit, and that bugged the hell out of him. "What's going on with you? You seem distracted."

"I just have a lot on my mind." She reached for the door, but he leaned over her and pushed it open, holding it as she walked through. "Thanks."

He locked the shelter door, and Sidney shoved her hands into the front pockets of her jeans, eyes trained on the ground as they headed across the yard toward the house. She put her hands in her pockets only when she was overthinking something.

"Anything you want to talk about?"

She shook her head.

"Did something happen at my mom's yesterday?"

"No. I just…It's nothing."

Bullshit. "Look at me, MOS."

She looked up, brows lifted. "Hm?"

There were too many conflicting emotions staring back at him to dissect. "A'right. Fess up. What's going on?"

"It's nothing important."

Granger, his white pit bull mix, barked as they approached the house, and all four dogs descended the porch steps. Opha Mae yapped as they bounded toward them.

"Do I need to drag it out of you? You know I hate that shit." Gunner petted Belleau and scooped up Opha Mae, kissing her furry head as Sidney petted Granger and Rosco, smiling as they licked her face.

"Stop staring at me," she said without looking at him.

"Then spill it."

She sighed dramatically and straightened her spine, looking a little bashful, which was unlike her, especially with him. "I've been thinking about what you said yesterday, and the thing is, there *is* a guy I'm interested in."

No wonder she was acting weird. He'd hated it when she'd brought *Pretty Boy* home, because that guy wasn't good enough for her, just like the other guys she'd gone out with. But who was he to stop her from living her life? He was her best friend, and he'd always have her back and keep her safe, but he didn't own her.

He kissed Opha Mae's head again and set her in the grass. "And you're worried about bringing him back to the house because you're afraid I'll interrogate him?"

"No. I probably wouldn't bring him here anyway, but he doesn't see me like *that*, and…" She pushed one hand into her pocket, looking at Rosco as she petted him. "I don't know how to get his attention. I was hoping you might be able to help me figure that out."

"What're you talking about? You're a great-looking girl with a killer personality. Just talk to him."

"You know as well as I do it's not that easy." She met his gaze. "Not many guys are into tough girls, and I'm not exactly great at flirting."

"Bullshit. You're awesome at everything, and if this guy doesn't want the best of the best, then the hell with him."

She planted her hand on her hip, eyes narrowing like the badass he knew her to be. "That's easy for *you* to say. You have flocks of women after you, but it's not like that for me. I look like a college kid and I'm almost *thirty*. Most of the guys who give me the time of day are twenty-four or -five and still playing video games and figuring out their lives. And the few that are my age are either not very interesting or just…I don't know. Not right for me."

"A'right. I can see your point. You can't be with someone dull or a guy who doesn't have his shit together."

"Then you'll help me figure out how to get his attention? You'll be my wingman? Because I know this guy is right for me, and if I can get him to notice me as a girl instead of just a friend, I know he'll see it, too."

"*Christ*, Sid. You want me to help you get his attention?" He scrubbed a hand down his face. "That'd be a little weird, don't you think?"

"Not nearly as weird as asking someone else to help me."

"Can't the girls help you with this? Isn't that what girls do?"

"*That* would be weird. It's embarrassing that I don't know how to catch a guy's attention the way they do, and asking them would make me even more self-conscious. You know Marly and Mads are always scouting guys they want me to go out with—"

"What? Since when?" *And why the hell didn't I know about that?* Marly Bowers was a close friend of theirs who'd founded the Head Safe motorcycle safety program. She was at most of the club's events and often hung out with them at the Salty Hog.

"Since forever, and if I do get his attention and he doesn't like me, I don't want the girls knowing. I trust them but not like I trust you. And you're a guy, so you know what guys want, and you know me better than anyone else. We make a great team, and like you said, you'd never judge me." She looked up at him with her big green eyes. *"Please?"*

He uttered a curse. *"Fine. I'll help you."* At least he could make sure the guy was worthy of her.

"Yes!" She did a fist pump.

"But in exchange, you're doing the calendar shoot."

Her brows knitted.

"That's the deal, MOS. Take it or leave it."

"Fine. I'll do it, but only because I really like this guy, and I need your help. From what I can tell, he's into curvy girls. Lots of them."

Gunner gritted his teeth. "Then why the hell do you want him?"

"Because there's more to him than that. He's loyal, smart, funny, and he's got to be the best-looking guy on the entire planet."

Gunner scoffed. "We both know *that's* not true." He spread his arms out like he was presenting himself as proof.

"I'm being serious. Besides, he's not a stranger, and I like that he knows me. I can see a future with him. I've never had that with anyone else."

"What the hell, Sid? You want a future with a guy who doesn't even notice you? Who is this asshole?"

"He's not an asshole." She paced, staring at the ground, and Rosco trotted alongside her.

"*Sid?*" He watched her pacing, wondering why she was holding back. "Come on, babe. Spit it out." His phone rang, and he pulled it out of his pocket as she wore a path in the grass. Looking at his phone, he grumbled, "Zander?" He pushed the green icon to answer the call and lifted it to his ear.

"*Yes,* okay?" Sidney threw her hands up and spun around. "It's *Zander.*"

Holy fucking hell.

"Dude, you there?" Zander said in his ear.

"Yeah," he said distractedly. "I can't go tonight." He ended the call, trying to wrap his head around Sid going after the biggest player of them all.

"Don't look at me like that." She started pacing again.

"Tell me I didn't hear you right. You want to get with Zander?"

She crossed her arms and lifted her chin. "Yes, that's right. Zander."

"Why *him,* of all the guys out there?" His blood boiled at the thought of her with his player cousin.

"I told you why. Does it bother you that he's your cousin?"

"*No.* But you *know* how he is. He's with a different woman every other week."

"So what?" she challenged. "Those women know exactly what they're getting into. It's their *choice* to be with him for a night or a week or whatever, just like the women you go out with. There's no shame in that. I didn't think you'd have an issue with it, given your revolving bedroom door."

"I'm not the one trying to go out with him."

She threw her arms up again. "Forget it. You said you wouldn't judge me, but you obviously are."

Damn it. Sidney had never judged him, and Lord knew he deserved to be judged. He'd had no right to say what he had. She turned to walk away, and he grabbed her by the wrist, tugging her back. The dogs ran over, and Rosco pushed between them, protecting Sidney. As if Gunner would ever hurt her. He would slaughter anyone who tried. "We're *not* forgetting it. You want to be with Zander? Fine. It's your life. I said I'd help you, and I will. But you gotta know what you're getting into."

"I know *exactly* what I'm getting into. You have to promise you won't say a word to him or anyone else about this."

Fuck. Fuckfuckfuck. He hated everything about this, and she just took threatening Zander off the table. He wasn't about to let her down, but he sure as hell wouldn't let her serve herself up on a silver platter to his wolf of a cousin. He was going to keep her as far away from Zander as possible. Maybe he could change her mind, or at least redirect her toward a more suitable guy, of which he could think of exactly *none.*

Clenching his jaw so tight it hurt, he gritted out, "Fine."

She held out her fist, and he reluctantly bumped it with his. Her smile lit up her eyes. How could something that made her so happy make him so mad? *Fuck it.* She was happy, and that was what mattered. What's done was done. "If we're doing this, you're feeding me."

"Okay." She took out her phone and ordered a large mushroom pizza for them and four orders of plain beef meatballs for the dogs.

As the sun dipped from the sky, he slung an arm over her shoulders, and they headed for the house with their brood in tow. "I can't believe I'm doing this."

Sidney rubbed her hands together, grinning like she did in their military days before going out on a mission. "Let Operation Get My Guy begin."

SIDNEY COULDN'T BELIEVE she'd made the mistake of saying she was interested in Zander, but she'd been on the verge of giving up on the whole idea when she'd thought she'd heard Gunner *guess* that it was his cousin. She'd been so flustered, she hadn't realized he was talking about a phone call, and she'd just gone with it. What was even more surprising was that Gunner had agreed to help her. But there he was, sitting between Belleau and Granger on the living room couch with Opha Mae on his lap, eating a slice of pizza and looking at her skeptically as they talked about their mission.

"You sure you want to do this, MOS?"

That was the second time he'd asked, and she gave that some thought. It was kind of a crazy plan, but wasn't it better to carry out a crazy plan than to go crazy wondering *what if?*

"Yes. One hundred percent." She finished her slice and broke the crust in half, giving one piece to Granger and the other to Rosco, who was lying on her other side with his head on her lap.

Gunner nodded curtly. "Then we need a plan. You know

you've got to go with the three-date rule, right?"

"Why would I do that when he obviously sleeps with girls on the first date?"

"That's *why* you're going to do it," he said firmly. "You don't want to be a once and done with him, do you?"

"No, definitely not." *I want forever, and I want it with you.* She also didn't want to toy with Zander's emotions, but she'd figure out how to avoid that when the time came. For now it might come in handy to have him as her pretend love interest because he and Gunner had similar dating habits.

"Then you've got to make sure he's into *you*, not just having sex with you." He stuffed the rest of his slice in his mouth, chewing angrily as he reached for another piece.

"But plenty of relationships start with one-night stands."

His eyes narrowed. "Not this one." His tone left no room for negotiation.

She liked that he didn't want her taken advantage of. "Okay, three-date rule, got it. But I'm not sure how to even get his attention enough for him to ask me out. You're a lot like Zander." Only hotter, less brash, and most importantly, he was *her* guy. He'd even said it, and she'd wrapped those words up in pretty little ribbon and tucked them away to revisit later. "What do you look for in a girl?"

His brows slanted. "I don't know. A pretty face, nice rack, good personality."

"Oh, you actually look for personality?" she teased, but it didn't surprise her. Gunner wasn't a pig. He respected women. He just respected *a lot* of them. That brought a bad taste to her mouth. She took a sip of her iced tea, then set the glass on the coffee table.

"I've got to be into the girl, for Christ's sake, and I don't want to hook up with someone who's looking for something long term."

"Ever?" slipped out before she could stop it.

"I don't know," he snapped. "We're not talking about me. We've got to figure out how to get Zan to want something long term, and I think that's going to be a hard sell."

"*Ouch.* Thanks for your vote of confidence."

"Not because of *you*. You're awesome." He ate half of his slice of pizza in one bite. "But you want Zander, and he's never said a damn thing about wanting a girlfriend. You've got to understand that guys who sleep around do it for a reason."

She shook her fist. "To conquer and come!"

He chuckled and finished his pizza. "Yeah, that's part of it."

"I've worked with men my whole life. I know the reasons, and they're not that different from why women do it. It's easier to be in control than to catch feelings and get their heart broken. Or they do it to boost their ego or because they're afraid of commitment. For some people, it's probably fear of getting bored and hurting their partner, or maybe they like variety. Am I close?"

"It can be some or all of those things, but I think Zan just enjoys it. I think he likes the challenge of the chase, the high of the conquest, and the ego boost that carries him to the next one. It's never-ending entertainment."

She petted Granger, wondering if that's all sex was to Gunner. Never-ending entertainment. But she was supposed to be going after Zander. "I get that, and I know Zander gets bored easily." She couldn't help asking, "Is that what you like about it? The challenge and the high?"

He shrugged one shoulder. "I've never really thought about it. It's just how I roll. You know how I feel. Life is short and meant to be lived, not analyzed. Besides, I'm not giving up our time together to try to have a relationship with some chick who doesn't know me, and if you end up with Zan, he damn well better know that we're a package deal. My ass and my dogs will be on his couch half the time."

Why can't you just want to be Zander in this equation? "Seriously? In what fantasyland do guys share their girlfriends fifty percent of the time?"

"In the one where he wouldn't even know you if it weren't for our friendship. It's grandfathered in, part of the brotherhood."

Why, *oh* why, couldn't he see her as a woman and not one of the guys? Maybe she needed to take a page from his playbook. Stop analyzing everything and get to the living part. "So, where do we start? Should I get a notebook and write down our plan?"

"Hell no. We're not putting this shit in writing. I'll catch hell if anyone finds out I'm helping you get Zander."

"Why? He's a great guy." She meant that. It wasn't Zander's fault Gunner had stolen her heart without even trying.

"I agree. He is an incredible person." His expression turned serious. "But you should be with a guy who hasn't been a player. You shouldn't have to fight for attention."

"I thought we weren't being judgy. Some of the best guys I know are players, and I'm looking at one of my favorites right now." She poked him in the ribs, but he didn't even crack a smile. "Gunner, I can't help who my heart wants, and the guy I like can't change his history, so are we doing this or not?"

He gritted out, "Yeah," and sat up straighter. "A'right, MOS. The mission starts now. We need a timeline. What's your kill date?"

Whoa, he'd switched into military mode so fast, it threw her off. "*Um.* Kill date?" Her pulse quickened as reality came slamming home. If she screwed this up, or if Gunner truly wasn't interested, it would most likely be a kill date to their friendship. "How about we call it the date I go in for a kiss, instead?"

His jaw clenched again. "Fine, whatever. When?"

She needed time for Gunner to show her how to win him— not Zander—over. "How about the fundraiser?"

"Okay. That gives us about seven weeks to get you ready. You need that long, MOS?" Why the hell was he bringing that up? The longer the better.

"I don't *know.* Don't pressure me."

"You're right. Sorry. Let's get our heads in the game. We don't need to do recon. We know Zan's territory. Phase one will be preparing and practicing, to make sure you're ready for phase two, which will be making your move, and we'll go over that once you've mastered phase one. Catching the attention of a player is different from trying to get with any other guy. You've got to let him know you want him without being too eager. That's key. Too eager is a turnoff, but we'll get to that in time. Let's start with the basics. What do we have to work on besides clothes?"

She looked down at her jeans and T-shirt. "I don't own many options."

"I'll call my cousin Dixie and get you some. Her husband joined forces with a big-time designer, and they put out a hot clothing line for women. You need to show a little flesh if you want to get Zan's attention. Every woman around him is your competition."

"That sounds impossible," she said more to herself than to

him.

"Hey, you're the one who wants to go after a player. You're walking into enemy territory and trying to take a hostage."

She swatted his arm. "I'm not kidnapping the enemy. You're supposed to help me show him that everything *he* wants is in this little badass package." She waved her hand at herself.

"Well, *that's* what it'll take. If you can't handle it and show a little flesh, you've got no business on the battlefield."

She narrowed her eyes, accepting his challenge. "For *him*, there's nothing I can't handle."

"Great," he snapped, his jaw clenching again. "What else do you need help with?"

"Flirting for sure."

His face contorted in confusion. "You know how to flirt."

"I never flirt."

"Oh, come on. You do that thing where you peek through your hair and that other thing where you…" He moved his shoulders up and down, angled his face, and lifted his chin while looking at her out of the corners of his eyes.

"What is *that*?"

"You know. Picture my hair longer and in front of my eyes." He held up his hand in front of his face and did the whole thing again. Opha Mae cocked her head from side to side, her ears standing at attention. She barked, and the other three dogs' heads popped up, while Gunner tried to flutter his lashes and moved his hand and head awkwardly.

Laughter burst from Sidney's lips, and the dogs' barked and jumped to the floor, causing Gunner to laugh, too. "You scared the dogs!" She bent at the waist, howling with laughter, and a snort rang out, making them both crack up even harder.

"That!" Gunner pointed at her, laughing. *"That's* an adora-

ble flirty thing."

"Shut up! It is *not*." She clapped her hand over her mouth, but Gunner was snorting and the dogs were barking and jumping, and she couldn't hold back her laughter.

"Do it again." Gunner laughed. "Come on, MOS. Do it for *me*."

She shoved him, laughing as he lunged, tackling her onto her back, making her laugh so hard she snorted again and again, which made them both crack up. The dogs jumped and barked, pushing their noses against her side and cheek as they tried to get in on the action. Gunner's head dipped beside hers, his laughter ringing in her ear. Sidney's laughter faded as awareness crept in with the feel of him straddling her, his thick thighs pressing against her hips, his weight bearing down on her, his strong hands gripping her wrists. Desire flared inside her as his rugged scent infiltrated her every inhalation.

His scruff brushed her cheek, sending hot pinpricks along her flesh as he spoke in her ear. "MOS, you fucking kill me."

His voice was rough, but she heard his smile louder than the dogs' ruckus, and she swore she felt that python between his legs thickening against her belly. But knowing her, she was imagining it. He bit her earlobe, and she *yelped* as he climbed off, laughing, and one by one grabbed the dogs' heads and kissed them. She always melted a little at how much he loved them, but she wanted him to climb back onto her, to feel his body pressing down on her again.

He stretched one arm over the back of the couch as she sat up and hauled her against him. "That snort is the cutest fucking thing."

Great. You're thinking about my snort and I'm thinking about your python. If she didn't get better at this, she was going to be in big trouble. "I hope I can pull this off."

He didn't say a word, his expression turning serious.

"*Hello?*" She nudged him. "You're supposed to build me up and tell me I've got this."

"There's nothing you can't do." He pushed to his feet, and the dogs looked up at him like the master he was. "I'll work on my cheerleading skills, and we'll find some unsuspecting fool at the gym Wednesday morning so you can practice flirting."

She was relieved he didn't expect her to practice on Zander. "Okay, but I'm *not* snorting."

He didn't respond as he picked up the empty food containers and headed for the kitchen. "I'm taking my bike out. Don't wait up."

Chapter Three

GUNNER WELCOMED THE familiar rush of adrenaline when they walked into the gym Wednesday morning. Only today that rush was accompanied by the uneasy feeling of Sidney's nervousness about practicing flirting and his own discomfort over helping her win his cousin's damn heart. But he'd agreed to do it, and he wasn't going to let her down.

She stopped by the doors and planted her hand on her hip, looking up at him from beneath the brim of her Wicked Animal Rescue baseball hat. She wasn't like the Barbell Barbies—her term, not his—who wore skimpy sports bras and skimpier shorts, their hair and makeup perfect, posing for selfies for their social feeds between each set. Sidney always wore her favorite sweatshirt, a threadbare black US Marine Corps crewneck, or her forest-green Wicked Animal Rescue T-shirt, one size too big—*God forbid she showed off her hot little bod*—and either black leggings or black spandex shorts that covered her thighs. Today she was wearing the sweatshirt and shorts and looking at him like she wanted to turn tail and run as she said, "Maybe this isn't the best idea."

"Since when do you back down from a mission?"

Her eyes narrowed.

"Come on, babe. Let's go choose your victim."

She spun on her heels and headed toward the door.

He grabbed her sweatshirt, tugging her back to his side. "MOS, you've *got* this. You met Pretty Boy here. Just say whatever you said to him."

It hadn't come as a surprise when Mark had asked her out. Gunner had seen him checking her out the week before, and Sidney, whose keen eyes picked up on everything, had noticed, too, and had mentioned it to him. Gunner had asked Cuffs to check the guy out, and he was squeaky clean. Gunner had known after Sidney's first few dates with him that he wouldn't last. The guy took her out to fancy dinners and to the movies and had never once included Rosco in their dates. Sidney wasn't a candlelight and wine, private-couple-date girl. She liked being with friends, hanging with the guys, and above all else, spending time with her dog. Like him, she enjoyed the outdoors and being active. When they wanted to escape, they'd pack up the dogs and head over to their favorite beach, where he'd taken her the first night she'd moved in. He'd declared it Wicked Beach with a homemade wooden sign he'd put on the dunes when he was a teenager. That sign still stood today, only he and Sidney had added CARVER at an angle between *Wicked* and *Beach*. She needed a man who understood her enough to know that as tough as she looked, she had a job that could overwhelm her emotionally, and sometimes she just needed to get out of her own head. A guy who would also challenge her when she was a pain in the ass, the way she would surely challenge him, because Sidney would get bored with a guy who tried to make her life perfect. At least Zander knew who she was and wouldn't try to change her.

"I didn't flirt with Mark. I spotted him when he was on the

bench and told him he wasn't lifting heavy enough."

He chuckled. "Then do that, and take off your sweatshirt."

"What? *No*."

He took off her hat and lowered his face so they were nose to nose. "I know you've got shit in your head from the military about being seen as a capable person and not just a woman, but it's time to *glow up*, babe." He pulled off her sweatshirt as she bitched, and holy hell, he'd thought she'd had a shirt on under it, but she stood before him in nothing but a black sports bra and skintight shorts, looking hot as sin, despite her scornful scowl.

"Are you happy? Now I look like every Barbell Barbie in here minus the boobs." She snagged her hat and put it on, tugging the brim low over her eyes.

"No, you don't. They look at me like they want to fuck me, and you look like you want to kill me."

She crossed her arms. "At least you got one thing right."

"Wipe that scowl off your face and act like you can't beat the hell out of anyone in here."

Half an hour later, Gunner was spotting her as she worked through a second set of incline flys with thirty-pound dumbbells. "Two more, and you're moving up to thirty-fives for the last set."

"I hate you," she gritted out as she finished her set.

"How about that guy?" He motioned to a well-built dark-haired guy who looked to be about their age. Gunner had seen him around a few times and assumed he was either a new gym member or usually worked out at a different time.

Sidney checked him out. "I don't know."

"Sid, you've turned down every guy I've suggested. You're not going to sleep with him. This is a mock drill so you can get your man. Now get your ass over there and flirt like your life depends on it."

"Fine." She pushed to her feet. "Fucking drill sergeant."

He gave her a gentle shove in the guy's direction, and she glowered over her shoulder. But then she straightened her spine and walked over to the guy as he climbed off the leg press machine. He looked confused for a second, but whatever Sidney said brought a smile. She chatted him up with the sweetest, flirtiest looks Gunner had ever seen. She took off her hat and shook out her hair, holding the dude's rapt attention.

Can't flirt my ass.

Behind her, a guy stopped working out to give her an appreciative once-over. Gunner's gut tensed as that guy said something to his buddy and motioned to Sidney. *Get your eyes off her, assholes.* He'd seen plenty of guys check her out, so why did he want to go over there and shut those assholes down? He didn't like this at all. What was he thinking, telling her to flirt with a stranger? He felt like he was throwing her to the wolves. From now on, she'd have to practice on *him.* He kept an eye on her as he put the dumbbells she'd used back on the rack and brought the thirty-fives to the bench. She talked to the guy for almost ten minutes before putting her hat on and heading back to Gunner.

She sighed heavily. "Well, that didn't go very well, but Kent seemed nice."

"What are you talking about? You killed it."

"Not really, but at least he's going to come check out the animals at the rescue."

"He's probably coming to see you, babe."

She shook her head. "He really didn't seem interested in me."

"What do you mean? I watched you do the hair thing and flash flirty smiles."

"I don't know what you're talking about," she snapped. "What *hair thing*? I went over and asked if I could slide in for a set. I said I hadn't seen him around and asked if he was new at the gym. He said he'd just gotten out of the army, and he's having a rough time getting back into civilian life, so I told him how much having Rosco helped ease my anxiety and how you have your dogs…"

As she rattled off the details of their conversation, he realized why she'd looked so comfortable. She wasn't *flirting*—she was helping out a fellow military guy and talking about the animals she loved.

"He didn't ask anything about *me*. But like I said, he's interested in seeing the dogs, and I think Cheddar would be perfect for him." Cheddar was a friendly six-year-old Labrador mix with a gentle personality.

"MOS, that's great, but you've got to turn up the heat and redirect the conversation if this is going to work."

"I told you I suck at flirting. I don't even know how to do those things. I need a drink."

"I'll show you how." He followed her over to the water fountain, and when she bent over to get a drink, he leaned closer. "You had great form on those flys."

"Thanks." She rose and went to wipe her mouth, but he beat her to it, wiping droplets of water from her lip with his thumb. Her brow furrowed. "What are you doing?"

Holding her gaze, he stepped closer, their bodies brushing, and lowered his voice. "I don't know." *I saw you flirting with that guy, and it did something to me.* He ran his hand down her hip, and her breathing quickened.

"Gunner…?"

He closed his hand around her hip, backing her up against the wall. "You can't blame a guy for noticing you're *gorgeous* and *sexy*." Her cheeks flamed, and *man*, he liked that. He ran his hand up to the dip at her waist, stroking his thumb over her warm flesh, and lowered his mouth closer to hers, wanting to taste her, to feel her lips on his.

"*Gunny…?*" she said breathily.

Her lustful, confused, and far too beautiful eyes snapped him out of wherever he'd gone. What the hell was he doing? He stepped back, clearing his throat to try to clear the desire coursing through him. But it was like trying to cool lava. *Fucking hell.* "*That's* how you flirt."

Silently cursing himself for getting lost in *Sidney*, he took a drink from the water fountain, hoping it would take the edge off, and said, "Let's hit the weights."

SIDNEY TRIED TO calm her racing heart as Gunner walked away. Was he serious, or was that part of their practice? Because holy mother of hotness, she'd never been so turned on.

"Let's go, MOS. We don't have all day," he called over from the incline bench.

She told herself to pull it together as she went to him.

He tossed her sweatshirt to her. "Put that on."

"But you told me not to wear it."

"Right, to *practice*, but you're done. We can't do that shit all day. We've got work to do. Let's go."

He was obviously frustrated with her flirting skills, clearing up any confusion she'd had about if he had been seriously flirting with her or just showing her how it was done. She put on her sweatshirt and sat on the bench.

He handed her the heavier dumbbells and got into position to spot her.

They were back to business as usual.

Except for that extra flutter in her chest as she pushed the weights up and his eyes met hers from above, a sexy smile curving his lips as he said, "You've got this, beautiful."

LATER THAT NIGHT Sidney sat in the living room eating popcorn and watching *Venom*. Rosco was stretched out to her right, and Opha Mae was sitting to her left, watching the movie. Sidney swore the little dog loved Tom Hardy as much as she did. Belleau and Snowflake were curled up on the recliner, and Granger was stretched out beneath the front windows, being eyed by Blizzard, perched on the sill above him. After the day she'd had, Sidney needed a good distraction, and there was no better distraction than her favorite hot British actor. She couldn't believe she'd thought Gunner might have actually been flirting with her at the gym. He'd acted perfectly normal as they'd gone through their workday, joking around and stealing half of her food when they ate lunch and again when they'd had dinner before he'd left for church, which was what the Dark Knights called their Wednesday-night meetings.

She ate a handful of popcorn, and Rosco looked at her with the same expression Gunner had given her when he'd wanted some of her corn bread at dinner. "Did Gunny teach you that?

Or did you teach him?" She put some popcorn on the cushion in front of Rosco, and he gobbled it up.

Opha Mae whined.

"I didn't forget you." She put her arm around the old dog's fuzzy, frail body, pulling her closer, and gave her two pieces of popcorn. Opha Mae was missing a few teeth and couldn't gobble it down the way Rosco could. Rosco pushed his nose against her arm, pleading for more. She put more popcorn on the cushion for him and went back to watching the movie.

Belleau barked seconds before Sidney heard Gunner's motorcycle coming down the driveway. Butterflies swarmed in her belly as the dogs scrambled to the door. She wondered why he was home so early. It was only ten o'clock, and he usually went out with the guys after their meetings and came home much later.

He cut the engine, and she pictured him throwing one thick leg over the bike as he climbed off. She loved riding with him, holding on to him, feeling his muscles work as he controlled all that power.

She heard his boots on the porch steps. When he walked in, the dogs whined and jumped, vying for his attention. He crouched to pet them, lavishing them with praise and *missed you toos*. Sidney turned her attention back to the movie. She heard him pushing to his feet, followed by kissing noises, and knew he was holding Opha Mae.

"Well, well, what do we have here?" He came around the couch, and she had no choice but to look at him in all his delicious glory, standing there in his black leather vest with the pooch in one arm, eyeing Sidney like he'd caught her watching porn.

"What?"

He scoffed and looked at Opha Mae. "*What*, she asks, as if she doesn't sneak off to watch Tom Hardy every time I leave the house, just like she secretly listens to Justin Bieber. And she's wearing that sweatshirt again, too."

"Leave Justin out of this." Justin Bieber's music was her guilty pleasure, but Gunner always made fun of it. "I'm hardly sneaking, and you got me this sweatshirt." She grabbed the front of her sweatshirt, which had TAKEN BY TOM in a red heart over a picture of Tom Hardy.

He set Opha Mae on the floor and shrugged off his vest, tossing it on a chair. "That was before I knew how far your obsession went." He flopped down beside her on the couch.

"You should be happy it's Tom Hardy. He's a lot like you." *Why do you think I like him?* "He loves dogs."

"Still don't like him."

"He rides motorcycles."

Gunner did not look impressed.

"And he has a British accent, and those lips…" *They're almost as nice as yours.*

Gunner was looking at her like she was nuts.

"Oops. Forget those two things."

"You know what he's *not?*"

"Ugly?" she teased.

He bumped her with his shoulder. "You're a pain in my ass, MOS."

"I'm proud of that." She ate a piece of popcorn.

"Tom Hardy will never be your best bud, and he'll never bring you your favorite candy." He handed her a king-size Kit Kat bar.

Her heart fluttered, which was probably ridiculous, but she loved the little things he did that told her she was on his mind.

"Thank you!" She tore open the wrapper and broke the candy bar down the middle, handing Gunner half. "Is it bad that sometimes I want to wring your neck and hug you at the same time?"

"I'd worry if you didn't." He waved the candy bar at her. "Let this be a lesson. Any guy who doesn't bring you your favorite candy isn't worth your time."

"Duly noted." She bit off a hunk of chocolate. "*Mm.* Tom and chocolate. A perfect combination."

Gunner scowled, and she laughed. They settled in, watching the movie as they ate their candy. A little while later, Gunner scooted closer, pressing his leg against hers, stirring those butterflies again. That in and of itself wasn't unusual, but her hormones were still on overdrive from the water fountain tutorial. She stole a glance at him, catching him watching her.

"Hold still." He reached up and cupped her jaw, brushing his thumb over the edge of her mouth. "Chocolate." Holding her gaze, he dragged his tongue slowly over the chocolate on his thumb.

Lord have mercy. She curled her fingers around the popcorn bowl to keep from pouncing on him and licking that chocolate off his tongue. The way he was looking at her made her nervous and hopeful.

He raised his brows, cocking a grin. "Mission practice. If you're gonna get with Zan, you need to get used to having someone in your personal space."

Utterly deflated, the air rushed from her lungs. *The stupid mission. Right...*

He went back to watching the movie, and she tried to remember how to function as someone who *wasn't* in love with her roommate. But she couldn't stop thinking about the pressure of his leg against hers, and when he stretched his arm across the back of the couch, pulling her tight against him, her loneliest parts threw a hopeful celebration. *Be cool. Don't make a fool of yourself.* She finished her chocolate and stared absently at the movie, trying to act normal, but he nuzzled against her neck, sending titillating sensations scurrying over her flesh.

"You smell amazing," he said huskily.

How could a fake compliment give her goose bumps? She didn't know how to respond. He started running his fingers through her hair, causing a flurry of nervousness and desire. Her emotions were ricocheting inside her. She was trying so hard not to move—not to frigging breathe—but it was all too much. She tried to wiggle out from beneath his arm, but he grabbed her shoulder, keeping her close.

"Think of the mission, babe."

She didn't want to think about the mission. She wanted him to *kiss* her, and that was bad. Very, very bad, given that now he was trying to *feed* her popcorn. She pushed his hand away.

"You're not going to get any guys doing that." He held the popcorn in front of her mouth. "Come on, sugar. Open up."

She reluctantly opened her mouth, and he put the popcorn on her tongue, then ran his fingers down her cheek. She leaned back, pushing his hand away again. "Would you stop?"

"No. I take my job very seriously." He pulled her close again. "You're so beautiful."

Oh, her heart! If only he meant it. "And you're being a parasite. Stop it."

"What did you call me?" He cocked a grin, eyes narrowing.

She knew he got the reference to the movie they were supposed to be watching, so she continued the ruse and couldn't help but smile. "It's a term of endearment."

He leaned closer, getting right in her face. "Take it back, MOS."

She giggled. "No."

"Sid," he warned.

She whispered, "Parasite."

He grabbed her ribs. She squealed and jumped up, dumping popcorn all over the floor. The dogs sprang to their feet, and Gunner caught Sidney by the waist. But she was too quick and spun around, jumping on top of him. She wrestled him down to his back on the couch, pinning his arms with her hands.

"Take it back, MOS."

"Never!" Using the maneuver he'd long ago taught her, she pushed her knees into the cushions and pressed the tops of her feet onto his shins, both of them laughing as the dogs gobbled up the popcorn.

"I will eat your face right off your head." They both cracked up at his movie reference.

"The way I see it, I can do whatever I want with you right now." It was a partial movie reference, but her laughter faded as her wishful meaning took hold, and she became acutely aware of their bodies touching from thigh to chest, his lips inches from hers. She could lean forward and take the kiss she so desperately wanted. He'd have to kiss her back, wouldn't he? Maybe he'd realize how much he wanted her, and he wouldn't be able to stop. His eyes were dark as midnight, drilling into her like he *wanted* to kiss her, too. Hope shot through her like a guiding light, and—his brows slanted, as if he knew what she was thinking and he didn't like it.

His entire body tensed.

Nononono. What am I doing? This is just a mission to you.

"That's enough practice for today, MOS." He grabbed her by the waist, lifted her off him, and set her down at the other end of the couch as he pushed to his feet. "I'll get the vacuum. Try not to drool over Tom Hardy."

No chance of that. I'm too busy trying to remember how to breathe.

Chapter Four

THE SHELTER WAS quiet late Friday afternoon. While Gunner worked on schedules for next month's meet and greets, Sidney fed the animals. Being around animals had always centered her, and she needed that today. Operation Get My Guy was supposed to make Gunner want her, but it was backfiring. Everything they did made her want him more, not the other way around. When they'd gone running yesterday morning, he'd acted normal, just as he had throughout the day. They'd bantered like the buddies they'd always been, but the whole time, she'd silently hoped he'd flirt with her again. She'd lain in bed last night wondering if she should give up on Gunner seeing her as more than a friend and put some distance between them to keep from getting her heart broken.

But giving up on them would break her heart, too.

She pushed those thoughts away and went into Cheddar's kennel to feed the big, lovable dog. He jumped off his bed, tail wagging, and she petted him. "Come on, big boy. Let's sit down and have a chat." She sat on his doggy bed, and he climbed up beside her, anxiously awaiting more pets, which she was happy to give.

"I think I might have found you a human. His name is

Kent, and he's super nice. I think you'll like him. He's been through a rough time, and he needs a sweet, playful boy like you." The family that had brought Cheddar to the rescue had said they were his third home, and they loved him, but they'd just had a new baby, and an energetic dog was too much for them. As much as it saddened her when families didn't put in the time and effort to make things work with their pets, she would rather they brought them to the shelter than neglect them.

"Don't worry, big guy. We're going to find you a great home." She played with him for a few minutes, fed him, then pulled the food cart down to the next kennel, where Chappy stood waiting, eyes bright, tail wagging.

"Hi, my strong boy." She went into his kennel and sat down so he wouldn't try to jump and hurt his leg. This was one of her favorite parts of the day, when she got private time with each of the animals. As she sat petting Chappy, her mind tiptoed back to when she and Gunner had first met.

They'd been stationed on the same military base, and he'd seen her working with Rosco and had come over to meet her. They'd hit it off right away, and they'd talked for hours about their families and the reasons they'd joined the military—her to follow in her father's footsteps and him because he wanted to give back in a bigger way. He'd sought her out every chance he'd gotten after that, and they'd spent hours learning the ins and outs of each other's lives. It had been easy to open up to him. He'd been raised with the same values she had, and he hadn't been as much of a player back then. He was all about family, hanging with the guys, and yeah, he got laid whenever he needed to scratch that itch, but he'd been far more discreet about it. It wasn't until a year and a half later, after Ashley had died, that he'd changed in that regard.

Sidney would never forget the day he found out about Ashley. She'd been brushing Rosco when he'd come around the corner of the building. His face was sheet white, and when she'd asked what was wrong, he'd opened his mouth to tell her, but sobs had racked his body, and he'd collapsed against her. She could still feel his weight hanging on her, still hear his heart-wrenching torment. She'd seen horrible things in the military, and watching the virile man she'd come to trust and love break down was one of the worst. It had taken a while before he could tell her that Ashley had overdosed and Tank had found her in their parents' home.

She teared up at the memory. Chappy whimpered and licked her cheek. "I'm okay, buddy," she reassured him, stroking his back as more memories trickled in.

Gunner had gone home for the funeral, and he'd come back a changed man. At least to everyone else. On the outside he was more gung ho over each mission, more arrogant and self-centered. But he'd sought out Sidney, and in those private moments, he'd broken down, confessing how much it hurt to think he'd never see his sister again and how worried he was about Tank and the rest of his family. It had taken months before he could talk about Ashley without falling apart, and Sidney couldn't count the number of times he'd lain in her bed at night fully dressed, telling her stories about the little sister he'd played *Baywatch* with, taking turns saving each other in the ocean. The sister who would steal half his dessert and who had made a pact with him to never lie to each other. Only she had lied. She'd spoken to Gunner the night before she'd overdosed, and he'd heard something in her voice that had worried him. But she'd sworn she was fine and was just sick of school. After she died, he'd learned the truth. There had been some asshole talking smack about her at school, and Ashley had wanted to forget him, which was why she'd bought ecstasy. She and Bethany were going to try it together, but Bethany had talked her out of it. Ashley must have changed her mind after going home that night, and the pills she took were laced with a more toxic drug. Her little body had never stood a chance. Gunner had believed that if she'd only told him the truth, he could have talked with her and convinced her that drugs weren't the way to go. He could have alerted his brothers so they could have watched over her.

Sidney felt like she'd known the sister who had shared their father's dimples and zest for life and had called Gunner *Dwayne the Pain*. Sidney had gone with him months later when he'd gotten Ashley's name tattooed over his heart. It had helped him to heal, and at the same time, it had drawn Sidney deeper into him.

"What am I going to do, Chap?"

Chappy cocked his head.

"I can't imagine my life without Gunny in it, but this is killing me."

Her phone vibrated, and she pulled it from her pocket and read Madigan's message. *My friend's band is playing at Common Grounds open mic night tonight. Want to meet me and Marly there after work?*

Boy, did she ever. Putting a little space between her and Gunner would be a good thing, and she loved the cute coffee-house where the Dark Knights held their annual suicide-awareness rally. Once again, she wished she could talk to Madigan about Gunner, but she'd probably think Sidney was nuts for wanting him and for letting him believe she was after

Zander.

She heard Gunner's footsteps coming down the hall. Butter-flies swarmed in her belly as he appeared before her, all big and sexy in worn jeans, work boots, and a gray Henley.

"Are you two shacking up now?" Amusement danced in his devilish eyes. "I wish you'd told me earlier. I just talked to Dixie and ordered you clothes for your *mission* from Jace's Leather and Lace line."

"Sorry about that, but Chappy doesn't care if I wear leather and lace, so you can cancel the order." She put her arm around the dog. "We make a great couple, don't you think?"

"Yeah, right."

"You have to admit, it would be a good life. You could lavish us with attention, feed us, and take us out to exercise, and one day a great family will adopt us and we'll be lap pups. Right, Chap?" She scratched Chappy's head, and he licked her cheek.

Gunner cocked a brow. "That might screw up your plan with Zan."

Ugh. I wouldn't need a plan if you'd just open your eyes. She got up to feed Chappy. "Dogs are easier than guys anyway."

"That's funny. I say the same thing about dogs and wom-en."

She stepped out of the kennel, locking it behind her. "I'm not difficult."

"Yeah, but you're different." He grabbed the handle of the food cart and slung an arm over her shoulder as they headed for the supply room. "You're cool, like a really cute dude. I'm going to the Salty Hog later to meet some of the guys. Want to come?"

She knew he felt that way, so why did hearing him say it

make her want to cry *and* punch him? "*No*, I don't want to go. I'm going to Common Grounds with Mads and Marly."

His jaw tightened. "You're going out with Mads and Marly?"

"That's what I said." *God, I'm such an idiot. Why did I think I could get you to see me differently?* "Maybe I'll get lucky and find a guy who's into cute dude-like girls. It seems like the perfect place to practice flirting. Which reminds me, Kent called. You remember him, right? The guy from the gym?"

His eyes narrowed.

"He's coming to see Cheddar at seven thirty tomorrow morning, so if you want to run with me, I'm going early. Maybe I'll practice flirting with *him*, too. Now, if you'll excuse me, I have to feed the cats." She went into the supply room and stalked out, pulling the cat food cart. "Don't wait up."

COMMON GROUNDS WAS an unassuming coffeehouse tucked away at the end of a one-lane road. It was owned by Gabe Appleton, a voluptuous and outgoing redhead. She employed several people with disabilities, including her brother, Elliott, who had Down syndrome, and she fostered an environment where everyone was welcome. They didn't serve alcohol, and there was a sign on the front of the building that read LEAVE YOUR BIASES AT THE DOOR. Inside there were several dining tables, a coffee bar, a small stage, and pool tables off to the side, and outside there was a patio with a masonry fire pit and more dining tables. Their open mic nights were called Say Anything, and they were always packed as people sang, read poetry, did stand-up comedy, and a host of other types of entertainment.

Tonight every table was taken, and there were people playing pool and milling about as a brunette stood at the mic reading a story she'd written. Sidney sat with Madigan, who looked cute in a blue minidress that made her eyes pop, and Marly, an exotic-looking brunette with almond-shaped eyes, a tiny waist that looked even tinier in her floral wrap dress, and a smile that brightened the room. Evie and Steph had shown up about half an hour ago, and Sidney was glad they were wearing jeans, like her. Sidney only wore dresses when she had no other choice. She always felt a little uncomfortable in them, like she was impersonating a more feminine woman. But she *had* taken a little extra time tonight to do her hair and put on makeup. Gunner had pissed her off, and she'd wanted to strut past him when she left the farmhouse looking like she was on the prowl, even if she wasn't.

Although that didn't seem to matter. If Madigan had her way, Sidney would be walking out on her friend Dante's arm tonight.

"Did I tell you guys that I booked another storytelling gig?" Madigan had many talents. She had developed the Mad Truth About Love greeting card line, which poked fun at the more difficult parts of relationships, and she was also a puppeteer and a guitar-playing storyteller.

"Only about five times," Marly teased, and Madigan stuck her tongue out at her. "I'm kidding. I think it was only twice."

"Three times if you include the other day when you came into my shop," Steph added. "But I'm excited for you, Mads, so say it as many times as you'd like."

"I don't know how you can keep up with different jobs,"

Sidney said. "I can hardly keep up with one."

"I love having three jobs," Madigan said. "I meet lots of fun people. The other day I did a puppet show at Corinne's, and I had as much fun as the kids did." Corinne Langley was Junie and Rosie's babysitter. "And Chloe said that since I started holding puppet therapy sessions at LOCAL, she's seen improvement in my clients' dexterity, and they have more energy and a more positive outlook on therapy days. It doesn't get more fulfilling than that. Grandpa Mike even pops into the puppetry sessions sometimes. But I think he does it just to flirt with the ladies."

"Of course he does. Where do you think his grandsons learned how to flirt?" Evie said.

"He's sneaky and shameless," Madigan said. "I swear if he isn't flirting, he's sneaking candy into his pockets." Gunner's grandfather had a major sweet tooth, but because of health issues, he had to limit his sugar intake.

"I love Grandpa Mike," Steph said.

"We all do," Evie added.

"He reminds me of my grandfather," Sidney said. "They're both curmudgeons, and they don't sugarcoat anything."

Applause broke out around them, and they all joined in, even though they'd zoned out on the story the girl coming off the stage had been reading.

"There they are!" Madigan nudged Sidney, pointing to four guys coming in from the patio. "The guitarist I told you about, Dante, is the one with the shaggy brown hair, wearing a leather jacket. I had dinner with him last night and told him all about you."

Marly said, "He is *hot.*"

"I'll say," Steph added. "Mads, where have you been hiding

him?"

"I haven't been hiding him. I told you I had a guy for Sid. He's really cool, and he hates people who act fake. He's into real women who are smart and down to earth, and he has three dogs."

Evie's eyes widened. "He's perfect for Sid, but I get second dibs."

Sid had to stop herself from saying, *You can have him.*

"Who's the blond guy with him?" Steph asked.

"That's Caleb. He just broke up with his girlfriend last week." Madigan lowered her voice. "But you know what they say. The best way to get over a girl is to get under another. *Wait.* That's not right."

They all cracked up, and Dante looked over, turning their laughter into *Whoa, he's so cute,* and *Now, that's a man.* Sidney remained silent, although she couldn't deny that Dante was incredibly handsome, with a strong jaw and dark eyes that probably left a trail of melted panties in their wake. But it was Gunner's face flashing before her, his heated words whispering through her mind. *You can't blame a guy for noticing that you're gorgeous and sexy.* She shuddered with the memory of his thumb brushing over her ribs, but those good feelings were obliterated as his more recent comment came back to her. *You're cool, like a really cute dude.*

Madigan waved to Dante and pointed to Sidney. "This is Sid!"

Oh God. Sidney looked down, hiding behind her hair.

"Say hi to him," Madigan urged.

Sidney looked up and waved as his friends walked past him. Dante lifted his chin, saying, "Hi," before following his bandmates onto the stage.

"Girl, I am *so* jealous of you right now," Evie said.

"Me too," Steph said.

"Would you *stop*? There's nothing there. He's just being nice." Even if he was staring at her as they set up their equipment.

"If you don't take him home, I will," Marly said. "*Wait.* Do you take guys home with Gunner there? Have we ever asked you that before?"

They were all looking at her expectantly. "*Um.* I don't know if you have or not. But I have taken a guy home before."

"Seriously?" Steph asked. "What did Gunner do?"

"He interrogated him and called him Pretty Boy behind his back."

"I knew it," Steph said. "I bet he *hated* that. I never told you this, because I know how much it annoys me when people say they thought me and Gunner were or should be together. But when he was in the military, he talked about *his buddy Sid* all the time, raving about how you two hung out and how cool you were. I swear it was always *Sid this* and *MOS that.* I thought he'd started batting for the other team, and then he got out of the military and went straight to see you instead of coming home, and I was sure there was more going on there. When he finally made it back to the Cape, I said if Sid is so great, set me up with him. That's when he showed me your picture, and I was like, *damn.* No wonder he couldn't stop talking about you."

"It's not like that between us." *I only wish it were.*

"I know it's not," Steph said. "But when he told me you were moving in, I thought he meant as his girlfriend."

Madigan nodded. "Me too, but I asked him about it, and he said to get my mind out of the gutter. That you were one of his best friends."

"He pretty much told me the same thing," Steph said.

"That's what he told Baz, too," Evie added. "And I only know that because I asked if you two were doing the dirty."

Sidney wondered if they could hear her heart being crushed. "The only dirty thing going on in that house between me and Gunner is the laundry."

"Speaking of Gunner." Steph pointed to the entrance, and they all looked over.

Gunner was walking in with his brother Baz, who was raking a hand through his longish blond hair. Behind them were three of Madigan's brothers, Blaine, Zeke, and Zander, who were all dark haired, like their father. They stood in the entrance, five broad sets of shoulders shrouded in leather, their blue-eyed gazes surfing the room. Sid's heart raced as Gunner's eyes locked on her. Did he bring Zander for her to flirt with him? God, she hoped not.

"What the heck are they doing here?" Evie asked. "Baz said they were going to the Salty Hog."

"Hi, everyone" boomed through the microphone. "I'm Dante, and these are my buddies, Caleb, Ragner, and West. Our band is called Carnal Beat, and this song is for the brown-haired beauty with bedroom eyes and the prettiest smile I've ever seen sitting right over there. This song's for you, Sid."

Gunner's and Sidney's gazes shot to the stage. Dante winked at her as the band started playing. Everyone in the place was looking at her, and her friends were talking excitedly about her. Sidney's head spun.

Madigan said, "Shh, you guys. Let's listen to the song."

Thank you, Mads.

Sidney's phone vibrated. She pulled it out of her pocket and saw Gunner's name on the screen. She held her breath as she read the text. *I thought you were into Zander. Who's the guy?* Holding the phone under the table, she thumbed out, *What are you doing here?* Her phone vibrated seconds later with his response. *That's not an answer. Who's the fucking guy on the stage?* Was he jealous? Sidney's heart raced as Gunner led the band of brawny men through the coffeehouse, making a beeline for Sidney and catching the attention of nearly every girl in there.

Gunner was looking down at his phone, probably waiting for Sidney's response as they arrived at the table.

Zeke leaned down by Madigan. His thick black hair was neatly combed, his beard trimmed, and his leather jacket covered his tattoos. "What's going on, sis?"

Madigan rolled her eyes. "Oh, *come on.* Can't we have a girls' night without being babysat?"

"We heard there was a new band playing tonight." Baz winked at Evie.

"Don't try to get me in trouble," Evie warned, and looked at the girls. "I swear I didn't tell him where we were going."

Oh crap. Was it supposed to be a secret?

Gunner lifted his gaze to Sidney, his jaw clenched tight. The air between them sizzled and sparked. Was she imagining it, or was her plan working? Was he jealous, or was he pissed and being protective of Zander? Hope bloomed inside her, and she went for the brass ring, turning her attention to Zander, with his tousled brown hair and flirtatious grin. She smiled coyly, knowing anything more would set off alarm bells with the girls. She was saving *that* smile for the stranger with the guitar, because if she was reading Gunner right, it would set off *his* alarm bells, too.

"Hey, gorgeous." Zander grinned. "You look hot tonight."

Gunner looked like he was going to explode, and it was all

Sidney could do to keep from cheering. "Thanks. You're looking pretty good, too. Have you been working out?"

"Ohmygod, *don't* encourage him," Madigan pleaded.

Sidney felt Gunner's eyes on her and lifted her chin, meeting his stare. Her heart thundered, and she could barely hear past the blood rushing through her ears, but she remembered what he'd said about not looking too eager, and she forced herself to look away.

Marly dragged her eyes down Blaine's body.

"*Marly*," Madigan chided her, and Steph and Evie laughed.

Blaine, a James Marsden lookalike with chiseled features, short dark hair, and shockingly bright blue eyes, ate up her attention. "How's it going, Marls? Want to go for a ride?"

"No, she does *not*." Madigan pushed to her feet. "Get out of here. Go play pool or something. Sid's missing the whole song, and it was dedicated to *her*."

Gunner's thumbs flew over his phone screen as Baz gave him a shoulder nudge toward the pool tables.

"Thank God." Madigan sat down. "Sorry about missing your song, Sid."

"That's okay. I actually think it's my fault," Sidney said. "I told Gunner where I was going tonight. I didn't know it was a secret."

"She's just tired of being policed by her brothers." Marly leaned closer and said, "But forget them, because tall, dark, and swoony Dante is still checking you out."

The girls talked about Dante as another text from Gunner rolled in. *Can't flirt, huh? What kind of game are you playing?* Sidney's nerves caught fire, and with renewed hope, she gave Operation Get My Guy her all, thumbing out, *You told me to practice flirting, and I take my missions seriously! I'm going to nail this flirting thing, so be ready to move to the next level of training when I get home.* She sent the text and watched him read it.

He turned slowly, looking over his shoulder at her.

She couldn't tell if it was lust or anger looking back at her, but either way, she was done dicking around and was ready to throw caution to the wind.

Watch out, Gunny. You're the only target on my radar.

THIS WAS THE worst fucking night in history. Gunner didn't know what the hell was going on with him, but when Sidney told him she was going out with Madigan and Marly, he'd remembered what she'd said about them trying to hook her up with guys, and something inside him had snapped. He'd gone to the Salty Hog to try to distract himself, but Zander was there, and all he could think about was Sidney's hands all over his cousin. He made the mistake of telling Blaine he was heading over to Common Grounds, and they'd all followed.

He'd thought he'd have to just keep Sidney away from Zander tonight, but that fucking guitarist and his bandmates had been at the table with the girls for the past forty minutes, and Sidney had the guy's guitar on her lap as he tried to teach her to play.

Zander sidled up to Gunner. "Sid's looking all kinds of doable tonight, bro."

"Shut the fuck up. That's *Sid,* man." *And I wanted to kiss her so badly the other night, I had to walk away.*

"Hey, I'm just telling it like it is, and I'm not the only one who thinks so. That Dante dude is making serious moves on her."

If she wants that dickhead, there's nothing I can do about it. Just like if she wants you. Gunner eyed his cousin. He'd never been jealous before, but hell if the green-eyed monster wasn't parked on his shoulder now.

"Why're you looking at me like that?"

Gunner took a deep breath, his hands fisting. "Are you into Sid?"

"Hey, if she were into me and she wasn't attached to you at the hip, I'd do her."

Fuck. "For more than a night?"

"Man, you're crossing dangerous territory asking me that." Zander looked across the room at Sidney.

She was tucking her hair behind her ear, fluttering her long lashes at Dante, who was definitely into her. *When the hell did I start noticing Sidney's eyelashes?*

"I think we're all a little crazy about Sid," Zander said. "She's the coolest chick around. I mean, Sid's the kind of woman you can go out drinking with, fool around on the beach with and wake up with the sun all sandy and shit, take a dip in the ocean, and go out for breakfast. She doesn't worry about her hair and clothes and all that other garbage women use as excuses."

Gunner gritted his teeth. "I asked you a simple question. I didn't need to know you've thought it all out."

"Don't tell me you haven't."

"No, I haven't thought about fucking my best friend." He'd probably get struck by lightning for that lie. The truth was, he'd thought about it a hell of a lot when they'd first become friends, but she'd quickly become his person. The one he could trust with anything and be himself with no matter what he was facing. He knew how rare that was outside of family, and he didn't want to complicate or mess up their friendship, so he'd locked down those feelings for good. Or so he'd thought, until she'd come up with this fucked-up mission to win Zander over.

"Hey, isn't this one of yours and Sid's songs?" Zander asked.

Pink's "Raise Your Glass" was playing through the speakers. The lyrics he and Sidney had made up the first week after she'd moved in with him came rushing back. *Raise your paw if you're awesome in all the best ways. All our superdogs, you will always be everything in our eyes.* That was their thing, making up their own lyrics to songs, and Sidney was usually the first to notice when one was playing. But she was too busy flirting with that fucking guitarist.

After another torturous hour, Sidney and the girls finally called it a night, leaving Gunner with emotions he didn't want to deal with. At least she didn't walk out with the guitarist.

Gunner stuck around with the guys for a while, trying to cool off, but no such luck. He took the long way home to clear his head, hoping Sidney would be in bed by the time he got home. When he finally drove down the long driveway, he surveyed the house. The porch light was on, but the rest of the house was dark. He breathed a sigh of relief as he climbed out of the truck, closing the door quietly so as not to wake the dogs, some of whom were probably sleeping with Sidney.

Great. Now he was thinking about Sidney in bed.

This was messed up. He'd never been so easily distracted by a woman. Especially not a woman he'd never even kissed. He tried to ignore those thoughts as he headed inside, but the suckers clung like leaches. The dogs barreled out of the kitchen, tales wagging excitedly.

"Hey, guys," he said softly. "Why aren't you sleeping?"

Opha Mae scampered back into the kitchen and Granger ran after her, but Belleau hung by Gunner's side, and Rosco whined, looking between Gunner and the kitchen. *Fuck.* Sidney was definitely in there.

He shrugged off his leather jacket and hung it on a hook by the door, reminding himself he was Gunner Wicked, and there was nothing he couldn't handle. Especially when it came to women. "Let's go, boys."

He followed the dogs into the kitchen and found Sidney standing at the counter eating ice cream out of the container, wearing a baseball shirt that covered only half her ass, and she wasn't wearing her usual underwear that looked like tight, skimpy shorts. She was wearing black panties that bared half her cheeks and standing in that adorable way she did, with her right leg bent and the toes of her right foot resting on the top of her left foot.

What had he done to deserve this type of hell?

She looked over her shoulder, her hair covering one eye. He'd seen her like that more times than not, but it was like he was seeing her through new eyes, because she looked so damn sexy his cock jerked behind his zipper.

She tilted her head, absently petting Rosco as she stepped closer. "How'd I do tonight?"

Her voice was so seductive, his thoughts stumbled. "Huh?"

"Flirting with Dante." She gazed up at him through those long lashes. "He was definitely into me. I saw Zander watching me, too. Do you think he likes me?"

The beach fantasy Zander had painted brought jealousy slamming into him. "Probably."

"Hm." Her eyes narrowed. "Maybe when I flirt with Zander, I should touch him more, like this." She dragged her fingers along Gunner's pecs. "And say something like, 'Hey, big guy. I've been thinking about you.'" She licked her lips, leaving them enticingly wet as her hand moved down his chest and stomach, bringing rise to a lot more than jealousy.

"*Sid*," he warned through gritted teeth.

"What? Should I get closer? I knew it. How's this?" She rubbed her body against him, speaking low and sexy. "I saw you checking out that girl the other night, and I *hated* it. Wouldn't you rather check *me* out?"

Fuuck. His legs carried him forward, boxing her in against the counter despite his trying to hold back. Heat flared in her eyes, turning him on even more.

"Do you think he'll do that?"

"Fuck yeah, he'll do that." His hips rocked into her, lust coiling inside him like a viper ready to strike.

"Then what?" she asked breathlessly. "Should I...?" She put her arms around him and grabbed his ass, grinding against his cock.

He didn't think as he lifted her onto the counter, wedging himself between her legs. One hand belted around her, holding her tight against him, the other dove into her hair, and he lowered his mouth toward hers, growling, "Then he'll kiss the hell out of you."

"*Gunner*," she panted out, and reality hit him like a slap in the face.

Fuck. She wanted *Zander.* What the hell was he doing? He pushed away, tripping over Granger. Granger yelped, and all the dogs jumped to their feet. "Shit." He reached for Granger. "Sorry, buddy." Sidney was sitting on the counter, cheeks flushed, legs still spread, and it took everything he had not to take up that space again and kiss her senseless. But he knew he wouldn't stop there. "*Fuck.* You okay?"

"I'm...*Yeah.*" A smile crept up her beautiful face. "I'm good. Now I know what to do. With Zan I mean."

"Right. I'm going to bed." *Before I fuck everything up.*

Chapter Five

AFTER A SHITTY night spent trying not to think about how close he'd come to kissing Sidney—and how badly he'd wanted to do a hell of a lot more than that—Gunner got up early Saturday morning bound and determined to get his head back on track and put Sidney firmly back in the off-limits zone. But they were a mile into their three-mile run with Granger, and it seemed the universe was working against him. She'd forgone her normal baggy sweatshirt and wore a tight Under Armour shirt and leggings that fit like a second skin. He'd caught himself running slower just to check out her ass too many times to count. She was also wearing gloves, and her hair poked out from beneath a black knit hat, which made her look adorable in addition to looking so hot he couldn't concentrate on anything other than the burning desire to strip her naked and feel her sweet, soft body beneath him as he thrust into her so deep, she'd never think of Zander again.

"I'm ready to move to the next level with my mission, don't you think?" She didn't give him time to answer. "I can't stop thinking about the way you backed me up against the counter last night."

Neither can I. He'd beat himself up about it, trying to figure out if he was interested in Sidney for *Sidney*, or if he was just being a competitive jerk because she suddenly had all these guys coming out of the woodwork—including him. That made him sound like an asshole, but he had no fucking idea who he was at the moment.

"That was *hot*, and I didn't expect this, but practicing with you is really helping me find my inner flirt. I think I can pull it off with Zan, don't you? It might really turn him on if I do that thing where I back him up against a wall or a counter. Would it turn you on if a girl did that to you?"

Any girl, no. You, absofuckinglutely.

"Don't answer that," she said quickly. "You're not Zander, so it doesn't really matter."

There it was again. The reminder that he wasn't the guy she was interested in. His cousin would eat that shit up and have her naked in the blink of an eye. There was no way in hell he'd lead her down that road. He was about to be a selfish prick, and he'd surely go straight to hell for it, but he didn't care. Until he got his feelings sorted out, this was how it was going to be. "After thinking about it, I don't think he'd be into you coming onto him. He likes to be the alpha dog."

"Really? Maybe I could just try. If I can make him feel half of what you made me feel, there's no way he'll be able to turn me down."

Shit.

"Depending on how things go with Kent, maybe I can practice on him."

Had she lost her mind? "You said he was interested in a dog. Are you willing to screw that up for Cheddar?" It was another asshole move, using her love for the animals to shut her down, but damn it, she was going off the deep end. She wasn't the type of girl to throw herself at men. That was one of the things he'd always admired most about her.

She wrinkled her nose. "Maybe you're right. I'll have to see how it goes."

"What the hell, MOS? You're not that person."

"What do you mean? You don't think I can do it?"

"*No.* You can do anything you set your mind to. But you don't need to throw yourself at Zan or Kent or anyone else. You're awesome just as you are, and any guy who can't see that doesn't deserve you."

"I appreciate that, but flirting with Dante caught Zander's attention, so I think your advice was spot on. Flirting *is* important. You really know how to play the game. I'm glad you're on my team. I can't wait to see the sexy clothes you picked out for me."

She was quiet for the rest of their run, which was probably a good thing, because between thinking of her in leather and lace and thinking about her flirting with Kent—and who knew who else she'd turn her charm on for during their meet and greets later today—he was fit to be tied.

They slowed to a walk at the gated entrance to the property, and she took off her gloves and hat, shaking out her hair. Gunner saw it in slow motion and wondered how he'd run with her three times a week for the past three years and a hundred times before that when they were in the military and had never noticed how insanely beautiful she was when the morning sun shimmered in her eyes.

Granger barked at a shiny blue truck coming down the road. "It's okay, boy."

The truck stopped at the entrance, and Kent came into view. Sidney flashed an eager smile at him and held up one finger, turning the bright eyes that would soon dance for Kent on Gunner. "Would you mind opening the gate? I'll drive down with Kent."

"You think that's smart? You don't even know the guy."

"What do you mean? I've talked to him a few times since the gym."

"I don't care if you talked to his mother, sweetheart, you're still not getting into his truck." He slung an arm over her shoulder.

"What are you doing?"

"*We* are going to say hi to our buddy, Kent."

She rolled her eyes. "You're such a brat. I doubt he'd abscond with me with my big-ass bodyguard right here." She poked him in the ribs and giggled.

Freaking *giggled*.

He wasn't sure who *she* was right now, either, but as they went to talk to Kent, he mentally added that adorable giggle to the list of things driving him nuts about Sidney Carver.

TWO HOURS LATER, Sidney waved as Kent drove away. She was glad Gunner had gone about his business, cleaning kennels and feeding the animals rather than following her and Kent around. It had given her a chance to relax and just be herself, which she desperately needed. Flirting was much harder than she'd anticipated, and being *on* all the time was exhausting. It hadn't helped that she'd stayed up half the night reliving the white-hot moment when she and Gunner had almost kissed. If he could make her nearly combust by almost kissing her, what would it be like if those lips ever landed on hers? A jolt of heat accompanied that thought.

She'd woken up desperate to make that kiss a reality, which was why she'd said all that nonsense about flirting with Kent when she and Gunner were running. But when he'd called her out on flirting with a potential adopter, she'd hated *that* more than anything, because he was right. That wasn't who she was or who she wanted to be.

As she headed back into the shelter, she didn't want to act fake or flirty. She didn't want to try to win him over or get him to notice her. She missed the comfort of their easy friendship. She heard Gunner and Tori talking as she neared the office and gave herself permission to take a step back from Operation Get My Guy for a day or two and just spend time with her best friend without any ulterior motive.

Tori was standing with her back to the door when Sidney walked up. Granger was asleep under Gunner's desk, and Rosco was lying on a dog bed across the room. Gunner was sitting with his booted feet propped on his desk and Opha Mae in his lap. He wore a black Henley-style shirt with the Wicked Animal Rescue logo on the upper left of his chest, dark jeans, and his black leather boots. Even from across the room Sidney smelled the woodsy scent of his body wash. He'd used the same body wash since they'd first met. *The rugged, fresh scent of Dwayne "Gunner" Wicked, the first guy who ever really got me.*

Rosco trotted over to greet her as she walked in, and she petted his head. "Hi, buddy."

Tori, a supremely organized blonde with a vibrant personality and black-framed glasses, turned around. "Hey, Sid. I was just telling Gunner that we have three volunteers coming in today while you're at the meet and greets. Steph is bringing a friend, and Everett is coming in."

"That's great," Sidney said. "It'll make things easier when we bring the animals from the morning event back and pick up the ones for the afternoon event."

"Exactly. We'll make sure they're clean and cute as can be with their bows and bow ties," Tori promised. "How'd it go with Cheddar?"

"Fantastic. Kent and Cheddar hit it off beautifully. He filled out an application, and he's paying the fee online, so you can get started on his references." She handed Tori the application Kent had filled out. "Most of his references are from the military, but he added some from family friends in Plymouth, where he grew up. He's got a good job in Hyannis, and he listed a reference from there, too, but you should check the others, since he hasn't been there long."

"Great. I'll get started as soon as his payment comes through." Tori glanced at the application.

Gunner set his feet on the floor. "You trust the guy with Cheddar?"

"Definitely. His family has always had dogs, and he really missed them when he was in the military. You should have seen the way Cheddar lit up when we took him out to the yard. Kent got right down on the ground to play with him. I think it's a really good match for both of them."

"What's his living situation?" Gunner petted Opha Mae, eyes on Sidney.

"He's renting an apartment, but it's pet friendly, so that shouldn't be a problem. He's working as a mechanic right around the corner from where he lives, and he can go home at lunch to let Cheddar out."

"Good. I hope it works out." His eyes narrowed. "Tell me

you didn't flirt with him."

Before she could answer, Tori said, "Why shouldn't she flirt with him? Where else is she supposed to meet guys? She's always here or hanging out with *you*."

"What's wrong with *me*?" Gunner held his hands out, and Opha Mae gave him the stink eye for stopping. "I'm the best friend a girl could ask for."

Tori rolled her eyes. "Got a few hours? I can make you a list, starting with that arrogance you're sporting."

Gunner lifted his chin at Sidney. "Tell her how cool I am, babe."

Sorry, Gunny, you walked right into this one. "He is a great friend, and he has lots of great roommate qualities. He can burp the alphabet after chugging just one beer, he can't make coffee to save his life, and let's not forget my favorite thing about him. He takes longer to shower than I do, and I do *not* want to know why."

"What? A guy can't exfoliate?" Gunner shook his head. "This is bullshit. I'm funny, easy on the eyes, good with animals, and…" He glowered at them. "Stop rolling your eyes."

Sidney and Tori laughed.

"Y'all suck."

Tori patted his shoulder. "You know we love you. Although I have no idea how Sid puts up with you twenty-four-seven. But we're not going there because we girls have something far more important to talk about. So, *Sid.* Did you get a date with Kent?"

"No, I did not."

Gunner cocked a grin. "Your flirting bombed, huh? Bummer."

"I *didn't* flirt with him. You were right. I didn't want to risk messing things up for Cheddar. But if I *had* flirted, it would have worked and *you* know it. I should smack that smirk off your face."

Gunner chuckled. "Go on, MOS. It'd be fun to see you go all ninja on me."

Tori held a hand up. "What's going on with you two? Why do I feel like this is about more than just flirting with Kent?"

"Oh, that's right," Gunner said with an attitude. "You don't know about all the guys coming out of the woodwork and going after Sid, do you?"

"No, but it's about time." Tori turned to Sidney. "Do tell, girlfriend."

"There isn't much to tell. I met Kent at the gym, and the other night I met a musician named Dante when I was at Common Grounds with Mads and the girls."

"Darn it. I knew I should've gone when Evie texted me," Tori complained. "But I was in a *really* good part of the book I'm reading for Chloe's book club, and I stayed home to finish it. I want to hear *all* about Dante. Does he live up to that sexy name? Are you going out with him?"

"He was really nice—"

"We don't have time to talk about this crap." Gunner pushed to his feet, carrying Opha Mae in one arm, causing Granger to pop to his feet and follow him as he shooed Sidney out the door. "You need to shower and get ready. We've got a morning *and* an afternoon meet and greet."

"Fine. I'm going." Rosco trotted along beside her as she called over her shoulder, "Let me know how Kent's references pan out."

"Okay, and you can fill me in on Dante later," Tori called back.

Gunner cursed, and Sidney grinned to herself as she headed out of the shelter, loving that things were getting back to normal.

Chapter Six

GUNNER HAD BEEN looking forward to the meet and greets all week. It was a chance for the animals to shine and let their personalities speak for themselves, which potential adopters couldn't experience when looking at their website. It was nearing five o'clock, and they were almost done for the day. Three of the four dogs they'd brought to the morning event and two of the three cats had gotten adoption applications. There was no better feeling than witnessing what he liked to call the *moment of impact,* when an animal and a person or family connected on that special level that was different from all others. Gunner had felt a similar moment of impact the first time he'd met Sidney. She was like the open road calling to him, drawing out his hidden parts he hadn't shared with others, as if they were two sides of the same soul.

If only he could stop noticing little things about her that he hadn't paid much attention to before she set her sights on his cousin. Like how she flashed a cute, slightly crooked smile when she thought he was being silly, so different from all her other smiles, and the way she gave a pep talk to each of the dogs before events. At least he hadn't been forced to watch her flirt with anyone today. She'd been her regular, cool, funny self, focusing on the animals and potential adopters. Unfortunately, that made all those other little things about her even more attractive.

He glanced at Sidney, helping a couple by the dog pen, and her eyes flicked in his direction. A sweet smile curved her lips, and he felt a tug in his chest. That had been happening a lot today, too.

"What kind of dog did you say he is?"

Gunner turned his attention back to the couple he was talking with. "Koda is a husky/shepherd mix."

"I like how laid-back he is." The woman flicked dog hair off her fingers with an unpleasant expression.

Gunner made a mental note of those red flags. "Don't let him fool you. He's a big, energetic boy, and he needs daily exercise. He's going to shed a lot, too, and he'll need to be brushed often."

"What happens if we take him and then it doesn't work out?" the man asked. "Will you take him back?"

Every time someone asked that question, Gunner wanted to ask if they'd give away a child after it was born because it cried too much or went through too many diapers, but he bit his tongue. "If we do our jobs right, hopefully that won't happen. But on the off chance it does, we require that the animals come back to us. It's in the adoption contract."

The guy looked at his wife and shrugged. "Then maybe we should fill out the application. What've we got to lose?"

This isn't about what you have to lose, buddy. It's about what Koda has to lose, and he's already lost enough. "Adoption is an emotional and stressful time for the animal and the family, and there are adjustment periods on both sides. It sounds like you're a little concerned that this might not work out, and I think you need to consider Koda's emotional well-being. Rehoming would be traumatic for him. Why don't you pick up the pamphlets on that table over there. They outline everything you can expect when adopting a dog, what you can do to make the transition easier, trouble signs to look for, that sort of thing, as well as estimated pet care costs and various other considerations you might not have thought of, like who will take care of him while you're on vacation. You can call me with questions, and if you're still interested in adoption after reviewing the materials, come back and see Koda at the shelter, and we'll talk."

"I think that's a good idea," the wife said. "Thank you."

"Sure thing." They took the pamphlets, but Gunner knew they wouldn't be back. He crouched to pet Koda. "You did great, buddy. Don't worry. Your people are out there, and we'll find them." He put Koda in the large dog pen and petted Angel, a pit bull. A blonde had filled out an application for Angel, but Gunner had his reservations about the woman. Some women used the animals as a way to get closer to him. It happened more than he cared to admit.

"Can we see the Chihuahua?" a brunette with two little boys asked Sidney.

"You sure can." Sidney went into the pen where they kept the little dogs to get him. She cuddled the tiny dog against her chest and kissed her head, as she always did with the little dog who peed on everyone. "This is Twinkles. She's seven years old, and she gets a little nervous, so don't worry if she trembles." She carried Twinkles into the empty pen where prospective adopters could visit with the dogs. "You can come in here to play with her."

The woman and her children followed her in, and the older of the two little boys asked, "Does she bite?"

"Nope. She just shakes." Sidney started to hand Twinkles to the woman, and Twinkles peed on Sidney's hands.

The woman jumped back as if she'd been burned. The younger boy giggled, and the older one exclaimed, "She peed!" causing more giggles.

Sidney cuddled Twinkles, not at all affected by the puppy pee wetting her shirt. "Sometimes she does that when she's nervous, too."

"Is that *normal?*" the woman asked, looking disgusted.

"For her it seems to be, but she might get over it when she's comfortable with you." Sidney petted Twinkles.

"I think we need to put some more thought into this. Come on, boys." The woman hurried her disappointed boys out of the play area.

Sidney kissed the pooch's nose as she carried her out of the pen. "It's their loss, Twinkles. Someone will adopt you."

"Yeah, *us.*" Gunner took Twinkles from her. "Why do you always insist on bringing her when you know she's going to end up on our couch eating meatballs with the others?" As he said it, he was hit with the reality that one day she might not be on that couch with them. He'd been joking around when he'd said he and the dogs would follow her to Zander's. Not because he wouldn't do it. He damn well would. But because he didn't think Zander would ever settle down. He'd never even considered that she wouldn't always be with him before her stupid mission. It wasn't that he took her for granted. He'd just never thought about his life without her in it. It hadn't come up. But Zander's beach fantasy had changed that, and now he couldn't stop thinking about it or seeing her as the beautiful, special woman she was, instead of just his buddy MOS.

"Because I love her, and it's hard to believe someone else

won't." Sidney reached for a wet wipe to clean her hands, drawing Gunner from his thoughts.

"You've been doing this for three years. You know better than that. It'll take a really special person to welcome a dog who pees on everything. We might as well change her name to *Tinkles Wicked* right now."

"You are *not* going to pee-shame her with that name." She scratched the pup's head, smiling at Gunner. "Would it be so bad if she was yours? I'll get her tiny diapers so she doesn't pee on everything."

There it was, that adorable crooked smile.

He lifted the dog so they were eye to eye, and Twinkles peed again. Gunner eyed Sidney, who laughed. Then he looked at the tiny dog again. She didn't shake when she was with either of them, and he knew damn well where she would end up. He had a soft spot for the pooch, too, but if he took in all the animals he had soft spots for, he'd never let any go. "You're getting diapers all right. Maybe *then* someone will adopt you."

Sidney rolled her eyes.

"I brought you an extra T-shirt, MOS." He always packed extra clothes for her, because if a dog was going to pee, poop, or puke, they always did it on Sidney, and she was always so worried about making sure they had everything for the events, she never remembered to bring extra clothing. "It's in the canvas bag in the back of the van."

"You're the *best*." She kissed Twinkles and whispered, "He really does love you, Twinkie, pee-pee and all."

God, this girl...

She'd really gotten under his skin.

When they finally finished for the day, they brought the dogs back to the shelter, walked and fed them, and put them in their kennels for the night.

"Let's go, MOS," Gunner called out as she said good night to Twinkles. He heard her phone ring and her murmured voice.

A few minutes later, she came out with the phone to her ear. "Love you, too. See you then." As she locked the kennel, she called down the hall to Gunner, "I'm going to skip the gym Wednesday and have breakfast with my dad."

"Cool." He liked her father. He was a no-bullshit guy, always willing to go the extra mile, and any father who would change his life for his daughter was a damn good man in his eyes. "Do you want to head to the Hog and grab a beer and some wings?"

"*Yes.* I'm starved."

As she came down the hall, he noticed the front of her shirt was wet. "What happened?"

"What do you think happened? TW peed on me. Give me a few minutes to rinse off and change." She flew out the door yelling, "I'll meet you at your truck!"

Gunner followed her out and saw Baz walking up from the veterinary office. "Hey, man."

"What'd you do that made Sid bolt?"

"It wasn't me. A dog pissed on her." Gunner locked the shelter door, thinking about how most women would bitch about that and need to get all dolled up before going out, but not Sidney. She really was the coolest. "We're heading to the Hog. Want to go?"

"Yeah, sounds good. Let me see if Eves wants to meet us."

As his brother thumbed out a text, Gunner said, "Can I ask you something?"

"Sure."

"Have you ever thought of Evie as more than a friend?"

Baz met his gaze as he pocketed his phone, brows knitted. "Of course I have. Probably a lot more than I should. But hey, she's gorgeous and she's got a killer personality."

"Then why haven't you made a move?"

"Because I'm not a fool." Baz crossed his arms. "I have things I want to accomplish that'd be much harder with a woman trying to tell me what to do all the time."

"I get that." But Sidney never told him what to do. They were usually on the same page. "How did you turn off those feelings if you didn't make a move?"

"I didn't make a move toward sleeping with her, but I kissed her a long time ago to get that shit out of my system."

"And that worked? A kiss?" If Gunner had kissed Sidney last night, he wasn't sure he would have stopped there.

"We're not hooking up and we're still best friends, so I'd say it did. Now she's in a different category in my head. She's the woman I compare all other women to." He grinned. "I set that bar sky-high so I wouldn't make a mistake. Why're you asking? Are things changing between you and Sid? Are you into her?"

"No, man, just curious."

"Bro...?" Baz gave him a disbelieving look. "You're not the curious type."

Gunner threw his hands up. "I don't know what's going on. I'm just noticing shit about her that I never used to, and I can't turn it off. I know I need to get past it, because it's Sid. She's my girl, my buddy. She's my fucking life, man. I can't screw that up."

"Maybe you should kiss her."

Gunner scoffed. "She's not into me. She's into another guy."

"Ah, now I see. The grass is always greener. You know damn

well you can change that if you want to, and if you *don't* want to, then going in for a kiss just might get her out of your system."

"Or get my ass kicked by a hot little ninja." Gunner scrubbed a hand down his face, more confused than ever. "I'll see you at the Hog. I've got to go get cleaned up."

GUNNER PULLED INTO the parking lot of the Salty Hog. His parents' rustic two-story restaurant and bar was a hotspot for locals and tourists and a favorite hangout for the Dark Knights. It overlooked the harbor in Harwich Port, and Gunner and his siblings and cousins had practically been raised there. Tank and Blaine, the oldest of the two groups of siblings, used to watch over the rest of them as they ran around in the grass by the water while their parents were busy inside. He felt closest to Ashley when he was at his parents' house, but the Salty Hog ran a close second. Gunner could still hear her high-pitched laughter and see her always-tangled strawberry-blond hair flying out behind her as she ran by and swatted him, yelling, *You can't catch me!* and then sprinted away.

"Hey, daydreamer," Sidney said, drawing him from his thoughts. "You owe me a drink." She pointed to Baz's truck. "I told you you took too long in the shower."

He wasn't about to tell her that the reason he'd taken so long was that he'd heard her shower running when he'd gone inside and couldn't stop thinking about her wet and naked. He'd had to take things into his own hands for fear of walking around with a boner all night.

"I don't like to rush when I manscape."

"*Ew.* Don't tell me that." She climbed out of the truck.

"What's the matter, MOS? Afraid you'll be thinking about it all night?" He chuckled, enjoying toying with her.

"Of a razor near your privates? I don't think so." Little Miss Tough Talk looked sexy as hell with her hair covering one eye, wearing her leather jacket over a gray T-shirt, dark jeans with a hole in the thigh, and her pink high-tops. His favorites. She called herself a tomboy, and yeah, she was tough, and she didn't dress like most of the women he knew, but there was no escaping her femininity, and those pink high-tops softened her outfit just enough to be *perfectly Sid.* Knowing her sensitive side, the part of her that acted tough during thunderstorms but practically sat in his lap every time they occurred, felt like a treasured secret.

He leaned closer, lowering his voice. "Of me and my *smooth jewels.*"

She rolled her eyes so hard it practically rocked the cars in the lot.

As they headed for the stairs that led up to the bar, he said, "I texted Steph and the guys. Zan might be here. Am I going to be forced to watch you flirt with him?"

"Nope. I'm not up for it tonight."

Thank God. As relieved as he was, he was curious about the sudden change. "I thought you took your missions seriously."

"I do, but it's hard to act so girly and flirt all the time."

"Are you telling me you can't hack it, MOS?" That was a first. He'd seen her work under unfathomable conditions in the military without losing her cool and calm ferocious animals without breaking a sweat.

"*No.*" She stopped at the bottom of the stairs, planting a

hand on her hip. "Even professional athletes get nights off to recover."

"Recover? What kind of bullshit is that? You're flirting, not playing football."

"Don't pretend that all the flirting you do doesn't take something out of you."

He shrugged. "What can I say. I guess I'm a pro."

"What*ever*. I need a night off, so don't give me a hard time about it. I just want to be myself tonight and have fun with your obnoxious ass." She started walking up the steps.

"I knew you were into my ass. You've got a nice ass, too." He swatted her butt, and she glowered over her shoulder. *So damn cute.* He followed her onto the landing. "I have great abs, too. You can touch them if you want." He lifted his shirt, and her cheeks pinked up, which was new...and *interesting*. Or was he reading too much into it because of his fucked-up head?

"Put your shirt *down*." She pushed his hand away from his shirt.

"You're right. I don't want to cause a stampede."

She headed for the door. "In your dreams."

That was another problem. She was infiltrating those, too. "We both know it's my reality." That little reminder was for his sake, not hers.

She spun around, eyes shooting daggers. "Can we *not* discuss your revolving bedroom door tonight?"

"Chill, babe. Why're you so touchy?"

"Because I just want to have a regular night with my best friend and not think about those things. Is that too much to ask?"

Whoa. This unsettled Sidney was new, too, and he didn't like seeing her uncomfortable because of shit he said. The mission must *really* be taking a lot out of her, and cousin or not, no guy was worth that trouble. He draped an arm over her shoulder. "I hear you, babe. Tonight we're just two buddies having a good time. Fuck everyone else."

They headed inside the dimly lit bar, greeted by music and the din of conversation. Gunner looked over the crowd. As usual, there was a mix of customers and no shortage of black leather jackets and vests with Dark Knights patches. He'd worn his leather vest, too, and he felt a familiar sense of pride as he lifted his chin in acknowledgment of other members looking his way. His father was across the room talking with Starr, a waitress who sometimes hung out with them. Leah was serving a table a few feet away, and he spotted Baz and Evie sitting at the bar. As he and Sidney made their way over, he caught his mother's eye at the far end of the bar, where she was making a drink for a customer. Her lips curved into a loving smile.

"It's about time," Evie said as they approached. "Did you get lost on the way here?"

"Sorry." Sidney shrugged off her jacket and climbed onto a stool as their father came through the crowd. "The diva took his time getting all gussied up."

Baz chuckled. "Gunner's always been a bit girly."

"And we love him for embracing his feminine side." Their father clapped a hand on Gunner's back, his ever-present smile shining in his bright blue eyes. "Good to see you, son." Conroy Wicked was a tough biker with collar-length silver hair, dimples his children had all inherited, and movie-star good looks, but he was playful by nature, like Gunner and Baz. Ashley had been that way, too. He put an arm around Sidney, hugging her against his side as he kissed the top of her head. "How's it going, sweetheart?"

Sidney beamed, her love for his father radiating off her. "I'm good. How are you?"

His father looked at his wife heading their way. "That gorgeous woman still lets me call her mine, which makes me pretty damn lucky. How'd the adoption events go today?"

"Great," Gunner answered. "We picked up a lot of applications."

"I'm pretty sure one isn't valid." Sidney eyed Gunner as his mother joined them at the bar. "The woman wrote *Dwayne can call me if he needs anything* and underlined *anything* three times. She also put three hearts around her phone number."

His father grinned. "Sounds like someone wants to adopt my boy instead of a dog."

Gunner rolled his shoulders back. "I'm not up for adoption, but I do enjoy playdates." As he said it, he realized he was in big trouble, because the only person he wanted a playdate with was rolling her beautiful green eyes.

"What is it with you Wickeds and fear of commitment?" Evie looked between Baz and Gunner.

"I can't answer for Baz," Gunner said. "But I like my life the way it is. I don't see any reason to look at tomorrow until the sun shines on the new day."

"Except where the animals are concerned," his father pointed out.

"Well, yeah. Sid and I are all they've got." Gunner winked at Sidney.

"It's *all* about the animals," Sidney agreed.

"I don't get it. You guys are all about love, loyalty, and brotherhood with the club, but when it comes to settling down, you're hands-off." Evie looked at his parents. "Did something happen to them when they were young?"

His mother smiled. "No, honey. Everyone moves at a different pace. These boys see all that the world has to offer, and they don't want to miss any of it."

Evie elbowed Baz. "You hear that? Even your mom knows you like to get laid."

"Ow." Baz rubbed his ribs. "It's not a secret."

"I don't think it's all about sex." His mother looked at his father and said, "Men are complicated, but when a wild one settles down, you know they're all in, heart and soul, because they found their special person more exciting, more grounding, and more *everything* than anyone else who has crossed their path. They've found their ride or die, and let me tell you, those men are worth the wait." She smiled at Leah as she approached behind Evie.

"I didn't say *I* wanted one of them," Evie said. "If I wanted a Wicked, I would have gone for Tank when he was single. He didn't flirt with every woman who walked by."

"Hey, now. That's my man you're talkin' about, and he is *very* taken." Leah put her hand on her barely there belly.

They all laughed.

"Speaking of Papa Tank." His mother's expression softened as Tank came up the stairs from the restaurant, carrying Junie in one arm and Rosie in the other. His serious dark eyes zeroed in on Leah. Junie's red spiral curls framed her adorably serious, fair-skinned face as her gaze moved scrutinizingly over the crowd, while Rosie's golden-brown curls were pinned up in two fluffy pigtails, her light-brown apple cheeks glowing as she bounced on Tank's thick arm, waving and calling out, "Mama! Connie! Gingy! Gunny! Bazzie! Siddy! Evie! We went on a date!"

"Wosie, stop yelling," Junie chided her.

Tank grinned. "It's okay, Twitch. Cheeky's just excited." He dipped his head to kiss Leah. "Hi, gorgeous."

Gunner hadn't seen his brother smile like that for too many years to count, and Leah looked at Tank with so much love, he could feel it billowing between them. Tank had two inches on Gunner and Baz, and a solid thirty pounds of muscle. Nearly every inch of him was tattooed. To say his appearance was intimidating was an understatement. Gunner hadn't thought anyone could break through the walls Tank had built around himself after they'd lost Ashley. Before he and Leah got together, Tank hadn't thought about tomorrow either, but now he was always thinking months ahead for Leah and the girls.

As Rosie reached for Leah, Tank said, "We're not staying. The girls just wanted to kiss you good night."

"I'm glad they did." Leah kissed Rosie, then leaned in to kiss Junie.

"Papa Tank's gonna wead to us while we're in the bath," Junie said.

"That'll be fun." Leah looked at Tank and the kids the way Sidney looked at every new dog they got at the rescue, like they were the most precious and spectacular beings on the planet.

"Look at our new stowies!" Rosie exclaimed. Tank had told the girls that each of his tattoos told a story, and they'd called them *stories* ever since. She and Junie held up their arms, showing off drawings of the Easter bunny holding flowers, surrounded by colorful eggs. "Papa Tank dwawed 'em!"

As everyone fawned over the girls, Rosie talked a mile a minute about their stories and their earlier visit to Tank's tattoo shop, Wicked Ink. Gunner glanced at Sidney as she took Junie into her arms.

Junie ran her hand down Sidney's arm. "How come you

don't have any stowies?"

"Sometimes stories are private." Sidney glanced at Gunner with a secret smile in her eyes.

Don't worry, babe, your secret's safe with me. He found himself cataloging that look just as he had her crooked smile and felt another tug in his chest.

Sidney nuzzled kisses on Junie's cheek, earning sweet giggles, and man, that tweaked something inside him, too. He'd spent countless hours talking with Sidney about their lives over the years, and she'd never talked about getting married or having babies the way other girls did. She'd been all about the here and now, like him.

Until Zander piqued her interest. She wasn't talking about marriage and babies, but she had mentioned seeing a future with him. He wondered what it was about his cousin that had spurred her into wanting more.

Tank sidled up to him. "Why do you look like you've never seen Sid before?"

"Do I? Hell if I know. I was just thinking that Junie's almost as big as she is."

"Is that what you're going with?" Tank smirked. "Yeah, I'm not thinking about getting my girl naked, either."

Damn, am I that transparent? "Shut up, asshole." They fell into feigned punches and joking around.

"A'right, you two," their father said.

Tank and Gunner turned those feigned punches on him, and their mother said, "Get 'em, Con."

When Tank left with the girls, Leah said, "I need to get back to work, but the corner table by the window is clearin' out. You might want to snag it before someone else does." She went to the bar to go over a drink order with his mother as Baz and

Evie pushed to their feet, drinks in hand.

"Sid and I will be right over. I'm going to make our drinks." As Baz and Evie went to the table, Gunner went around the bar.

"You're waiting on me for a change?" Sidney teased. "I like this."

"I'm kind of liking it, too," his father said. "It's been a long time since I've seen you wait on a girl."

Gunner knew his father was thinking about Ashley, the only other girl he'd ever waited on. He leaned on his palms, and in his best old-school bartender voice, the one he'd used when he and Ashley were kids, he said, "What can I get you, *shhweet-heart?*"

A knowing spark flared in Sidney's eyes. "The usual." She smacked the bar and leaned forward. "And make it a double, *bah-tendah.*"

He'd told Sidney all of his stories about Ashley over the years, but they hadn't talked about when he used to play bartender for her in forever. Damn, he loved that she'd remembered what his sister used to say and exactly how she'd said it. Emotions brimmed in his father's eyes, warring with his confused expression as his gaze moved over Gunner's shoulder. Gunner didn't need to look to know he was looking at the picture of Gunner at ten or eleven years old, standing where he was now, grinning like a fool, his hair hanging in his eyes as Ashley, who would have been eight or nine, sat on her knees on the stool, leaning over the bar as she'd said, *And make it a double, bah-tendah,* meaning put two cherries in her drink.

When his father's gaze landed on him with a question in his eyes, Gunner said, "Sid knows all my secrets, Pop."

Sidney's eyes widened. "I didn't know that was a secret, but I'm honored that you shared it with me."

His father put his hand on hers, giving it a squeeze. "Thanks for the memory, darlin'." He hiked a thumb at her, looking at Gunner. "Ash would have loved this one."

Sidney had been such a big part of his life for so long, it felt like she and Ashley *had* known each other. "Yeah, she would've."

"Con." His mother waved his father over to the other end of the bar.

"Work calls. You kids have fun tonight."

Gunner made their drinks, and as he carried them around to Sidney, she waved to Steph, coming through the door with Blaine and Zander, and pointed them toward the table where Baz and Evie were sitting.

Zander winked at Sidney, and she smiled.

Gunner gritted his teeth and handed her a glass with two cherries in her beer. "Ready?"

She turned that infectious smile on him. "You do everything a little better than anyone else, you know that?"

"A *lot* better. In *and* out of the bedroom." He couldn't stop his competitive side from coming out. And that wasn't the worst of it. There was no denying the part of him that wanted to show her just how much better he was, and he knew he had to get that in check before it got out of control.

SIDNEY'S WORLD FELT right again. The table was covered with baskets of fries and half-empty platters of wings and nachos. She sat between Gunner and Steph, bobbing her head to the beat of the music and talking with Baz and Blaine.

Madigan and Marly had shown up a little while ago, and they were on the dance floor with Evie. Zander was chatting up a brunette at the bar, and Gunner was eating nachos off Sidney's plate. This was *exactly* what Sidney had needed. A normal night with Gunner and their friends without trying to be someone she wasn't. Only this was better, because girls had been checking out Gunner all night, and he hadn't given them more than a cursory glance. She couldn't remember him ever doing that.

"I heard you got Justice and Cuffs to do the shoot," Blaine said.

"She sure did." Gunner reached in front of her to grab fries from Steph's plate.

"Cuffs asked if he could wear a holster and his underwear, and when I said no, he said he'd be happy to forgo the underwear." Sidney shook her head.

Blaine laughed. "That'd sell a lot of calendars, but not as many as my picture will sell."

"Nobody's wearing underwear or a holster. This is a family-friendly calendar." Sidney leaned back as Gunner reached for more of Steph's fries.

Steph slapped his hand. "Get your own fries. You've been stealing mine since we were six."

"Exactly." Gunner reached for more, and she smacked him again. "Come on, Steph. Yours taste better than mine."

"Know what really tastes good?" Steph shook her fist at him. "A knuckle sandwich."

Baz chuckled. "Sid, you'd better rescue your boy before Steph takes him down."

"Blaine, hand me that basket." Sidney pointed to another basket of fries at the far end of the table. When Blaine handed it to her, she put it down in front of Steph and took Steph's basket and plopped it in front of Gunner. "Okay?"

Gunner put his arm around her. "My girl *always* has my back."

That made her feel good all over.

"She just knows how to placate a child." Steph ate a few fries from her basket, frowned, and reached for Gunner's fries.

He pulled his basket out of her reach. "Admit it. They taste better when they're someone else's."

"Never." Steph plucked a fry from her own basket and ate it in pure defiance.

"Ohmygod, you two." Sidney took the two baskets and poured them onto her plate. "Share nicely, or you're both going to time-out."

As they all laughed, Marly, Madigan, Evie, and Zander returned to the table.

"I bet the blonde that's been eyeing Gunner all night would like to give him a time-out," Blaine said.

Sidney's stomach knotted, and she steeled herself for Gunner to get up to flirt with the girl.

"What're you talking about?" Gunner asked.

Blaine motioned toward a buxom blonde standing by the bar openly eyeing Gunner. As everyone else turned to check her out, Gunner tightened his hold on Sidney's shoulder, winked at her, and ate more fries. She was as floored as she was relieved, and she knew she was grinning like a fool. But there was no stopping it. After the week they'd had and that *almost* kiss that was still wreaking havoc with her emotions, she didn't know if she could handle watching him pick up another woman.

"Okay, *wow*. She is gorgeous," Evie said.

"Dude, you should definitely tap that," Zander said.

Gunner popped another fry in his mouth. "I'm not feeling

it tonight."

Sidney wanted to do a happy dance, to spin this into the beginning of something bigger for her and Gunner. But she knew better and took it for the night of friendship that it was, even if her heart was hoping for more.

"Sid, check his temperature. Is he sick?" Madigan teased.

"Seriously. What's up with you?" Zander asked.

Gunner took a drink of his beer. "Can't a guy hang with his friends without needing to get laid?"

The guys exchanged perplexed glances.

"The rest of you should take lessons from him." Evie looked at the girls. "Am I right?"

They nodded in agreement.

"Think of our extracurricular activities as promotional efforts for the calendar," Zander suggested. "You know all the women I get with will buy it, and that's just about every woman in here. You signed me up for February, right, Sid? I've got my cupid thong all picked out."

"*Ew!*" Madigan cringed, and everyone laughed.

"Nobody's going to be looking at you," Gunner said. "They'll be too busy lining up to get an eyeful of this." He flexed his biceps. "I'm sure Sid is giving me December, because no other page would do my package justice."

"That little thing?" Baz scoffed. "They'd need a microscope to find it. The sad thing is, you guys need to rely on sexual promises that I bet you don't live up to, to get girls. All I have to do is look at them and they fall to their knees."

Evie rolled her eyes. "Puking, maybe."

"Only if they *choke* on you-know-what." Baz laughed, and Evie swatted his arm.

Gunner pointed a French fry at Baz. "For the record, pretty

boy, I've never broken a promise in my life."

"And we all know my reputation is stellar." Zander flashed a big-ass grin. "You tell women I'm going to be in the calendar, and you'll sell out, like always."

"I'll settle this once and for all." Blaine pushed to his feet and held his hands up. "Excuse me, ladies. I'm going to be featured in the Wicked Animal Rescue calendar that goes on sale in June. All proceeds will go to the rescue. Who's buying one?"

The women in the bar cheered, calling out, "Me" and "I am," and Blaine blew them all kisses.

"As good-looking as we are, I'm afraid we might *all* get blown away this year." Gunner looked at Sid. "You want to give them your news?"

"What news?" She had no idea what he was talking about.

"That you're going to be in the calendar," Gunner reminded her.

She rolled her eyes.

"That's awesome," Madigan exclaimed. "It's about time you showed yourself off, hot stuff."

"I'm not showing myself off. I'm wearing jeans, a rescue T-shirt, and my leather jacket, like always."

Marly waved a finger at Sidney. "You are *not* hiding those assets."

"You're right, she's not." Gunner cocked a grin. "I called Dixie and asked her to put together a few outfits from Jace's Leather and Lace line for her."

"Now we're talking." Zander set a lustful gaze on Sidney. "You, all wrapped up in leather and lace? *Mm-mm.* I'll buy a calendar for every room in my house."

She was about to make a smart-ass comment when she remembered she was supposed to be into him. Before she could figure out something else to say, Gunner glowered at him. A shiver of delight ran through her. She didn't know if he was jealous or just being protective, but it didn't matter. She loved it either way.

"I want new Leather and Lace clothes for the shoot, too," Madigan said. "It's the hottest clothing line around. Would it be rude if I called Dixie, too?"

"If you call her, order me some. I could use a little more leather and lace in my life." Marly took a sip of her wine.

Blaine raised his brows. "I'd like to see that."

"That makes two of us," Baz added.

"Would you two stop drooling over Marly?" Evie snapped.

Zander chuckled. "Yeah, Blaine. One at a time. Get in line behind me."

"Dream on, Zan." Blaine put an arm around Marly. "She doesn't want a kid."

"You're right. I want a *man* like *that* one." Marly pushed to her feet, and they all followed her gaze to a tall guy wearing a black leather jacket and carrying a motorcycle helmet breaking through the crowd, his jaw tight, brooding eyes trained on the bar.

Madigan jumped to her feet. "You guys go back to drooling over Marly and keep her busy."

"*Hey,*" Marly complained.

Madigan giggled. "I'll flip you for him."

Marly put her hand on her hip. "You're not even looking for a boyfriend."

"Who said anything about a boyfriend?" Madigan dramatically flicked her hair out of her face. "Love's not for me, but I'm not dead."

"*Madigan*," Blaine warned. "Anyone know who that is?"

Zander shook his head.

"Never seen him before," Gunner said.

"I'll go find out," Marly said.

Blaine rose to his feet and put a hand on Marly's and Madigan's shoulders, pushing them down to their seats, his eyes never leaving the guy at the bar. "That's *not* the guy for either of you."

"What the hell, Blaine?" Marly snapped.

"He's right. That dude looks shady," Baz said.

Madigan crossed her arms. "To people who don't know you, you guys look shady, too."

"Not like him," Sidney said. "Mads, he looks very guarded."

"I agree," Steph said. "He's hot, but he definitely gives off a don't-fuck-with-me vibe."

"As if Tank doesn't?" Madigan pointed out. "Zander, help me out here."

"No can do, sis. That's not a guy who's looking for company." Zander took a drink and glanced across the room at a cute brunette. "But *that* beauty looks like my date for tonight." He finished his drink and stood up. "Catch y'all another time."

Tension rolled off Gunner as Zander walked away. Sidney looked at him curiously, but he just sat up taller, jaw clenched tight.

"There is *such* a double standard around here." Madigan grabbed her glass and took a drink.

Blaine put his arm around her. "You're right. Because you're important to us, and we want to protect you."

"If you start spouting biker-princess shit, I'll punch you," Madigan warned.

Sidney laughed.

"Come on, let's dance it off." Marly pulled Madigan up to her feet, and they headed for the dance floor.

Blaine followed them, planting himself at the edge of the dance floor between the brooding stranger at the bar and the girls.

"Mads is gonna love that," Steph said under her breath.

Sidney knew how the guys' overprotectiveness bothered the other girls, but she also knew they were thankful for it, the same way she was. Gunner had been that way with her since they'd first met, and while it had taken some getting used to, she'd grown to appreciate it. But then again, she'd never really been on the hunt for a guy, so she never felt hindered by his protective nature. But plenty of guys had hit on her in the military, and he'd let it be known that if they messed with her, they messed with him. It brought her a certain level of safety, and that was never a bad thing.

Baz continued watching the guy at the bar, and Steph moved to the chair beside him, giving Baz her thoughts on the guy.

Sidney ate a fry, and Gunner leaned closer, talking quietly. "Sorry about Zan."

"What do you…?" *Crap.* She was supposed to act interested in Zander, so she mustered as much disappointment as she could. "It's okay. Old habits die hard, I guess."

"You sure you've got your sights set on the right guy?"

She gazed into his thoughtful eyes, hating that she was keeping a secret from him and wishing she could pour her heart out. But she couldn't take that risk. At least she didn't have to lie to answer. "I'm certain that the guy I want is the perfect man for me."

His jaw tensed, and he reached for his beer.

The song "What I Got" by Sublime came on, and she gasped, at the same moment Gunner said, "That's our song, babe." The tension she'd seen only seconds earlier disappeared as they began singing the lyrics they'd made up forever ago. *"Every single morning, running 'round the streets. Looking for those four-leggeds to bring home with me. Gotta find a dog, a dog who needs a home. Gotta find a dog who don't wanna be alone."*

Sidney rocked to the beat, singing, "I got a German shepherd, and I bought him some bling."

Gunner smacked his chest with both hands, keeping up the beat. "I can ride a bike like a motherfuckin' king."

They laughed, dancing in their seats as they sang. Sidney whipped her hair around as Gunner played the air guitar. Baz and Steph joined in, singing the real lyrics and laughing hysterically when Gunner sang about crying if his dog got lost and Sidney sang about promising to find his dog because *friendship is what we got.* When the song ended, everyone sitting around them applauded, and Sidney realized half of the bar had been watching them. She buried her face in Gunner's chest, all of them laughing.

"You guys are a riot," Steph said.

"You really are two of a kind," Baz said.

Sidney took a drink. "Two fools, no doubt."

"Hey, we're the coolest fools around." Gunner hooked an arm around her neck.

"I'm the coolest," Sidney said. "*You* make fun of Justin Bieber, and that takes you down a notch."

"I can see you guys fifty years from now," Steph said. "You'll still be living together in that old farmhouse with twenty dogs and thirty cats, singing made-up lyrics. Gunner's revolving bedroom door will have broken off the hinges, and Sid will still be making his coffee."

"He'll still be eating off her plate and scaring off her boyfriends," Baz added with a chuckle.

"And she'll be picking up his little blue pills from the drugstore." Steph giggled.

"I will *not* be picking up his little blue pills." *Unless they're for our benefit.*

Gunner smirked. "That sounds like an absolutely perfect life to me."

She scowled. "I am *not* buying your Viagra."

"You won't have to. I'm a Wicked." He high-fived Baz.

Sidney couldn't help but laugh at the man who had no idea he held her heart in those very big hands.

Chapter Seven

"WE'RE GOING WITH full names again on the calendars, the way we usually do, right? Real name, road name, and then the name of the dog they're holding?" Tori asked.

"Yes, and Madigan wants her name to read *Madigan 'Mads' Wicked.*" It was Tuesday afternoon, and Sidney was at the front desk with Tori going over the details for the calendar and the schedule for the photo shoot. It had been a great week so far. Tori had worked through several of the applications that had come in during the meet and greets, and two of the families had already picked up their new pets. Three more, including Kent, were coming tomorrow and Thursday.

As they went over the schedule for who was posing with which dog, Sidney thought about the other reason she was having such a good week. She hadn't been trying to gain Gunner's attention the last few days, and they'd been spending even more time together. Sunday afternoon they'd gone for a long motorcycle ride along the coast and had come home after dark and watched a movie. When they'd seen Zander at the gym Monday morning, Gunner had told her *not* to flirt with him. He'd said that Zander was used to women throwing themselves at him, and it would be more intriguing if she played hard to get. It was a good thing she wasn't trying to use Gunner's advice on him over the last few days, because she didn't even know how to play hard to get with him. Especially after last night, when they'd gone shopping for Easter presents for Junie and Rosie. They'd decided to get Junie a stuffed animal, and Gunner had cuddled at least ten of them against his broad chest, making sure to find the softest one that wasn't too big or too small. Seeing her big, burly bestie doing something so sweet and thoughtful had only made her want him even more. They'd chosen a stuffed bear and had found a black leather vest in the doll section to fit it. Since Junie wanted to be a tattooist, they'd also bought her washable markers to draw on the bear's arms. For Rosie, Tank and Leah's little chatterbox, they'd found a talking doll with light brown skin and pigtails that looked so much like her, they had to get it.

Tori looked over the list. "You gave yourself Twinkles. I love her."

"I do, too. But she'll have to wear a diaper for the shoot. I don't want to have to change my clothes a bunch of times. Which reminds me, I asked everyone to bring a change of clothes just in case."

"Remember last year when Bubba peed on Preacher's leg?" Tori laughed. Bubba was an old bulldog that had been turned in to the rescue after his owner had passed away.

"Yeah. Poor Bubba didn't know what to think when Preacher got down on all fours and went nose to nose with him. But it made for a cute picture."

Just as they turned to look at the picture of Preacher and Bubba hanging on the wall by the door, the door opened and Gunner walked in.

Sidney's pulse quickened.

His brows slanted. "Why are you two staring at me?"

Because you're everything I want and so much more, and I want to kiss you so badly I dream about it every night. A sly grin curved Gunner's lips, and for a split second Sidney worried she'd accidentally said it out loud.

"Here, let me give you a better view." He turned around and wiggled his butt.

"Get over yourself," Tori said. "We were looking at the picture of Preacher and Bubba."

"Yeah, right." He handed Sidney an orange Gatorade. "You've been running around so much, I thought you could use this."

Melt. Melt. Melt. "Thanks." Suddenly parched, she opened it and took a sip, wondering how he'd known before she had.

He glanced at the papers on the desk. "Did you figure out everyone's months yet?"

"Yeah. It's all done. You have October." *The month we met.* "And I gave you Chappy, since he has to be handled more carefully than the others."

"Cool, babe. That's our month, and I love Chappy."

She was thrilled that he'd remembered.

"What month are you taking?" he asked.

"December, with Twinkles. I ordered diapers and the cutest red-and-white holiday diaper cover for her."

"That's great. *Tinkles* needs them."

She glowered at him.

He chuckled. "I won't call her that as long as you don't give Zander February. I don't want to see him in a damn cupid thong."

Neither do I.

"I do!" Tori giggled.

Gunner looked empathetically at Sidney.

Ugh. She didn't know how much longer she could keep up this ruse. She tried to sound disappointed. "Doesn't everybody?"

"Every girl with a beating heart," Tori said. "I can't wait to see Justice, too. Can you imagine that man shirtless, with a tie hanging over one shoulder and an adorable dog in his arms? *Yum.* I'd be happy to oil him up for the shoot."

"Do we really need to hear this every year?" Gunner asked.

Sidney had never been one to drool over men the way other women did. But as she admired Gunner's sharp jawline and the alluring blue eyes that had been looking at her a little differently lately, a little closer, she thought, *Until you.*

"Justice wasn't even in the calendar last year," Tori reminded him.

"No shit." He pulled his ringing phone from his pocket and glanced at it. "But you said the same thing when we had Roman in the calendar." Roman was a Nomad, a member of the Dark Knights who didn't claim affiliation to any particular chapter.

"I *love* Roman. He's so big and muscly. I'd like to oil him up, too." Tori sighed dreamily as Gunner answered his phone.

"Hey, Steph, what's up?" Gunner paced, listening. "Did you call Cuffs?" He paused. "Good. I'll be right there." He stopped pacing, eyes narrowing as he listened to Steph. "I'm sure you are, but I need to see it with my own two eyes."

"Is everything okay?" Sidney asked after he ended the call.

"Steph got a text from Bethany. She said she's thinking about coming home for good."

"That's great news," Tori said.

"I hope she means it this time." Sidney knew how disappointed Steph had been in the past when Bethany had said the same thing but hadn't even shown up.

"I'll believe it when I see it," Gunner said. "I'm going to see Steph."

"Can I do anything?" Sidney asked.

"I don't think so. Steph sounded fine. She doesn't get her hopes up anymore. I just want to make sure, you know?"

"Yeah. I get it. Tell Steph I'm thinking about her."

"I will." He headed for the door but glanced at Sidney over his shoulder. "I should be back in a couple of hours. I'll grill some burgers tonight. Sound okay?"

Another night with you? "Perfect. But if Steph needs you, you should hang out with her. I can whip something up and bring you guys dinner later if you want."

"You're the best, MOS. I'll text you if I'm going to stay."

After he headed out, Tori said, "I love how he'll do anything for his friends. Is it weird that in my head I see him falling for you or Steph?"

"Yes, it's weird." *If I have it my way, he's going to be mine. He just doesn't know it yet.*

BY THE TIME Sidney finished with the animals for the night, it was almost seven. Gunner had texted a while ago to say Steph was doing fine and he was heading home, and she'd been looking forward to hanging out with him. As she walked up from the shelter, his truck came into view, filling her with happiness and reminding her of the first time she'd driven down the driveway and set her eyes on the magnificent property. The old farmhouse with its wide front porch was just like they'd talked about, surrounded by acres of lush grass and pockets of trees. Sidney liked to take the dogs to a private shady spot in the hours before they went home with their forever families to tell them how much she'd enjoyed caring for them and how wonderful their new lives were going to be. It might seem silly having that kind of conversation with a dog, but she liked to believe it helped them to know they were loved. She also liked to believe that her mother had done the same with her before she'd left for the last time.

As she crested the hill, she looked back at the buildings, which were also exactly like they'd talked about. Except they hadn't imagined Baz's veterinary clinic on the premises. But the clinic, and having his brother and Evie close by, made it even better. Gunner had made the dreams she'd thought she wouldn't live out for another thirty years a reality. If that wasn't love, she didn't know what was. If only he could see it, too.

Belleau ambled off the porch to greet her. "Hiya, big boy. What do you think? Will your daddy ever love me the way I love him? Or is all of this his definition of friendship?" She swore the old dog smiled. "I hope so, too." She kissed his snout. "Come on. Let's go eat."

When she walked through the door, the other dogs ran out of the kitchen. "Hi, guys." Granger went paws-up on her chest. "Whoa, buddy. I missed you, too."

Gunner walked out of the kitchen. *Granger.* He patted his thigh and Granger dropped to all fours and trotted over to him. "You're just in time to try on your clothes."

"What clothes?"

"The ones I ordered for you." He went into the kitchen and returned with a large box. "I expect a fashion show."

He handed it to her, and she looked at the black and gold

Leather and Lace logo on the label. Her nerves caught fire. She'd gotten curious after hearing Madigan's and Marly's reaction to the clothing line and had googled it. She'd never seen such sexy clothes. "You're kidding, right?"

"Nope."

Wickedness rose in his eyes, making other parts of her catch fire, which made her even more nervous. "I need to shower, and you're already making dinner. I'll try them on another day." *Or never.*

"I just got home. I haven't even started up the grill yet."

Why was she so nervous? They were just clothes. She could wear anything around Gunner, couldn't she? She wore her underwear around him, for Pete's sake.

He stepped closer, and a heat wave stroked over her skin. "No time like the present, MOS."

No way. Nope. She couldn't do it. "They probably won't fit. You don't even know what size I wear."

He cocked a brow. "Have you forgotten that I've had my hands *all* over your panties?"

"That is *not* something I'd forget." If her cheeks burned any hotter, she'd go up in flames.

"Come on, MOS. You know I've been inside your shirts, your jeans…"

The way he was talking, slowly and seductively, was turning her on, but that tease in his eyes had her scrambling to figure out what he—*laundry.* "Stop making laundry sound like"—*everything I want from you*—"like something else."

He laughed.

"I need to take a shower." *A very cold one.*

He put a hand on her lower back, guiding her down the hallway that led to her room. "Go do your thing, babe." He leaned against the wall and crossed his legs at the ankles. "I'll wait here for my fashion show."

"I thought you were going to make dinner." *Please go make dinner.*

"Dinner can wait."

It was obvious he wasn't going to let her off the hook. "I hate you right now." She stalked toward her room.

"You'll love me when all the girls are jealous of you at the photo shoot."

She didn't care if the *girls* were jealous. She only cared if he...*My mission!* She stopped walking, inhaling deeply, filling her lungs with as much courage as she could muster, and glanced over her shoulder at her pushy man. "Who cares if the girls are jealous? The only one I care about is—"

"*Yeah*, I know who it is." He pushed from the wall and strode away.

She was shocked that it had worked.

But now she had to wear the clothes, and if they were anything like she'd seen on the website, she was screwed. She grumbled at herself as she showered, unable to believe she'd agreed to do the photo shoot at all, much less let Gunner buy her clothes to wear from *that* place. After her shower, she wrapped a towel around herself and went into the bedroom, staring at the box like it had a disease. She reminded herself that she was doing this to win over Gunner and opened the box, peering hesitantly inside.

The clothes were wrapped in black and gold tissue paper. *Nice touch.* She carefully unwrapped a sexy black dress with a deep V that plunged from the low-cut neckline to about navel height and laced up the center. That was not going on her body.

She set it aside and unwrapped leather pants, strappy leather bralettes, and a leather miniskirt with zippers down both sides. She imagined Gunner unzipping them and shuddered with desire. She couldn't believe he'd bought all of this just so she could get Zander's attention.

She unwrapped another tissue-wrapped item and found a leather-and-lace bustier with a zipper down the front and a long strip of leather wrapped around the middle several times and secured in the front with a sexy silver clip that looked like a dagger. Everything was gorgeous, but she'd never worn anything like these clothes. She withdrew the last package from the box, and there was a card sticking out of the tissue paper. She opened it and read the handwritten message. *Sidney, these are not from the Leather and Lace line, but they're my favorite items outside of the line. Guaranteed to get you noticed by your special guy. Good luck! Dixie*

Sidney tried not to think about whether Gunner had told Dixie she'd set her sights on Zander and unwrapped the package, revealing skimpy black leather shorts with BIKER BOOTY stitched across the ass in silver. *Holy cow.* They were smaller than her boy shorts underwear. She couldn't imagine wearing them in public, but she'd met Dixie, and she knew the tall, tatted redhead wasn't afraid to strut her stuff.

Sidney was tough and confident, but these clothes took a different type of confidence. She needed to channel Madigan or Marly to pull these off.

Or even better, *Dixie.*

If that were Jace out there waiting for her, Dixie wouldn't mess around. She'd get her ass into the sexiest outfit she could find and get her man.

Sidney took a deep breath. *It's just like any other mission.* Only this time her heart was on the line. This was a chance to really turn Gunner's head, and she knew she couldn't half-ass it. She had to push away her insecurities and go *all in.*

Bees swarmed in her chest, bringing a wave of anxiety, but she forced herself to push past it all. Who knew if she'd ever get another chance like this? She closed her eyes, hands fisted, and tipped her face up, whispering, *"Please don't let me regret this."*

She went to her dresser and dug out a thong Madigan and Marly had convinced her to buy on one of their shopping excursions. They were so pushy. She tore off the tags, dropped her towel, and stepped into the thong. She felt naked, but that was the point, wasn't it? She snagged the booty shorts from the bed and held them up, trying to calm her racing heart. "Okay, Dixie, let's put your guarantee to the test."

She put them on, and they fit like a second skin. They felt *good.* Now she needed a shirt. Eyeing the tops spread out on her bed, she went for the corset. It fit like a glove, and she wound the strip of leather around her tiny waist about ten times, securing it with the sexy dagger clip. She wanted to see how it looked, but she was pretty sure she'd look like she was trying too hard. It took a ridiculous amount of courage for her to turn around and look in the full-length mirror.

"Holy shit." She looked *hot*, and that made her feel sexy. She ran her hands over the dip at her waist and the curves of her hips. When had she developed an hourglass figure? Even her boobs looked amazing. She palmed them and laughed at herself, but they felt good, too! She turned her back to the mirror— *Please look good, or at least passable*—and looked over her shoulder. The shorts revealed the curve of her ass and made her legs look a mile long. Excitement bubbled up inside her. Who knew she could look like that?

She ran to the dresser to get socks, and then into the closet to get her chunky black leather boots. After putting them on, she took one last look in the mirror, shook out her hair, and as she reached for the doorknob, she tossed a prayer up to the universe. *Please don't let him laugh at me.* She was so nervous, her skin prickled, but she forced herself to open the door and walk down the hall.

She heard Gunner pacing, and as she stepped into the living room, the dogs ran over, vying for her attention as Gunner turned around. She froze as his eyes widened, then narrowed as they raked slowly down her body, leaving a trail of heat that bowled her over.

His jaw tightened, and his chest expanded as his eyes shot up to hers, burning with unmistakable desire. "What the…? *That's* what she sent you?"

"Yeah." *And Dixie was right! It's working!* She tried to act cool despite her excitement. "Isn't it cute?"

He splayed his hands, tension rolling off him. "Where's the rest of it?"

"What do you mean?"

He motioned toward her. "I told her to send a few sexy outfits, not *lingerie.*"

She giggled, loving his frustration. "You don't like it? I think it's super cute. Look." She showed him her butt.

"Biker booty?" He groaned and turned his face to the side, cursing. *"No.* Just…*No."* He crossed his arms. "No fucking way are you wearing that to the photo shoot."

Loving the way his entire body flexed with restraint, she stepped closer, turning up the heat with feigned innocence that came far more easily than she could have hoped. "What do you mean? Don't you like how the corset hugs my waist? And check out my boobs. Don't they look amazing?" She wiggled her chest, and he gritted his teeth, looking up at the ceiling, bolstering her confidence even more. "You have to feel how soft the leather is." She grabbed his hand and put it on her hip.

His fingers tightened around her, and he gritted out, "*Fuck.*"

Sexual tension roared off him, and her body vibrated with it, spurring her on. "It feels nice, doesn't it?"

He tore his hand away like he'd been bitten. "Go put more clothes on, and cover your ass."

"My *ass*? Why? Zander's a total ass man. I think he'd really like these shorts." She had no idea where this brazenness was coming from, but she loved pushing his buttons.

His eyes narrowed. "So would every other asshole at the photo shoot."

"They're not assholes. They're your brotherhood."

He looked like he was either going to explode or pin her against the wall and kiss the hell out of her. *Yes, please!*

He pointed to the hallway, jaw clenched so tight it had to hurt.

Giggling, she turned to walk out with the dogs on her heels and glanced over her shoulder, catching him staring at her ass and *biting* his knuckle. It took everything she had not to cheer, *Yesyesyes!*

He cursed under his breath and barked, "Come." The dogs trotted over to him.

Sidney headed into her bedroom, wishing he'd give her the same command—and even more determined to make Gunner hers...*tonight.*

GUNNER WAS GOING to slaughter Dixie for sending those boner-inducing outfits. What the hell was she thinking? What was *he* thinking calling her in the first place? He was already having a hard time keeping his emotions in check, and now his cock was begging for a ride. He looked down at his hands, still able to feel Sidney's perfect hips in them. He paced, trying to get the image of her looking like his every fantasy out of his head. Only she wasn't just his fantasy. She was better, because she was *Sid.*

He heard her bedroom door open and her footsteps nearing the living room. He tried to rein in his emotions and looked down at his dick. *Behave.*

She walked into the room wearing a black bra-like leather top with several straps crisscrossing over her chest, bringing thoughts of other things he could do with those sexy leather straps. Her legs were wrapped in tight black leather pants riding low on her hips, exposing planes of sweet, tender flesh. This was not the girl he'd slid into the friend zone all those years ago. This was Sidney Carver 2.0, and he had the greedy desire to drag his tongue along her stomach and take those pants off with his teeth. His traitorous cock rose to greet the smoke show before him as she lifted one shoulder, eyeing him seductively and just a tad bashfully. *Hot. As. Sin.*

"What do you think?" She turned slowly, showing him her ass again.

"Leather has never looked so good" came out before he could think to stop it.

"Really?" Her eyes lit up, and she stepped closer.

Drawn to her like metal to magnet, he felt himself reaching for her hips again, needing to feel them filling his hands. He stopped short, fighting those carnal desires and silently cursing himself, gritting out, "Yeah. You look great."

Her eyes narrowed, and that bashfulness fell away, replaced with raw seduction. "Great, or too hot to resist?" She closed the gap between them, thrusting her chest forward so it skimmed his body, and her hips followed.

"*Sid*," he warned, gritting his teeth against the burning desire to touch and kiss and *take*.

"Don't *Sid* me. This is *my* mission, and it's time I took it to the next level." She grabbed his shirt, tugging him down so their lips were a whisper apart. "*Gunner—*"

The plea in her voice shattered his restraint, and he crushed his mouth to hers. Her lips were soft and eager, her mouth hot, wet, and so fucking addicting he couldn't get enough. Her mouth was exquisite. It was heaven and hell, innocence and sin. These weren't just kisses. They were the fucking master of all kisses. *She* was a fucking masterpiece, and he needed *more*. He lifted her into his arms, and she wound her legs around him, clinging to him as they ate at each other's mouths. His cock throbbed greedily, but his whole body was on fire. *Oh yeah, baby. You feel good.* She moaned and mewled, her sexy sounds sending electricity searing through him like lightning, unleashing the animal in him. He gripped her ass tighter with one hand, grabbing her hair with the other, kissing her rougher, more possessively, losing himself in the taste and feel of her. Feasting deliriously. He needed to strip her naked and devour every inch of her, to be buried deep inside her and feel her sweet, hot body wrapped around him. He wanted to hear her moaning his name, feel her clawing at his skin, begging for more. He headed out of the living room, stumbling over a dog, who yelped, sending the other dogs into a flurry and jerking him back to reality. He tore his mouth away, and it took a second for his brain and eyes to focus. Sidney was panting, her lips swollen and red from the force of their kisses. *Holy fuck. What have I done?* He lowered her feet to the floor, backing away from her, his head spinning.

She gazed at him as if in a fog and lifted her fingers to her lips. "That was—"

"A big fucking mistake."

Hurt flashed in her eyes.

"*Shit.* It's not you, Sid. It's *me.*" *I sound like a fucking cliché.* "I got carried away and wasn't thinking. I can't ruin our friendship just to get my rocks off." She looked like she was going to cry, and that made him sick. "I'm so sorry, babe." His mind scrambled for a way to erase what he'd done, but he could no sooner take it back than deny he wanted more. So much more, he didn't trust himself. He needed to get the hell out of there. "It'll never happen again. Just please don't fucking hate me."

He stormed out the front door and climbed onto his motorcycle, flying down the driveway, hoping to lose the motherfucker who might have just ruined things with the most important person in his life.

Chapter Eight

SIDNEY THOUGHT SHE'D used up all her courage last night, but after hours of trying to piece together her broken heart, she realized that was nothing compared to the courage she needed to muster this morning. When Gunner had kissed her, it hadn't been anything like she'd imagined it would be. She'd pictured a slow, sensual kiss where he'd look at her afterward with wonder, asking himself why it had taken so long for him to see her as his perfect match. But he'd kissed her rough and greedy, bringing out a part of her she hadn't even known existed. She'd felt the earth move. Hell, her heart had sprouted wings and she'd *soared* to the top of the world in the arms of the man she loved. She hadn't even tried to hold back and had kissed him with everything she'd had. Nothing had ever felt so good or so right.

But her *everything* hadn't been enough or had been all wrong, because he'd shattered her heart into a million painful pieces when he'd said that kissing her wasn't just a mistake but a *big fucking mistake*. If that wasn't enough to annihilate her, knowing if they'd taken it further, he would have just been *getting his rocks off* sure was. She'd tossed and turned all night, futilely trying to spin his words into something less hurtful. But even now, as she stepped out of the shower and dried off, the truth cut like shards of glass.

When she walked into the bedroom, Rosco whined and brushed against her leg. "I'm okay, buddy," she lied, petting him. All of the dogs had sensed something was wrong last night and had stuck to her like glue. It would have been hard to miss, considering after he'd walked out, she'd crumpled to the living room floor completely, utterly devastated.

She got dressed and put on her lucky black high-tops. She needed something to help her get through the day. Embarrassed that she'd brought this nightmare on herself, she avoided looking in the mirror as she dried her hair.

How was she going to face him when she couldn't even face herself? Why couldn't she just be like other girls who crushed on guys and never did anything about it?

She didn't have to search for the answer.

She wasn't raised to sit back and wait for life to work itself out. She was taught to go after what she wanted, and that lesson had never failed her until now. If only she could take it all back and find another way. She could have moved out and stopped hanging out with Gunner after work to avoid hearing about or seeing him with other women. But *no*, she'd wanted it all—a life she was passionate about with the man she loved.

In her head, she *knew* it was just a kiss, and Gunner was just a friend who wanted to remain that way. There was no crime in that. She should be thankful that he'd stopped them. It would have hurt more if they'd gone further and *then* he'd told her how he felt. She should be able to deal with it and move on, right? But her heart wasn't rational. That stupid organ had gotten her into this mess in the first place, and it was vying for even more heartache, desperately fighting against giving up, wanting to *convince* Gunner to love her as she loved him. But it was one thing to try to open his eyes to seeing her as a woman rather than just as his buddy. She'd truly believed that if he saw her that way, he'd realize how right they were for each other. It was a whole different ball game to try to convince his heart of something it didn't want, and *that* was a line she wouldn't cross.

If only it didn't hurt so bad.

Her grandfather would say, *Ain't no use fretting over a flooded pasture. Pick a new place and make it work.* She couldn't fathom a new place without Gunner in it.

Maybe she didn't need to.

She was a freaking marine, for Pete's sake. There was nothing she couldn't get through. She just needed to take it one minute at a time. She considered not making Gunner's coffee and slipping out the front door to go see her father, but she wasn't a jerk or a coward. She hadn't heard him come downstairs yet, so there was a good chance she could make his coffee and be gone before he even got up.

"Come on, Rosco." *Time to pull up my boy shorts and face the music.*

With her heart in her throat and determined not to let things get weird if she saw Gunner, she and Rosco headed down the hall, stopping abruptly at the entrance to the living room. She put out her hand, settling Rosco by her side as she took in Gunner, asleep on the couch, wearing the same clothes he'd worn last night. He was lying on his side with Granger tucked against him, Opha Mae sleeping on his stomach, and Belleau stretched out between his legs. Belleau's head rested on his crotch, and one leg lay on his thigh. Seeing all that love and not being part of it nearly took her to her knees.

Forget making coffee. She had to get out of there. Belleau

lifted his head, awakening Granger and Opha Mae. Snowflake popped up behind Belleau, and Gunner groaned as the animals hopped off him. She hurried toward the door.

"*Sid?*"

She froze, squelching the urge to dart outside, and *tried* to act normal, focusing on the dogs as Gunner climbed off the couch. "Come on, guys, let's go out."

Gunner came to her side as the dogs went out the door. "I'm glad I caught you. Can we talk about last night?"

"There's no need. We're good." Avoiding eye contact, she grabbed her keys from the table and reached for her leather jacket, but he snagged it.

"You're not having coffee?"

I'd probably choke on it. "No. I'll get some at my dad's."

He stepped between her and the door. "Look at me, MOS."

She reluctantly lifted her eyes, and her knees weakened at the storm of emotions looking back at her. His jaw tightened, and she swallowed hard, telling herself to hold it together.

"You're everything to me, Sid. I hate that I kissed you and jeopardized our friendship. I don't even know what I was thinking. You're into my *cousin*, and more importantly, you're an endgame girl, while I'm a fucking once-and-done, twice-at-best guy. I just got lost in the moment, and I'll never—"

"I *get* it," she snapped, gutted. "You don't have to spell it out for me. We made a mistake. Let's move on. I've got to get to my dad's. Can I have my jacket, please?"

He held it open, helping her put it on. Then he pulled her into his arms, hugging her so tight she could barely breathe. If his words weren't enough to destroy her, being in his arms was.

"I love you, MOS, and I'm glad we're cool."

Nail, meet coffin. "Me too," she managed, and headed out

the door, calling Rosco from the other side of the yard, needing his unconditional love now more than ever.

As she put him in the car, Gunner jogged down the porch steps. "Wait."

Her breath caught on a flutter of hope that maybe he'd changed his mind.

"Rosco didn't get a chance to eat." He handed her a brown paper bag she hadn't noticed he was carrying. "I put his bowls and some food in there."

Disappointment swamped her. "Thanks. I can't believe I forgot to feed him."

"Don't feel bad." He opened her car door, and as she climbed in, he said, "One kiss from me can rattle a girl for weeks."

It would be easier if she could hate him for that arrogance, but *that* was who he was, who she'd fallen in love with. Besides, she couldn't hate him for being honest. The most she could do was try to save her pride. "Dream on, Gunny. It wasn't that good."

"You're not a very good liar." He winked and closed her door.

Tell me something I don't know.

As she drove away, she realized she'd never lied to him until she'd tried to get his attention—and she'd done far too good a job of both.

BY THE TIME Sidney drove down her father's quiet lane, she was as sad and confused as she was pissed off with herself. None of which made for good breakfast companionship. She tried to tuck all those emotions away as she parked behind his motorcycle in the driveway. Her father had taught her to always do the right thing. He'd probably be ashamed of her for lying, even though she knew he'd done his fair share of wrong things. Her grandfather had told her stories about when her father was young and rebellious. He'd gotten into trouble at school, and every day after helping on the farm, he'd take off on a beat-up motorcycle he'd bought and restored the summer after he'd turned seventeen and stayed out carousing most of the night. That rebellious streak was what had hooked her mother into marrying him. It was only after her mother had gotten pregnant with Sidney that her father had straightened up, which, according to her grandfather, was one of the reasons her mother had abandoned them just two years later.

They'd moved so often when she was growing up, she'd learned not to get attached to houses or neighbors. But in the last three years, her father's quaint cedar-sided cottage, with its spotty-grass-and-sand yard, pitch pine trees, and massive rose hip bushes had become his home, and in turn, the place that most felt like *coming home* for her, second only to Gunner's farmhouse.

She grabbed the bag with Rosco's food. "Let's go, buddy."

As they made their way up the walkway, her father came out the front door. He was wearing one of his old flannel shirts over a black T-shirt, jeans, scuffed black boots he'd probably had for twenty years, and a warm smile that nearly brought tears to her eyes. Brian "Colonel" Carver was tall and athletic with pitch-black hair, save for around his temples, which had more gray than black. He had a salt-and-pepper beard and mustache, and beneath his shirts were broad, tattooed shoulders that had already carried a lifetime of burdens. He had keen dark eyes that had brimmed with worry when Sidney was injured. He'd stayed by her side at Walter Reed National Military Medical Center in Bethesda, Maryland, and had rented a house near the hospital for them during her recovery. She'd been his entire world forever, but she'd always hoped that one day he'd find love again.

Although if her current state was any indication of how love made a person feel, maybe he was better off without it.

Rosco hurried onto the porch, and her father got down on one knee to love him up, studying Sidney as she climbed the steps. He leaned closer to Rosco. "Hey, buddy, who pissed off Mom this morning?"

"I hate that you can still size me up in seconds."

"You've been my shadow since you were yay high." He pushed to his feet, holding his hand at his thigh, and then he embraced her. "I've missed you, Sidekick."

"Me too, Dad." She couldn't remember a time when he hadn't called her Sidekick, because that's what she'd always been to him. When she was growing up, he'd taken her everywhere he went: to the barbershop, the grocery store, to see friends.

He kissed the top of her head and continued hugging her for a minute longer, as he always did when they'd been apart for a while. He'd just gotten back from a two-week trip to Peaceful Harbor, Maryland, where he'd been consulting with a military contractor and had spent time with Reba's brother, Biggs Whiskey, the president of the Peaceful Harbor chapter of the Dark Knights, which Biggs's grandfather had founded.

She felt like a ten-year-old girl again, clinging to him after he'd come back from deployment, wanting to stay there just a little longer and soak in his surety. But she wasn't a kid anymore, and she was too pissed off at herself for screwing things up with Gunner to stand still, so she stepped out of his arms. "I want to hear all about your trip."

Her father's brows knitted. "Is that how you're playing it? Avoidance? That's not like you."

"There are certain things a father doesn't need to know."

He eyed the bag in her hands. "You got clothes in that bag?"

"*No.* Why would I have clothes? It's Rosco's food. I didn't have time to feed him."

"That's interesting."

"*Dad*," she warned. "Stop trying to psychoanalyze me."

"Just tell me this. Are we hiding your guns or hiding a body?"

She had to smile, because she knew the man who had taught her to always do the right thing would stand by her no matter what she'd done. "Neither *yet*, but if you don't stop questioning me, your body might need hiding."

"Attagirl. Stand your ground." He leaned closer, lowering his voice. "But whatever it is, you can trust me to keep it quiet."

He opened the door, and a heavenly scent surrounded them as they followed Rosco through the cozy living room into the kitchen, where the table was set for two.

"What did you whip up this morning?" Her father loved to cook.

He motioned to the pan on top of the stove, which held a concoction of eggs, pieces of bacon, and other savory ingredients. "Baked eggs with Swiss chard and green olives." He grabbed an oven mitt and pulled muffins out of the oven.

"*Mm.* Blueberry?" Her favorite.

"You know it."

"Everything looks amazing." She fed Rosco and petted his

head. "Go ahead, buddy. Dig in."

Her father transferred the food onto plates and carried them to the table. "Coffee or juice?"

"Coffee, by IV please."

"I thought it might be one of those mornings." He poured two cups, and they sat down to eat.

"Thanks for cooking." Sidney took a bite and closed her eyes for a second, savoring the taste. "Dad, this is so good. It tastes familiar, but I don't remember you making it for me. Have you?"

"Not since you were a little girl."

There was something in his voice that made her curious. "Well, I love it. What made you decide to make it again?"

He set down his fork with a thoughtful expression. "This was your mother's recipe, and last night when I was picking up groceries, I saw a woman who looked a lot like I'd imagine your mother might look now. One memory led to another, and I remembered how much you liked this dish."

"Really? I didn't even know she cooked."

"She was a phenomenal cook, and she taught me what I know." He ate a forkful of eggs. "She made this dish for me the morning after our first night together."

She wrinkled her nose. "That's a little too specific."

He smiled. "Sorry. You're right. But you should know that your mother was great at everything she did—except the thing that mattered most." He reached across the table and squeezed her hand. "That's her loss, baby. You're the best thing that has ever happened to me."

"Thanks, Dad." They'd never talked much about her mother. At least not that she could remember beyond her father saying that he'd loved her more than he'd ever loved anyone until Sidney had come along, and he hated that she'd left. She'd never reached out to Sidney, and Sidney had never had the urge to try to track down the woman who'd chosen to leave her behind. As they ate, it dawned on her that her father had been in a similar situation to the one she was in.

Sidney pushed her food around on the plate with her fork. "Can I ask you something about her?"

"Anything. You know that."

"You've always said that you loved her, but we've never talked about what it was like for you after she left. How did you move on?"

"It wasn't easy, but I didn't have a choice. When I got back from deployment, you were with my parents and she was gone without a trace. We were pretty wild kids. She'd been estranged from her parents for two years when we'd met. She was a teenage runaway, and she never talked about them or where she was from, and I was too overwhelmed to even think about trying to figure out how to track her down."

"Have you ever since?"

"No. I figured if you ever came to me and wanted to find her, we'd do it together. Do you want to?"

"No. Not at all, actually. That must have been so hard for you."

"It was rough. But she was like a fantasy who blew into my life, gave me *you*, and disappeared like the wind. I probably should have expected it based on her background. But we were just two kids who met at a concert when I was on weekend leave. We took each day as an adventure and never really looked back or talked about the past."

"I don't think we've ever talked about how or where you met."

"That's because I didn't want you knowing we met when we were sneaking into a concert, and the police caught us. We talked our way out of getting arrested and spent the rest of the weekend together. I fell madly in love with her that weekend, and we were married a month later."

"I can't picture you breaking into a concert."

"Back then I was just a reckless kid with no responsibilities." He was watching her intently, the way he did whenever they talked. "You asked about how I moved on, and to be honest, your mother saved me a lot of heartache by disappearing. I don't think I could have moved on if she'd stuck around. It would have been too hard to see her all the time and know I couldn't be with her. I loved her *too* much. That said, I'd have gladly suffered through it if it meant you could have her in your life."

"I know you would, but you've always been more than enough for me. I mean, I've had fleeting moments of wishing I had a mother to talk to or seeing Ginger and Reba with their kids and realizing what it might have been like to have a mom. But my mother wasn't like them. They'd never leave their kids or their husbands. Plus, I always had the coolest dad around *and* the best birthday cakes."

He chuckled. "That you have. Remember when you turned seven, and all you wanted was a cake that looked like one of your grandparents' foster dogs?"

"Millie." She laughed. "She was the sweetest poodle, and you did a great job on that cake."

"I had to make three just to get it right. But that's what you do for the people you love."

She thought about what he'd said. "You said you loved my mother too much. I didn't think that was possible." *But now I know better.*

"Neither did I. But on the flip side, I wouldn't want to be with someone who didn't want to be with me."

"I can understand that." *But I still want to be around Gunner, even if he doesn't love me like that. I just don't know how to make it stop hurting, or how to stop being angry at myself for royally screwing us up.*

"Do you want to talk about whatever you're not telling me?"

She met his concerned gaze. "I'm just mad at myself. I did something stupid that messed things up with a friend, and I don't know how to fix it." Gunner might have been joking around by the time she'd left, but she wasn't okay, and she couldn't imagine things not being awkward between them when she got back.

"What kind of something?"

"I'd rather not say." She didn't want to put him in the middle of their sticky situation. When she'd first met Gunner, her father had had him checked out, *because that's what fathers do.* He'd met him a few weeks later and had been pro-Gunner ever since.

"Okay. I respect that. How good of a friend is this person?"

The best. She trained her eyes on her plate, hoping her father wouldn't notice how much it hurt to think about it. "A really good one."

He was quiet for so long, she could feel him staring at her and knew he wanted to ask more questions. But she also knew he wouldn't push too hard.

"Well, in my experience, if this person is really a good friend, then whatever you did will be forgiven. It might take some time, but you'll get there."

"I know you're right, but how can I get from here to there if it hurts to see them?"

"That's tough without knowing how often you see this person."

"A lot." She met his gaze, and something in his eyes told her he knew who she was talking about.

His brows knitted. "In that case, a little distance goes a long way to bring perspective. You're welcome to stay here if you'd like."

Oh God, you do know.

"No, I'm fine where I am. It's not Gunner." She hated lying, but he and Gunner had church tonight, and she didn't need him going all protective father on Gunner in the middle of a Dark Knights meeting. "But maybe getting away to clear my head is a good idea." Putting some distance between her and Gunner might give her a chance to wrap her head around the reality that they were never going to be a couple. As awful as that was, she needed to come to grips with it, because Gunner and the rescue were her life, and she didn't want to give up their friendship or her job. But even if she *was* able to accept it, she knew she had to start thinking about moving out because her feelings weren't going to change, and she couldn't handle being in the same house with him while he was with someone else.

"I think that's a good idea," her father said. "You work seven days a week, and you never take time off."

"That's because I love what I do." *And who I do it with.* "Maybe I'll give Gram and Gramps a call. Do you think they'd mind if I visited?" Her grandparents' house had always been a safe place for her. She wouldn't be mollycoddled or bombarded with questions about why she needed to get away. Her grandparents were from a different generation, one where feelings were *worked out* on the farm, not talked out with others, and that sounded perfect to her.

"They'd be thrilled to see you. When are you thinking of going?"

"I'm not sure. I'm working with a dog that's recuperating from surgery, but he's far enough along that Gunner can handle working with him. The calendar photo shoot and Easter are this weekend." She couldn't imagine trying to act like everything was normal at the Easter egg hunt or at Easter dinner with Gunner's family. "Would you mind if I missed Easter?"

"Of course not. You need to put yourself first for a change."

She couldn't believe this was the turn her life had taken, running away from the people she loved. "I'll talk to Tori to see if she can line up extra volunteers for next week. If she can, then I'll call Gram and Grandpa to see if I can come Sunday and stay for a few days." She had a feeling even a few years wouldn't be enough time to come to grips with her new reality, but she had to try.

"Do you want me to go with you to see your grandparents?"

"No thanks." Rosco wandered over and put his chin on her leg. She kissed his head, thankful that he always knew when she needed him. "We've survived much bigger tragedies than"—*a broken heart*—"a bruised friendship. We'll get through this." *Even if I'm just not sure who I'll be when I come out the other side.*

If I come out the other side.

She looked at her father, still alone after all these years, and wondered if the pain of unrequited love ever really went away.

Chapter Nine

GUNNER SAT AT a table with his brothers and cousins in the old brick schoolhouse that had been converted into the Dark Knights' clubhouse, trying to focus on anything *but* the noise in his head about Sidney. His eyes were trained on the front of the room, where his uncle Preacher, the club president, and his father, the vice president, sat at the head table with the club secretary and treasurer, discussing club finances, prospects, and upcoming obligations with the members.

Gunner enjoyed everything about being a Dark Knight, from the black leather vests with patches signifying their brotherhood to the work they did to keep the community safe and the way they had each other's backs twenty-four-seven. Normally he listened to every word said at church, but tonight his thoughts kept spinning back to Sidney. He couldn't stop thinking about the kiss that had rocked his world or the look on her face afterward. She'd acted strange after coming home from seeing her father that morning, and Gunner had felt her father eyeing him since he'd walked into church. He wondered what had gone down over breakfast. Had she told her father that Gunner had crossed that line? He looked at Zander and felt even more like a dick.

Why couldn't Sidney go after some asshole he didn't know? And why the hell couldn't he stop *wanting* her? This was all Baz's fault for putting the idea of kissing her in his head in the first place. He leaned closer to his brother and whispered, "Your fucking advice sucked."

"What're you talking about?" Baz whispered.

"You know *exactly* what I'm talking about. Evie and Sid...?"

"What about them?"

Gunner gritted his teeth. "*Jesus*, don't play stupid. *Kissing?*"

"Eves kissed Sid?"

"No, you idiot. Did you get knocked in the head? *I* kissed her, and it's your fucking fault."

"You kissed Evie?" he seethed. "I'll fucking kill you."

"Not Evie. *Sid!*"

"*Ladies*," Preacher said gruffly, drawing their attention to their uncle's ice-blue eyes. His salt-and-pepper hair was slicked back, his beard trim, and his tattooed arms were crossed over his broad chest. "Would you girls like to share with the class?"

Chuckles rose around the room. *Fucking hell.*

"No, sir," they said in unison, and Baz knocked Gunner's knee under the table, glowering at him.

"Then let's get down to business," Preacher said. "I'm sure some of you have heard that Steph Lockwood got a text from her sister, Bethany. It was another dead end, sent from a burner phone that was bought with cash in a Pennsylvania store. Security cameras were broken, so there's no record of who purchased the phone."

Cuffs had already passed that information along to Gunner and Steph, but it still sucked to hear it.

"Bethany's message indicated that she was thinking about coming back for good, so let's keep our eyes peeled," Preacher said. "There are flyers on the table by the door, so please pick some up and distribute them to local businesses, gas stations. You know the routine." Murmurs rose around them about finding Bethany. Preacher gave everyone a minute to talk before continuing the meeting. "The next order of business is the Easter egg hunt, taking place at the Salty Hog on Sunday…"

He spoke authoritatively, demanded attention, so different from Gunner's father's easygoing nature. But Gunner knew just how badass his father was. All it took was the scent of a threat to flick his switch from easygoing friend to savage beast to protect the people they loved and their community.

"Ginger, Reba, and a number of the girls have made goody bags and stuffed hundreds of eggs with candy, so bring your kids, nieces, nephews, the neighbors' kids and plan on having a hell of a good time. Let's move on to this year's fundraising rally and ride to benefit the Wicked Animal Rescue." Preacher went over the details for the ride, then turned to his brother. "Con, you want to take this?"

"Sure do. First I'd like to say thank you to Justice and Cuffs for stepping up and taking part in the calendar that Gunner's rescue is putting together this year." Conroy searched the faces of the members, landing on Justice, a handsome black man, and Cuffs, the tough-looking white guy sitting across from him. "It's about time you young bucks took over. Preach and I don't need any more ladies chasing after us."

Everyone chuckled.

"Damn straight," Preacher said. "I've never seen my wife stare down so many females as she did last year at the rally. Man, that was hot. Actually, that was a rockin' night. Maybe we *should* be in the calendar again."

"Watch yourself, Preach," Blaine called out. "That's our

mama you're talking about."

Preacher cocked a grin. "I raised you right, boy. But you keep in mind, I'm the *only* man allowed to talk about your mama that way."

More chuckles rose around them.

"And while we're talking about our ladies," Preacher said, "Madigan is going to be in that calendar, along with Colonel's daughter, Sid, and Steph and Evie. I want you to treat those girls' pictures as if they were pictures of your own daughters."

"I second that," Sidney's father said loudly. "Disrespect my daughter and I *will* break your legs."

Fuck. Gunner gritted his teeth.

"In case I wasn't crystal clear," Preacher said. "Disrespect any of them and you'll have the Wickeds and the Colonel to deal with. Got it?"

A chorus of *Yes, sir*s and *Got it*s rang out.

"Now that *that's* settled," Gunner's father said with a nod, "let's get to the fundraiser. Thank you to everyone who has either donated something to be raffled off or has signed up for a booth at the event. Ginger and Reba have taken the helm again, and they've set up lots of fun stuff for the kids. We've put out a sign-up sheet for anyone who might have missed it last week." He motioned to a clipboard on the edge of the table. "Gunner, do you have anything you'd like to add?"

Gunner pushed to his feet, trying to jostle his brain into gear. "You all know how much the rescue means to me and Sid." There she was again, but he couldn't get hung up on that while her father and everyone else was watching him. "We wouldn't be able to help so many animals without your support, and I think y'all know it's greatly appreciated. We'll have as many of the adoptable animals at the fundraiser as we can, so please bring your friends and family and anyone else you think could benefit from the love of an animal."

As Gunner sat down, someone yelled, "I thought Tank was off the market," inciting a round of laughter.

"Damn right I am," Tank called out.

Zander pushed to his feet, hands splayed. "But Gunner and I are still single, and we're the biggest animals of them all."

"Sit your ass down." Zeke pulled Zander down to his seat, earning a rumble of laughter.

Normally Gunner would be riding that wild-child train, talking himself up like he was God's gift to women. But all he could think about was how Sidney was trying to change herself for his fucking oblivious cousin and how wrong Zander was for her. That kiss had really messed with his head, because as he looked around the clubhouse at the guys he trusted and respected most, he didn't think a single damn one of them was good enough for her.

After the rest of the club business was discussed and the meeting was adjourned, everyone began milling about, grabbing drinks, heading to the pool tables, and catching up with one another.

"Who's hitting the Hog tonight?" Zander asked.

"Tank's got three ladies waiting for him at home, and Maverick's wife-whipped, so we know they're out, but I'm in." Blaine eyed Maverick with the tease. Maverick had been fostered and later adopted by Preacher and Reba. Although with his dark hair, blue eyes, and magnetic personality and given the way he and Blaine used to compete and were now as tight as two guys could be, Gunner was pretty sure he was born to be a Wicked.

"Hey, I do what I want." Maverick cocked a grin. "And

tonight I want to do my gorgeous wife."

"I've got a date, so I'm out." Zeke raked a hand through his thick dark hair.

"A date?" Baz arched a brow. "You scoring with one of the moms at the community center?"

"Hardly. I met her at Tank's shop." Zeke had been a special ed teacher until he'd gotten into a fight with a guy who had made derogatory comments about the kids and had lost his job. Now he worked with Preacher and Zander at their family's renovation business, and he also tutored middle schoolers and volunteered at the community center. "She's one of Aria's clients. Aria was finishing my sleeve when she came in, and she asked me out." Aria Bad was a tattooist at Wicked Ink. Zeke had tutored the cute blonde when she was in high school. She suffered from social anxieties, and Zeke had remained close to and protective of her ever since.

"How did Aria feel about that?" Gunner was fairly certain that sweet, shy Aria Bad had a crush on Zeke.

"Why would she care?" Zeke asked.

"Get with the program, bro. I keep telling you she wants you to tutor her in the *bedroom*." Zander pushed to his feet, and as usual, Zeke ignored the barb. "I need a drink. Anyone else?"

"Grab me one," Tank said.

"The countdown is on for your ball and chain, bro," Baz said to Tank. "I heard Mom and Aunt Reba talking about throwing Leah a bridal shower. You might need a bigger house for all the gifts she gets."

"Good. Hopefully they'll throw her a baby shower before our little one is born, too. I want my girl to experience every-thing that goes along with getting married and having babies." Tank nodded to their father as he sidled up to the table.

Conroy put a hand on Tank's shoulder. "Then you'd better buy her some Preparation H and earplugs."

They all laughed.

"You boys going to the Hog in a bit?" Conroy asked.

As the others answered, Gunner wrestled with the urge to go home and see Sidney, but he didn't trust himself not to kiss her again, and once he did, he knew he wouldn't want to stop. Which was exactly why he *needed* to go to the bar. *Fuck.* Why was it so fucking stifling in there tonight? He pushed to his feet. "I'll be right back. I need some air." He strode through the clubhouse and out the doors, filling his lungs with the brisk night air as he headed across the gravel lot.

"Gunner, wait up," Baz called as he came out the door and jogged over to him. "You okay?"

"My head's pretty fucked up about Sid right now."

"That's understandable. You kissed your best friend."

"No shit. I think I wanted to kiss her for days before that, which is also messed up." He pointed at Baz. "You'd better keep this between us, or I will fucking destroy you."

"Chill out, bro. Your secrets have always been safe with me, but I'm worried about you. When did this happen?"

"Last night. She was trying on the clothes Dixie sent. Sid's always beautiful, but she was a fucking smoke show in tight leather, showing all that skin and acting like a *girl*." He started pacing.

"Maybe we should talk about *that*, because Sid always acts like a girl."

"You know what I mean. Yeah, she's a girl, but she's cool like a guy."

"Dwayne, do you hear yourself?" Baz only used his given name when he was trying to make a point. "You totally friend-zoned her and fooled yourself into thinking she *wasn't* hot as hell."

"I just *said* she's beautiful."

"Yeah and cool like a *guy*." Baz shook his head. "You've had her as your screen saver on your phone for as long as I can remember. You call her *buddy* and *MOS*. You two walk around in your fucking underwear, for God's sake. If Evie pranced around in underwear, I'd be all over her ass, and I mean that in the dirtiest way."

"It's different between us," Gunner insisted, wearing a path in the gravel.

"I hear ya, but I think it's because you've put her in this box where she sure as hell doesn't belong."

"You're *wrong*, Baz."

"Okay, then. What's the problem?" Baz stepped in front of him. "Do you *want* to be with her?"

"How the fuck should I know? All I know is that I can't stop thinking about her in ways I shouldn't because she's my best friend. We *just* kissed, Baz. We didn't fuck. She wasn't on her knees. We just…" He paced, his body igniting at the memory of her in his arms, her mouth on his. "I've *never* felt like I did when I kissed her. People talk about fireworks and shit, but it wasn't like that. It was like…" He held his hands beside his head and made an explosive sound.

"Damn. That mind-blowing, huh?"

"I can't even describe what it was like. Kissing her, *holding* her. It fucking changed everything. It changed who I *am*. This is going to make me sound even crazier than I already do, but it was like suddenly the world made sense, and at the same time, nothing made sense. Which is totally fucked up because I never thought the world *didn't* make sense in the first place. What the hell is *that* about? What is wrong with me?"

"Before we go there, the other night you said Sid was into another guy." Baz's tone was dead serious. "Where does she stand on this?"

"I told her it was a mistake and apologized. She says we're cool, but it's been a little weird between us."

"Okay, well, that's to be expected. So she thought it was a mistake, too? Because I've got to tell you, when we were all at the Hog the other night, I was watching you two, thinking about how good you were together with your made-up songs and the rest of the shit you do with each other."

"We've always been good together. We've got an unbreakable bond from the military and with the rescue."

"I think it's a hell of a lot more than that. She's the only one you'd talk to after Ashley died. Remember how upset Steph was because you didn't want to talk about it? You couldn't wait to get back to your post."

Gunner stopped pacing as those memories rolled in. When he'd come home for the funeral, he'd felt like he'd left a piece of himself behind. Baz was right. He'd been anxious to get back because he could be one hundred percent himself when he talked to Sidney without worrying about whether he'd look like a pussy if he broke down or needing to be strong for everyone else. She knew how it felt to have someone she loved ripped from her life. She might've been too young to remember her mother leaving, but she'd told him she'd felt an emptiness inside her that her mother had left behind. That was the night he'd promised never to abandon her. She'd given him the same type of security after Ashley had died, when she'd promised never to lie to him.

"Dwayne, how do you feel about Sidney right now? Right

this very second?" Baz asked.

Gunner crossed his arms, needing the barrier between him and the truth. "I don't know. I might've fucked us up beyond repair, but I also want to go home and do it again."

"Jesus, Gun. You're playing a dangerous game."

"That's just it," he snapped. "It's not a game. It's not like with other women. I don't want to go home and just fuck her and have her leave. There are all these other feelings and thoughts messing with me. Yes, I want her in my bed. I want to do *everything* to her, with her, *for* her, but even thinking about *that* messes with me. Because what the hell? *Right?* She's into someone else, and we both know she's the girl you marry, and I'm the guy you fuck." He swallowed the acidic taste of that truth. "What the hell am I going to do?"

Baz looked at him for a long moment, as if he were choosing his words very carefully. "The way I see it, you have two choices—"

"I need to protect her."

"You'll do that no matter what. You can't help it. She's your best friend. You love her. But as far as all the rest of this goes, you either do what's best for her or what's best for you, and only you know if they're one and the same."

"I don't even know what that means."

"You're a smart guy, and I know how much she means to you. You'll figure it out."

The door to the clubhouse opened, and their brother and cousins walked out. Zander yelled, "Hey, Gunner. Are we doing blondes or brunettes tonight?"

The only brunette Gunner wanted had her sights set on a guy who was choosing women by hair color. It was like looking in a mirror at himself a few weeks ago, and he didn't like what he saw. His phone rang, jerking him from his thoughts. He pulled it from his pocket, and adrenaline rushed through him at the sight of Sidney's name on the screen. "Give me a sec, guys."

Baz whispered, "She's not a dude."

Gunner gave him the finger as he put the phone to his ear. "Hey, MOS"—*damn it*—"*Sid*. What's up?"

"We just got a call on the emergency line from an older lady in Yarmouth. She and her sister live near a guy who has a dog chained to a tree, and as far as she can tell, he's not feeding it. She said the dog showed up a couple of weeks ago and barks all the time. She's heard the guy yelling at it, but she thinks she heard him beating it tonight, because the dog was yelping and whining."

"*Fucker.* Text me the address. We're on our way." That caught the attention of the other guys, and they gathered around him, arms crossed, chins low, ready for whatever battle lay ahead.

"I'll meet you there with the van, but there's more," Sidney said. "She said the guy is bad news, and there are people coming and going from his house all the time."

"A drug runner?"

"Maybe," she said.

"Sid, I want you parked way the hell down the street, and do *not* get out of the van. We will come to you—do you understand?" He knew she was tough enough to handle just about anything, but he didn't like the idea of her anywhere near trouble. He never had, but she'd set him straight when she'd first come to the Cape and they'd gotten a similar call. He'd told her to hang back and let the men handle it, and she'd chewed his ass out.

"Yeah, fine."

Gunner turned to the guys. "Get everyone out here."

Zander ran into the clubhouse. Zeke and Tank took out their phones, and Gunner knew they were clearing their night, because club business took priority over dates and bedtimes.

"Gunner," Sidney said softly. "Please be careful."

She'd said that hundreds of times over the years, but it hit differently this time. "Always, babe." He wasn't worried about himself. He was worried about *her*, the dog, the woman who had called it in, and every other person on that guy's block. He would try to handle the situation with a conversation and a show of force from the brotherhood. The sheer number of Dark Knights usually did the trick, but things could go south quickly.

As he ended the call, his father and Preacher came out of the clubhouse, followed by the rest of the Dark Knights. They had more than thirty members from all walks of life, but when they accepted those patches, differences fell away and they became a brotherhood of fiercely dedicated men willing to give their lives to protect others.

Gunner explained the situation and gave them the address. As Cuffs called the station to see if the guy had any priors, Gunner said, "We need protection for the woman who called it in and her sister."

Four guys stepped forward, and Fish, one of their older members, said, "We'll cover the ladies."

"Sid's got her number. You can start there." Gunner gave Fish Sidney's number. "Chaos, can you pull together some guys to patrol the neighborhood for a few weeks after this goes down? If this guy is a dealer, it could get ugly."

"I'm on it," the bearded and bespectacled chemist said.

Cuffs filled them in on the guy's priors, all misdemeanors. "Christopher Kile has been on local police radar for a while.

Two cars are on their way to back us up. They'll wait in the shadows until I give the signal."

"Let them know Sid will be there in our van." Gunner knew the police would be focused on the house, but if things got bad, he wanted them to be aware she was there. "A'right, guys, let's be safe and see if we can talk some sense into this guy."

GUNNER LED THE Dark Knights down the quiet residential street, the rumble and roar of the motorcycles announcing their presence. Porch lights came on and front doors opened, curious faces peering out. Zeke and Zander took up the rear, telling the neighbors to go inside and lock their doors, while the rest of them continued on to Christopher Kile's house. Gunner surveyed their surroundings as they approached the rundown rambler. There were two trucks and a motorcycle in the driveway and an old SUV parked at the curb. The curtains were drawn, but the lights were on, and he saw shadows of movement through the curtains. As Gunner parked, he spotted two police cars a few houses down and the rescue van at the far end of the street.

They climbed off their bikes, and Gunner motioned for Baz and Justice to go around the right side of the house and Maverick and Blaine to go around the left. Baz would verify the location and condition of the dog and report back to Gunner. If the dog was there and in need of help, they would cover the back and get the dog out if shit went south. Gunner kept his father, Tank, and Preacher on the front lines with him for pure intimidation. The three of them followed him halfway up the walk and stopped. Cuffs waited with them, although he wouldn't make a move unless the police were needed. The rest of the brotherhood stood shoulder to shoulder a few feet behind them.

Gunner's phone vibrated with a text from Baz. He opened it, and a picture popped up of a skinny, cowering dog chained to a tree. Gunner's gut twisted, rage piercing him as another text from Baz rolled in. *There's a guy smoking on the patio and two more inside the patio doors.*

Gunner thumbed out, *Sending more your way.* He shoved his phone in his pocket, pointed to four of the guys and motioned for them to head around back. Gunner met his father's gaze, his silent *Careful, son* heard loud and clear. He caught the same message from Preacher.

Tank growled, "Let's shut this fucker down."

With his cavalry at the ready, Gunner headed up to the porch alone and banged on the door. Heavy footsteps approached, and a bald man peered out the sidelight window. Gunner stared back at him. *Come on, fucker. Open the door.*

The door opened just enough for Gunner to get a good look at the thick-bodied, bald man staring back at him.

"What do *you* want?" the guy asked.

"Are you Christopher Kile?" He always let them know he had their number.

The guy's eyes narrowed. "Who wants to know?"

"I'm Gunner Wicked from Wicked Animal Rescue. My buddies and I were driving by and noticed you had a dog tied up out back." The guy peered over Gunner's shoulder. "I'd be happy to take it off your hands and give it a good home."

"Fuck off." He went to close the door, and Gunner stuck his booted foot inside, stopping him. "What the *hell* do you think you're doing?"

"Saving an animal's life." A young, scrawny guy and a bigger man who looked to be about forty appeared behind the bald guy. Gunner held up two fingers behind his back, keeping his foot in the doorway. "Animal abuse is a felony punishable by imprisonment. You can save your own hide by just giving me the dog. There's no need for it to suffer any more than it already has."

"Like I said, *fuck off,*" the bald guy seethed.

"That's not happening. Come on, man. There are only two ways this ends, and you know it. One with you in prison and one with you free." It was a lie. Gunner was damn well going to press charges against this asshole, but his goal was to get the dog out of the yard safely first. "I suggest you hand the animal over and be done with us."

The guy looked him up and down. Gunner couldn't imagine what he thought he'd do to him with thirty-plus bikers backing him up.

"What's going on, Kile?" the scrawny guy asked.

Bingo, baldy.

"This asshole wants to take my mother's dog," Kile answered.

"That ain't right, man," the fortysomething guy said. "Your mama just died two weeks ago."

"It was your mother's dog?" Gunner didn't wait for an answer. "Listen, man, your mother wouldn't want the dog to suffer, would she? I bet she loved that dog."

Kile's jaw clenched.

"She'd think you were doing the right thing by giving it to me so I can give it a good home, some food, and love. Wouldn't your mother want that?" Gunner urged.

"Who the fuck cares what she'd want?"

Gunner pushed the door open wider, getting right in his face. "Your mother brought you into this world, and *that's* the way you repay her? With disrespect and torturing her dog?" He heard Tank, Preacher, and Conroy ascending the steps, and the rest of their cavalry pushed forward. Tank towered behind Gunner, flanked by Preacher and Conroy.

"My mother was a fucking cunt," Kile barked.

It took every bit of Gunner's restraint not to beat the guy to smithereens. "All the more reason to give me her dog. So you won't have to see it anymore. Don't let that dog's death be on your conscience, man. Give me the fucking dog." *Before I tear you apart.*

A large tattooed man came into the foyer waving a gun. "Kile doesn't want to give you the fucking dog. Now back off."

Gunner didn't flinch, having lost his fear of guns years ago. "Nice *gun*, dude," he said loudly.

Cuffs and two other cops hurried up the steps, pushing past Tank and the others, firearms drawn. "Drop your weapon," Cuffs demanded.

Gunner arched a brow. "I guess I forgot to mention that some of my buddies are police officers. There are more cops out back. So, what's it going to be, Christopher? Are you going to play nice and hand over that dog, or do we have to shoot it out? Your buddy might get *one* bullet off before all of y'all are dead and gone, and in the end we're taking that dog anyway."

The man with the gun looked between Christopher and Cuffs, and two more guys appeared behind him in the foyer. One urged him to shoot; the other told him to put the fucking gun down.

"Put the gun *down*," Cuffs demanded.

"What'd'ya want me to do, Kile?" the guy with the gun asked.

Gunner kept his eyes trained on Kile, leaning closer. "Don't be stupid. You don't want to die over a dog, do you?"

Kile's jaw clenched, and he spoke through gritted teeth. "Put the gun down. Let 'em take the fucking dog."

The guy with the gun lowered it to his side.

"Put the gun on the *floor*," Cuffs shouted, and when he did, Cuffs and the other officers rushed in, pinning Kile and the guy who had held the gun against the wall, reading them their rights as Gunner yelled, "Get the dog," and he, Tank, their father, and Preacher stormed in, forming a barrier between the other men in the house and the officers, while the dog was cut free from the chain and carried to safety.

HOURS LATER, AFTER Baz had checked out the dog and everyone had gone home, Gunner grabbed one of the sweatshirts he kept in the office and a Gatorade and headed down to the Healing Room. Sidney had named it that after the first time they'd rescued an abused dog together. She'd outfitted the room with the comfiest of dog beds and a cot for herself, because when they had dogs like the abused terrier/pit bull mix they'd rescued tonight, Sidney stayed with them twenty-four-seven to build trust.

Gunner peered through the window into the room. Sidney was sitting on the floor with her back against the wall, her legs crossed at the ankles. There was a bowl of water beside her, and she had two silver dog bowls on her lap, one with potato chips and one with kibble. The dog cowered a few feet away. They'd gotten to her just in time. She was thin but not painfully so. She had a few lacerations, and she was bruised and tender, but thankfully she had no broken bones. Baz estimated her to be about five years old. She had a white face with a tan spot around her left eye that went up to the base of her ear. The backs of her legs and the rest of her body were tan, and the fronts of her legs were white.

Sidney picked up a potato chip and looked at the dog as she ate it. She was talking, but Gunner couldn't hear her through the glass. She took a piece of kibble out of the other bowl and put it on the floor a few inches from the dog. He'd seen Sidney do this with enough dogs to know she'd gain this one's trust in time. Conflicting emotion warred inside him—admiration at the love emanating from his best friend, sadness for the dog who had suffered so harshly she was afraid to accept that love, and anger at the sadistic men who had caused and/or allowed it to happen.

Sidney looked up, and a sweet smile spread across her face, but it didn't reach her eyes, and that sent another uncomfortable feeling through him, reminding him of how he'd fucked up.

He mouthed, *Can I come in?*

She nodded, and he slowly entered the room. He sat beside Sidney, handing her the Gatorade and his sweatshirt, whispering, "What can I do?"

"Throw prayers up for our new little girl."

He loved that no matter what else was going on in their lives, the dogs always came first. "Already doing it, babe." *For the dog, and hoping you don't hate me.* He put his hand on hers, like he always did in situations like this. Usually, she'd lace her fingers with his and rest her head on his shoulder, whispering about how hopeful she was for the dog. But she didn't this time, and he got a sinking feeling in his gut. "Are you okay?"

"Just sad for her. I don't think that guy's mother abused her. Look at her eyes. She *wants* to trust us. I can see it behind the fear."

He studied the dog for a moment, seeing what Sidney had mentioned. "I think you're right. She needs a name."

"Liberty," Sidney said softly. "Because she's free now."

"I like that. It's a great name." He looked at the fearful dog. "Don't worry, Liberty. You're in good hands now. The best hands." He curled his fingers around Sidney's hand, and they sat in silence for a few minutes. But he missed those hopeful whispers, and he knew their absence was his fault. "Sid, are we okay?"

"Yeah."

"Are you sure? I feel horrible about last night."

"Don't. It's fine." She turned her hand over and laced her fingers with his.

How could something so little mean so much? He held on tight, breathing a little easier.

"I was thinking about going to see my grandparents for Easter," she said softly. "But I don't want to leave Liberty. Once she's settled, would you mind if I took a week or two off?"

"Of course not." He must be getting good at lying, because he hated the idea of her going away. They hadn't been apart that long even once in the last three years. "Are your grandparents okay?"

"Yeah. I just want to clear my head. I think when I come back, I'll look for a new place to live."

His thoughts came to a screeching halt. "Sid, you don't have to move out. I'm sorry I kissed you—"

"It's not because of the kiss. It's just time. We're almost thirty years old, Gunny. I don't want to be ninety years old buying your little blue pills, and you don't need me hanging around when you're entertaining women."

Every ounce of him wanted to fight her on this, but his conversation with Baz echoed in his head. *You either do what's best for her or what's best for you, and only you know if they're one and the same.*

"Is that what you really want?" he finally asked.

She stared at the bowl of chips, running her finger absently along the rim. "Yeah. Like I said, it's time."

He felt sick. Lost at the thought of her moving out. "If that's what you want, then I'll find you a place."

"No. I can do it. It's time I took control of my life and grew up."

Fuck. "Are you going to quit the rescue?"

"Not if you'll let me stay," she whispered.

"I wouldn't have it any other way. This place is as much yours as it is mine." He struggled to push away his emotions and support her decision, regardless of how awful he thought it was. He put his arm around her, pulling her against him, his chest aching at the thought of her not being there in the mornings or at night, but he wasn't going to let his selfishness hold her back. "If you need to spread your wings, you go right ahead. But I get to check out your new place and make sure it's safe before you sign a lease."

"Okay," she said softly.

"And I'm putting in security cameras so I can see you at any time."

"That's considered stalking."

He heard her smile. "Best buds are allowed to stalk. I'll be over every morning for coffee."

"Okay, but wear pants, please. I don't want the neighbors talking."

He chuckled. "Can we still go to the gym and run together?"

"Sure. Just don't make me flirt with guys, because I suck at it."

"Actually, you're a little too good at it." *I found you irresistible, which is why we're in this mess.* He hated what he was about to say, but she was his friend above everything else. "Flirt with Zan the next time you see him. You'll see."

"I'm done flirting and working angles. You can't force attraction."

Even better. "I'm sorry about Zan. Men are stupid sometimes." *As I've proven.* "Are you okay?"

"Yeah. I don't want to talk about it."

He kissed her temple. "Okay, then, back to your new place. Will you still come over and watch movies with me?"

"Only if I can watch Tom Hardy without catching hell."

"I hate that guy."

"I guess Rosco and I will watch at my place."

He spoke directly into her ear. "The hell you will."

She smiled up at him, and *fuck him sideways*, it took everything he had not to press his lips to hers. He may not be the right partner for her in a romantic relationship, but if he could keep his lips to himself, they'd always have the best friendship around.

Liberty sniffed the kibble, and Sidney squeezed Gunner's thigh, hope dancing in her eyes as Liberty looked at them, then sank back to the corner. A few minutes later, she sniffed the kibble again.

Sidney said, "It's okay, baby. You can eat it."

Liberty stared at them for a long time before sniffing the kibble once more and finally picking it up and huddling in the corner as she ate it. Sidney looked up at Gunner with tears in her eyes, and as the dog took her first step toward her future, Gunner saw his falling apart.

Chapter Ten

GUNNER WAS UP before dawn and full of anxious energy the morning of the photo shoot. It had been three days since Sidney told him she was moving out, and he thought he'd have come to grips with it by now and that his feelings for her would naturally wane. But the feelings that had plagued him to the point of distraction hadn't lessened. They'd magnified. Sidney was all he could think about. Things were a little awkward between them, and her sleeping in the shelter with Liberty for two nights hadn't helped. He was used to hearing her rattling around in the kitchen in the mornings, and sometimes in the middle of the night he'd hear her padding around downstairs with Rosco.

The silence was deafening.

He told himself he was being ridiculous. She'd slept in the shelter plenty of times over the years, and he'd never felt like this. It wasn't like she was quitting and moving out of the state. She was just looking for a new place to live. Logically, that made sense to him, but there was nothing logical about how he felt lately. Now that Liberty was eating and settling in, Sidney had finally slept in her own bed last night, and Gunner realized he didn't just like knowing she was there. He liked knowing she was *safe* under *his* roof, where he was just a few steps away in case she needed him, and he liked starting the day with her sassy comments and shared breakfasts.

He headed downstairs with the dogs, excited to have a normal morning with her before the chaos of the photo shoot this afternoon. He opened the door to let the dogs out and found Rosco on the porch. "Hey, buddy. I missed you last night." Rosco had been sleeping with him when Sidney had stayed at the shelter. "Want to come in and see your mama?"

He and Rosco headed into the kitchen, but Sidney wasn't there. "Did she go back to bed, buddy? What do you say we make her some breakfast and surprise her?" He whipped up eggs and bacon and headed down the hall to Sidney's bedroom. Her bed was unmade, and her sleeping clothes lay in a pile on the comforter, but she was nowhere in sight. Rosco sniffed his way around the room, and Gunner looked out the window. He saw the lights of the shelter glittering against the dusky sky and knew she was with Liberty.

"Found her, buddy."

Rosco was sniffing Sidney's mystery novels and a big fluffy pillow on the dog bed that Rosco had never used because he slept with her. She'd put the cushion against the wall by the window and used it as a reading spot. Gunner smiled as her voice whispered through his mind. *Not everyone needs a window seat.* He glanced at the dresser. Two drawers were open with clothes sticking out. He pictured her blindly grabbing a shirt and jeans to wear down to the shelter. Her closet door was open, her sneakers and boots lying messily on the floor because she usually kicked them off.

Soon all traces of her would be gone.

Rosco looked up at him, and as Gunner stroked his head, he

realized Rosco would be gone, too. A painful knot formed in his chest. If he had a dollar for every time that had happened recently, he'd be a rich man.

"Come on, buddy. You can hang with your brothers and sister while I bring her breakfast." She and Rosco would always be part of his family.

Gunner fed their dogs and headed down to the shelter with Sidney's breakfast. He put her plate in the office and found her lying on the cot in the Healing Room curled around Liberty, fast asleep. *Lucky dog.* Sidney must have sensed him watching her, because her eyes opened and immediately found his. He felt an electric jolt, but she shifted her eyes away as she sat up, causing that painful knot to tighten even more.

She kissed Liberty's head and said something he couldn't hear, and then she joined him in the hallway.

"Is she okay?"

"Yeah." She pushed her hands into the front pockets of her jeans, shifting her eyes away. "I couldn't sleep, so I came down about an hour ago. Why are you up so early?"

"Same reason. I made you breakfast. It's in the office."

"Thanks."

She was trying so hard to smile and act normal, it hurt to watch. As they made their way to the office, he realized why it was so painful. Because he was doing the exact same thing.

THEY SPENT THE morning cleaning kennels and feeding and caring for the animals, and he made a point of working side by side with Sidney, chipping away at the awkwardness, making her smile and laugh, until that discomfort finally fell away. It felt incredible to get back to being the real *them*. They were outside bathing Rocky, a Saint Bernard/husky mix, while Tori, Steph, and Evie were inside with the groomer, drying and prettying up the seven dogs they'd already bathed.

Sidney stood in the baby pool with Rocky. Her jeans were rolled up to her knees, and she had suds on her chin and in her hair. She looked adorable, working shampoo through the dog's fur on his chest and legs. Gunner made the fur on Rocky's back stand on end all the way down to his tail. "Hey, MOS. What do you think?"

Sidney laughed. "I think you should stick to rescuing, not doggy hairdressing."

"Why? Rocky loves a Mohawk. Don't you, boy?" The dog licked his face.

"Rocky loves attention, like the rest of us. We have four more dogs to bathe."

"*Aw.* Are you jealous of the attention he's getting?"

She gave him a deadpan look. "I was making a point."

Gunner picked up the hose and flicked it at her, wetting her face.

"*Gunner!*" She dragged her forearm over the water dripping down her forehead and got suds on her cheek.

"You've got some suds on you. Let me get that." He leaned forward like he was going to wipe them off and sprayed her with the hose again.

She scowled.

Fucking adorable.

"If you value your life, you will *not* do that again," she warned.

He couldn't stop laughter from bubbling out as he flicked

her with the hose again. She shrieked and lunged at him, causing Rocky to bark. But Gunner was too fast, and he turned the hose on her, soaking her shirt as she chased him around the grass.

"You are so freaking dead!" she shouted, running after him.

"I'm feeling pretty alive." He nailed her with the water again.

She slipped and fell but pushed to her feet and sprinted after him like the warrior she was, and he sprayed her again, cracking up. She dove on the hose trailing behind him, yanking it out of his hand, and shot to her feet, nailing him with the water. "How do you like that, *Dwayne?*"

He stalked toward her. "Some guys like getting *wet.*"

Her jaw dropped, and she blasted him with the water again. He darted toward her and she screamed, sprinting away. He snagged her waist from behind, both of them cracking up as she yelled one threat after another, wiggling and flailing, pushing her ass back as she tried to break free. Holy hell, he was an idiot for starting this, because the feel of her grinding against him and the sound of her sweet laughter and harsh threats made him want her even more.

"I swear to God, Gunner, I'm going to—"

"What're you going to do, tiny one?"

"Get *you!*" She put one foot between his legs and twisted her whole body, grabbing him by his shirt. "Now I've got you."

Hell yeah, more than you know.

He tried to escape those feelings by joking. "You think so?" He belted his arms around her, pinning her hands against his chest, and she wiggled from side to side, feeling *all* kinds of good. Her laughter filled the air, and she tried to stop it by making a straight face, but laughter burst from her lungs, and her eyes glittered with it. She squirmed, rubbing against him in all the best places.

He gritted his teeth. "Give it up, MOS."

She looked up, and their eyes collided with the heat of a thousand suns, turning her laughter into heavy panting. His body flamed, but it was his heart whispering in his ear. *Kiss her. Just fucking kiss her. Tell her how you feel.* He was definitely losing his mind. He needed to let her go, but he didn't *want* to, and he thought he saw the same desire in her eyes. She opened her mouth to say something but snapped it closed, making a sexy little noise full of want and need and—

"I can't leave you two alone for five minutes," Tori shouted, startling him from his lustful thoughts. "The dogs are waiting and you're goofing off."

Sidney pushed at his chest and he stumbled backward, his arms still locked around her as he tripped over the baby pool. Sidney shrieked as they hit the water, and Rocky bolted away. Tori cracked up as Sidney tried to stand, but slipped, falling with her elbow between Gunner's legs.

"Oomph!" He rolled onto his side in the water, pain shooting through him.

"Ohmygod!" Sidney doubled over, cracking up. "I'm sorry!"

"This video is going to be great for our social feeds!" Tori circled them, holding up her phone, while Rocky ran around them barking.

Gunner hooked his arm around Sidney's neck, pulling her down beside him in the water, making her laugh even harder. As he lay cringing in pain, she tried to cover her mouth to stop her laughter, but she was laughing too hard. If he died right then and there in that dirty pool of water, he'd die a happy man with his favorite person by his side and his favorite smile beaming back at him.

THE AFTERNOON FLEW by in a flurry of upbeat conversation, barking dogs, biker banter, and unsolicited photography advice. Sidney ran in and out of the shelter getting dogs where they needed to be, and when she was in the yard, she tried to rein in the guys. She'd worried about how Erika, the photographer, would react to all the commotion. If the guys weren't hitting on her, they were making suggestions for different angles and locations for the shots. But the auburn-haired beauty seemed to eat up the attention, flashing her Julia Roberts smile and joking around with them. Taking pictures of animals could be frustrating, and Erika was patient and kind with them and didn't seem bothered whether it took a dozen or a hundred shots to get a good one, and they'd already gotten some amazing pictures. After she'd finished shooting each animal-human pair, she showed everyone a few shots from the session.

She'd taken great pictures of Tank straddling his motorcycle with Chino, the chow/bulldog mix, sitting in front of him, both man and dog wearing sunglasses and the same serious expressions, and another of Madigan wearing a low-cut white shirt beneath a black leather jacket, along with jeans and black boots. She was sitting on her pink Vespa holding Bubbles, a dachshund/terrier mix, both wearing pink scarves around their necks. It was the perfect shot for February. Baz looked like a model in his pictures, with his longish hair swept to one side, wearing an open dress shirt and a stethoscope around his neck, holding Goose, a black-and-tan mutt. They'd taken his pictures in the veterinary office. The man sure knew how to work his puppy-dog eyes. Zeke was every woman's dream in his pictures, which were taken on the couch in the rescue office. He was stretched out, shirtless, wearing his wire-framed glasses instead of his contacts, and reading to Muffin, a playful labradoodle with a penchant for chewing anything and everything in her path.

But while Erika was good with the animals, the way she'd captured Gunner's attention was downright annoying.

Sidney stole a glance at him, standing with Blaine, Tank, and Zeke, watching Erika take pictures of Steph as she moved through different poses beside a tree with Taboo, a German shepherd mix. Steph looked incredible in a Wicked Animal Rescue T-shirt, denim shorts, and knee-high black boots. She wore bright red lipstick that matched the red streaks in her hair, giving her a sexy edge. Madigan stepped in between shots to move Steph's hair over her shoulder or out of her face, per Erika's directions.

"Hold on." Gunner grabbed a red bandanna from the accessories table and tied it around Taboo's neck. "There you go, handsome. Now you match your girl."

Erika lowered her camera, flashing a coy smile at Gunner. "You have an exceptional eye for detail. I could use someone like you."

"Most women can." Gunner strutted back to the guys, who chuckled.

Sidney swallowed the jealousy that stirred and turned away.

Zander took a break from hitting on Marly, their official oil-up girl, as she smeared oil on his torso, and called out, "I've got something exceptional you can use," starting a round of raunchy jokes and laughter.

"I've never heard anyone call a cocktail weenie exceptional,"

Gunner hollered.

Sidney fought the urge to look over and catch his smirk, focusing instead on Chloe, who was lovingly applying oil to Maverick's torso. Chloe stopped to kiss him, and Maverick pulled her against him, deepening the kiss. Chloe came away grinning from ear to ear as she looked down at the oil on her shirt, then went up on her toes for more kisses. That was what Sidney wanted. To give and receive that easy, all-consuming love, and instead, she'd broken her own heart.

Tori sidled up to her. "Erika's great, isn't she?"

"Yeah. She's a fantastic photographer, and she's excellent with the dogs." Sidney couldn't even muster dislike for the woman. It wasn't her fault she was a Gunner magnet.

"She's great with the guys, too, don't you think?" Tori said. "She's got them eating out of the palm of her hand."

"You can say that again." Sidney glanced at Gunner, wishing she could rewind time and go back to the morning fun with the hose, when she would have bet her life he'd been *this close* to kissing her before Tori had interrupted them. But that was Gunner, wasn't it? Kissing one girl, then turning around and hitting on another? She clung to that uncomfortable thought, hoping it might take the edge off her feelings for him.

After Erika was done taking pictures of Steph, she moved on to Evie, who looked badass in leather pants and a rescue T-shirt, holding an adorable old pug named Ricky, and then she took pictures of Justice, who Tori practically drooled over when he went shirtless with a tie, holding Willie, a tan mixed-breed puppy who spent the entire time licking Justice's face. Sidney had suggested that shot just for Tori. Evie and Baz headed back to their office after Evie's shoot, and Tank, Justice, and Zeke also took off.

"Maverick, you're up," Tori announced.

Maverick headed over to his motorcycle, where he was going to pose with Boon, the howling hound dog, and Gunner headed for Erika. Sidney tried not to give any credence to the stab of jealousy seeing them together caused, and she got Boon out of his crate. She crouched in front of him to straighten the blue bow tie she'd put on him earlier. "You're going to do great. Just remember not to—"

Boon howled.

"I hear ya, Boon. I'd howl at that hottie, too." Zander winked at Sidney as he sauntered by.

Gunner stayed close to Erika during Maverick's and Zander's shoots, saying things that made her nod, laugh, or smile, annoying Sidney even more. When it was Cuff's turn to be photographed, Sidney got him situated with Rocky. Cuffs started to unbutton his jeans, and Sidney waved her hands. "Whoa. What are you doing?"

Cuffs grinned. "Stripping down to get a picture in my skivvies and holster, like we talked about."

"I said *no* to the skivvies and holster, remember?" Sidney said firmly.

"I think you're mistaken, sweetheart," Cuffs said. "Women *always* say yes to me taking off my clothes."

The guys laughed.

Sidney rolled her eyes. "I'm sure they do, but this isn't that kind of calendar."

"But it could be." Cuffs waggled his brows.

These guys loved pushing the envelope. "We're not doing underwear shots, and we're not having guns in the pictures with the dogs, but you *can* wear your jeans and dangle a pair of handcuffs. What do you think, Gunner?" She turned just in time to see Zander nudging Gunner, who was engrossed in a conversation with Erika.

Zander said something to him, and Gunner's brows slanted. Gunner looked over and said, "Cuffs, are you giving my girl trouble?"

"No, man, we're good." Cuffs draped an arm over Sidney's shoulders. "Your girl wants to use my handcuffs."

"I'll be happy to oblige." Gunner winked at Sidney. "But Sid's too good for your ugly ass. Let's get this show on the road before the sun goes down."

An hour or so later, it was Gunner's turn to be photographed. He took his shirt off, and Erika said, "Someone needs to oil him up."

Tori looked around. "Where's Marly?"

"She and Blaine went up to the house to get a drink," Madigan said. "They've been up there a while."

Great. They'd better not be in my bedroom.

Gunner hollered, "Sid, oil me up."

Don't you want Erika to do it? "No thanks. Tori can do it."

"He's my *boss*," Tori said sharply. "That's just wrong."

"He's my boss, too," Sidney pointed out. "Where's Steph?"

"Steph left. She had to get back to her shop, and Gunner is my cousin, so that would be weird." Madigan shoved the bottle of oil into Sidney's hand. "*Go.* You were in the military together. You're probably used to putting war paint on each other."

"Come on, babe." Gunner patted his chest with both hands and spread his arms out to the sides. "You know you want to touch me."

"With a two-by-four, maybe." Sidney reluctantly went to oil him up. She didn't need to look at his face to feel the heat of his stare as she poured oil into her hands and began rubbing it along his shoulders and down his chest. Why did he have to feel *so* good?

"I want in on this action," Zander hollered. "I'm next, Sid."

Gunner's jaw clenched.

"I hate you right now." Sidney glowered at him.

"No you don't." He spoke low and gruff, stirring the butterflies she'd thought his flirting with Erika had permanently smothered. He flexed his pecs, his lips curling into a devilish grin.

Her pulse quickened, but she managed to keep a straight face. Or at least she hoped she did. She was so busy trying *not* to enjoy the feel of his heartbeat quickening, his nipples pebbling beneath her fingers, and the hard curves of his muscles, she couldn't concentrate on anything else. She wanted to kiss his chest, to tease his nipple with her tongue and teeth. His rough hand covered hers, pushing it slowly down his abs.

"Like what you feel, MOS?"

Oh, yeah, that's nice. I want to feel you pressing me into the mattress—ohmygod. She blinked several times as her brain started firing again and looked at his face.

He was smirking! What the hell was wrong with her? He was just being the flirtatious big mouth he always had been. She yanked her hand out from beneath his, mortified to have gotten lost in him in front of everyone. "Nope. I didn't feel anything special."

She heard Erika laugh and wondered if the flirtatious photographer and Gunner would joke about this in his bed later. Anger whipped through her. How was she going to make it through the next few weeks under the same roof as him? She looked at Erika. "He's all yours."

She turned to walk away, but Gunner grabbed her wrist, yanking her back, his eyes boring into her. "I think you missed a spot, MOS."

"Get it yourself." She shoved the bottle of oil into his hand. "Remember to be gentle with Chappy. I'm going to change."

"Send Blaine out so we can get his pictures done," Tori said as Sidney stalked past.

"Wait for me!" Madigan ran after her. "I want to see the clothes from Dixie."

Sidney hadn't planned on wearing those clothes for the photo shoot, but her pride needed a boost.

It was time to level the playing field.

Chapter Eleven

AS SIDNEY AND Madigan entered the house, Rosco and Granger ran out of the kitchen to greet them. Belleau and Opha Mae were snoozing in the living room, and Marly's voice trailed out of the kitchen. "*Stop*, Blaine. I can't take any more."

Madigan grabbed Sidney's hand, stopping her in her tracks.

"Sure you can," Blaine urged. "Open your mouth wider. I'll go slow."

Madigan wrinkled her nose in disgust.

"I swear if you get it on my face, I'll kill you," Marly warned.

"*Ew*," Madigan whispered.

If Sidney couldn't get down and dirty with Gunner in their kitchen, she wasn't about to let Blaine and Marly. "Hey, you two!" she shouted. "Put your clothes on."

Blaine walked out of the kitchen fully dressed, holding a can of whipped cream. "I haven't even gotten her naked yet."

"Thank God," Madigan said dramatically. "Do you know what it sounded like you were doing?"

Marly giggled as she came out of the kitchen, looking cute in what she called her oil-up uniform: skinny jeans and a gray long-sleeved V-neck shirt. "We were getting drinks and helped ourselves to your whipped cream. We'll buy you more."

"Don't worry about it," Sidney said. "Tori needs Blaine for his pictures."

Marly rubbed her hands together. "Oil-up time."

Blaine put the whipped cream away, and the two of them headed outside while Sidney and Madigan went into Sidney's bedroom with Rosco on their heels.

"I *really* need to find another place to live." Sidney grabbed the box of clothes from Dixie out of the closet.

Madigan petted Rosco. "Yeah, right."

"I'm serious, Mads." She set the box on the bed. "If you know anyone who has an apartment or a room to rent, let me know."

Madigan's brows knitted. "You're really going to move out? Does Dwayne know?"

"Yup." Sidney had noticed that Madigan only called Maverick and Gunner by their real names when she was worried about them or pissed off at them. "Steph was right the other night. If I don't do something to change my life soon, I'll be sleeping alone and listening to women leave his bedroom in the middle of the night forever."

"I totally get it." Madigan began picking through the clothes. "But is he okay with you moving out?"

"Yeah. I mean, he'll miss me making his coffee in the mornings and us hanging out together when he's not entertaining some random chick." *But he didn't try to stop me.* Which was another indication that she was doing the right thing.

"I can't imagine you two not living together. It makes me sad. You get along better than most couples."

"That's because we're not a couple." Sidney dumped the clothes out of the box onto the bed. "Like I said, if you know of anyone who has an affordable place to rent, let me know."

"Hello...?" Madigan waved. "I'm renting Chloe's house all by myself, and there's plenty of room for you and Rosco."

"Really? I don't want you to feel like you have to offer me a room just because I'm living with Gunner."

"Don't be silly. You're one of my closest friends, and I'd love the company. It'll be fun, and you know I love Rosco." She grabbed Rosco's face and kissed his snout. "You'll never be bored with me around."

Madigan went on about how much fun they would have, and as they talked about rent and splitting household chores, Sidney tried to imagine herself living someplace other than there, with Gunner. But her mind refused to do it.

"What do you think? I promise not to drink out of the milk carton or burp the alphabet."

Am I really doing this? Sidney looked out the bedroom window and saw Gunner posing with Chappy by his motorcycle as Erika moved around him taking pictures. The thought of hearing Erika slink out of his bedroom turned Sidney's stomach. "Okay, I'll take it." Her heart broke as she said it, but it was the lesser of two evils.

Madigan squealed and hugged her. "When do you want to move in? You don't have that much stuff. I bet it won't take too long."

Sidney had never thought much about the things she owned. When she'd lived with her father, she'd had him and had never longed for material things. Military life had been necessities only, and when she and Rosco had moved in with Gunner, she had *them* and had never needed more. As she looked around the room, she realized that other than Rosco's bed, she didn't even have her own furniture. Gunner had furnished the bedroom for her before she'd moved in.

A lump formed in her throat at the thought. "I need to buy furniture."

"No, you don't. Chloe left her master-bedroom furniture, and I had my own, so I put it in the second bedroom."

"Oh, good." Since she wasn't going away, she might as well make it happen fast. "Then how about if I start moving stuff in after work this week?"

"Perfect! We'll have to celebrate. But *first*." Madigan held up the leather miniskirt with zippers down both sides and the strappy leather bralette. "Do you have black high heels? Let's show my brothers and cousin that they're not the only ones with abs and arrogance."

Oh boy. "Arrogance?"

"You can do arrogant, can't you?" Madigan asked hopefully.

"I can barely do *confident* dressed like that." Except she'd had all sorts of confidence when she was trying to seduce Gunner, which pissed her off and made her angry for sounding weak. *Fuck that.* She was confident. She was freaking *badass*, no matter what clothes she was wearing, and there was no way in hell she was going to let Gunner one-up her with his ripped abs and insane sexual energy. "On second thought, give me that." She grabbed the skirt. "Can you get my black combat boots from the closet?"

"No heels?"

"Nope." She dug her black Wicked Animal Rescue tank top out of her drawer. "You want arrogance? We're doing it *my* way."

Ten minutes later, with Madigan by her side, giddily encouraging her, Sidney strutted across the lawn in her rescue tank top, torn up the middle and tied beneath her breasts, the leather miniskirt, and black boots, carrying her leather jacket over her shoulder. Sidney appreciated Madigan's support, but she could have saved her breath. Gunner was standing so close to Erika as they looked at pictures on her camera, he might as well be *wearing* her. If that wasn't motivation enough for Sidney's arrogant strut, nothing was.

As they approached the group, Zander looked over and did a double take. "*Damn*, Sid. You look *hot*."

"Whoa," Tori said with awe. "You need to wear skirts more often. You have gorgeous legs."

Gunner's gaze hit Sidney like a freight train, sending her heart into a tailspin. But she refused to give in to her nervousness and planted her hand on her hip, lifting her chin as he checked her out, his jaw tightening.

Blaine whistled. "Now, *that's* how you sell calendars."

Gunner looked like he was going to explode, but he turned back to Erika, speaking too low for Sidney to hear. Erika looked at Sidney, brows knitted. Knowing she was being talked about was an awful feeling, so she turned away from Gunner and his newest conquest before her broken heart stole every ounce of her confidence.

"Where have you been hiding *this* little vixenish side of yourself?" Marly walked around Sidney, eyeing her up and down. "Girl, you look incredible."

"Doesn't she?" Madigan said excitedly. "And guess what? Sid's moving in with me this week!"

Gunner's gaze shot to Sidney again, and everyone else looked at *him*. Sidney swallowed hard at the angry look in his eyes.

"You're moving?" Tori asked.

"Yeah." Sidney tried to sound like it wasn't killing her to say it. "I can't live with Gunner forever."

"Um. Okay," Tori said uncomfortably, looking between Sidney and Gunner.

Gunner said something to Erika, who smiled, driving Sidney's jealousy deeper. Scrambling to get his attention off Erika, she said, "Do you think my stomach needs oil?" shocking herself.

"Oh, *yeah*." Zander grabbed the oil from the table and strode over. "My hands were made for this."

"She's doing *December*. She doesn't need oil," Gunner said gruffly. "Let's go. The sooner we get this done, the sooner we can all get out of here."

"What crawled up your ass and died, fun sucker?" Zander walked away shaking his head.

Sidney was *this close* to asking Gunner if he was in that much of a hurry to get laid, but she bit her tongue. It was none of her business who he slept with. He wasn't hers. She was his biggest fucking mistake. *That's your loss, Gunner, and I hope one day you realize it.*

"I'll get Twinkles." Tori headed down to the shelter.

Sidney turned to Erika. "Where do you want me? On the hill, or are we doing the pictures inside?"

"Behind the shelter," Erika said, and she headed in that direction.

Blaine and the others followed her, but Sidney stayed rooted in place and crossed her arms, looking at Gunner. "Why are we taking pictures *behind* the building? We never take pictures back there. There's nothing to see but woods."

"It doesn't matter where we take them." He sounded annoyed. "All anyone's going to be looking at in the calendar is you in those clothes."

How dare he get annoyed with her. "I know *you* told me not to wear them, but obviously other people appreciate it. I think we should go with the shots I came up with on the hill by the prettier trees."

"It'll be fine, MOS. Erika knows what she's doing."

I bet she does.

"Come on," Gunner urged. "We've been out here all day. Just go with it."

"Fine." She fumed as they made their way down to the shelter.

"You're really moving in with Mads?"

"Yes." *Tell me not to. Say kissing me wasn't a mistake and you want me to stay.*

"Okay. I'll help you move."

That hurt more than the explosion that had cost Sidney her military career. It was all she could do to put one foot in front of the other.

Tori came out of the shelter with Twinkles as they walked past the entrance. "Perfect timing. Here's your favorite little girl." She handed her to Sidney.

"Come here, baby." Thankful for a distraction, Sidney kissed her furry head. Twinkles was adorable in her holiday diaper cover, but even that wasn't enough to pull Sidney from her heartache.

"I'll meet you back there." Tori hurried around the corner of the building.

Sidney cuddled Twinkles. "It's just you and me in the woods, princess. It's a good thing I bought you something pretty to wear."

"You might like the woods," Gunner said coaxingly.

She gave him a deadpan look.

"Let's do this, babe." He slung an arm around her, as if he hadn't slayed her with four words minutes ago, and petted Twinkles. "You're mighty cute in that diaper, TW."

The sun was just beginning to set as they walked around the building. "It might be too dark to get good pict—" Her voice fell away as colorful lights bloomed to life, illuminating a beautifully decorated tree with a red tree skirt with gold trim beneath it, littered with wrapped presents. Speechless, Sidney looked at Gunner.

"Every year you put this calendar together and you make sure everyone has a dog that matches their personality, and you come up with great ideas for the pictures, but I knew you wouldn't come up with something spectacular enough for yourself. We couldn't have you and TW representing the holidays without a little flair." He pulled a Santa hat from his back pocket and put it on her head. Then he pulled a tiny one from his other back pocket and put it on Twinkles, tying it with a red bow beneath her chin. "Perfect."

Oh, her heart! She had no idea how it could fill up when it had so many cracks. "You did all of this for *me*?"

"Nothing but the best for my buddy."

There it was. The single word that defined her in his mind.

"Dude, let's go," Zander yelled.

Sidney looked around for him. "Where is he?"

Gunner pointed to Zander and Blaine sitting on the limbs of another tree a few feet above the pine tree, holding buckets. "They're going to make it snow."

He'd thought of *everything*. She felt like she might cry.

"Hey, D, are we ready?" Erika asked.

That wiped away her mushy feelings. "D?" Sidney whispered.

"She wanted to call me something special. Can you blame her?"

No, but I wish I had a seat belt for this emotional roller coaster ride.

THEY TOOK DOZENS of pictures, with and without snow. Some with Twinkles standing inside a gift-wrapped box, her front paws perched on the edge, and others with Sidney sitting, standing, or kneeling, holding or cradling Twinkles and/or presents, and some with Twinkles and Sidney peering into gift boxes. They even took one with Sidney standing with one leg kicked up behind her, holding Twinkles in one hand and reaching up to hang an ornament with the other. She'd felt ridiculous posing for it, and she hated that Erika made her move her hair out of her face for nearly every shot, but she wasn't going to argue in front of everyone. The girls and Zander and Blaine cheered her on, but her sweet roommate stuck like glue to his *flavor of the night.*

Every few shots Erika showed Gunner the pictures she'd taken. The way he gushed and they talked quietly among themselves, Sidney had a feeling he was using her photo shoot to get in even deeper with the beautiful photographer. She wondered if Gunner had seen Erika before today, because that would explain this whole holiday set he'd put together. He never went out of his way to impress women, but there was obviously something about Erika that had gotten under his skin.

It hurt knowing she hadn't had that effect on him but a stranger could.

Every time Sidney thought they were done, Erika or Gunner would suggest another pose. When Erika asked Tori to get a white blanket out of her trunk, Sidney was seconds from putting her foot down and being done with it, but Erika said since the sun was setting, the white blanket would make the shots stand out even more, and everyone encouraged Sidney to do it *for the rescue*. She reluctantly agreed, and Erika took a dozen pictures, including one with Sidney lying on her stomach, propped up on her elbows, her chin resting on her palms, with Twinkles standing in front of her, their noses touching, which Sidney had to admit would probably be a super-cute picture.

"Okay, last one," Erika said.

"Thank God for small favors," Sidney said under her breath.

Erika draped the blanket around Sidney's shoulders and arms and handed her Twinkles. "Hold her up like you're going to kiss her nose."

Sidney felt silly, especially after taking so many other pictures, but the way Marly and Madigan *awwe*d made her feel like it was worth it.

Gunner sauntered over after they were done. "Great job, MOS. The whole calendar is going to look amazing."

"Thanks." She waited for him to say more, but he headed over to Blaine and Zander. She escaped into the shelter with Twinkles to put her in her kennel, then checked on Liberty. She'd been glad when the volunteers had told her that Liberty had eaten all of her meals and had done well with them.

Liberty greeted her with bright eyes and a wagging tail. What a difference a little love made. She spent a few minutes giving her extra attention, then checked on the other dogs before heading back out to help clean up.

There was no time to stew as the sun went down and every-one hurried to put everything away. When they finally finished, Madigan said, "I just got a text from Chloe. Everyone's going to the Salty Hog. Who wants to go?"

As Marly, Blaine, and Zander jumped on the invitation, Sidney looked around for Gunner and saw him heading up to the farmhouse with Erika.

Zander sidled up to her. "Hey, beautiful. You don't want to watch that go down, do you? Come to the Hog with us."

"No thanks. I don't feel like partying."

"Then let's go for a ride. We'll grab dinner and head over to the ocean. We can talk about your move and what an idiot my cousin is."

Little did he know how well his comment fit her current situation, but she couldn't blame Gunner for not liking her that way. "He's not an idiot. He's just a guy doing what your species does."

"My *species*? You act like we're aliens."

She raised her brows.

He chuckled. "I still think he's an idiot. If you were my roommate, you'd never leave my bedroom."

"It's not like that between us, and I'm not sleeping with *you*, so don't get any ideas."

"That's good, because I'd ruin you for all other men."

She laughed. "I swear cockiness runs in the Wicked genes."

"If you didn't love it, you wouldn't have lasted around Gunner for five minutes." He slung an arm around her. "Come on. I don't feel like partying either. Let's go see what other kind of trouble we can get into. You want to change out of that skirt?"

Sidney glanced at Gunner and Erika on the farmhouse

porch. "No. I'm good." She put on her leather jacket and climbed onto the back of his motorcycle.

"Damn, girl." He handed her a helmet. "I'll be the envy of every guy around tonight."

Except the one that matters.

Chapter Twelve

GUNNER PACED THE living room, checking his phone for the millionth time. It had been three hours since Sidney had taken off on the back of Zander's bike, and neither of them had responded to his texts. His skin crawled at the thought of his cousin getting up close and personal with her. The dogs were looking at him like he was losing his mind, and he was pretty damn sure he had already lost it. He'd never pined after a woman. Much less been stuck in the clutches of jealousy all fucking night.

The sound of a motorcycle approaching broke his train of thought. He glanced out the window. Zander was parking in front of the house. His chest tightened as Zander helped Sidney climb off the bike in that sexy-ass miniskirt and took off her helmet. *Gunner's* girl, his best friend, the only woman whose kisses had ever consumed his every thought was looking at his cousin like he was her favorite breed. Gunner's hands curled into fists as Zander reached for her. *You'd better not fucking kiss her.* Zander pulled her into his arms, and Gunner turned away, unable to watch.

He paced furiously, jealousy stacking up inside him. He wanted to kill his cousin, and he knew he had no right to feel that way since Zander was the guy she wanted. He heard footsteps on the porch and tried his damnedest to tamp down the torturous battle going on inside him as Zander drove away. But when Sidney walked in and the dogs ran to greet her, "*Did you fuck him?*" came out before he could stop it.

She glowered at him. "Why do you care?"

He closed the distance between them, teeth grinding. "Because I *do*. Is that why you didn't return my texts?"

"I didn't bring my phone, and it's none of your business who I sleep with." Anger billowed off her.

"No shit. But I need to know."

She scoffed, eyes throwing daggers. "Why do you care who I'm with? Kissing me was your biggest fucking mistake, remember? Or did Erika literally screw you senseless?"

"What the hell are you talking about? I didn't screw Erika."

"You mean a woman actually told you *no*? Well, *that's* a first."

He stalked forward, backing her up. "She didn't tell me *no*, MOS, because I didn't ask. You want to know why? Because I don't want *her*. I want *you*."

She stared at him, confusion rising in her eyes, but it was quickly wiped away by anger. "If you do, it's only because you think I fucked Zander, and you have some warped competitive shit going on in your head that I don't even want to know about. I'm going to bed."

She turned to walk away, but he grabbed her hand, tugging her back, honesty spewing from his lips. "I thought so, too, at first, but I was *wrong*, MOS, and so are you. I said that kiss was a mistake because I knew you wanted to be with Zander. But that was the best fucking kiss of my life. It changed *everything*. It changed *me*, Sid. *You* changed me, and I know how crazy that sounds."

"Because it's not real," she said sternly.

"Bullshit. When we first met, I wanted to be with you more than I wanted anything else in my entire life, but I was afraid I'd fuck it up, and I'd never had a friend like you, so I closed that door." He didn't mean to raise his voice, but the words came too fast. "I didn't realize that when I closed it, I also turned off the part of my brain that I allowed to see you as the incredible *woman* you are. I didn't even know that was possible, but that kiss opened that door, and I can't stop thinking about you. *Wanting* you. Wanting to see if there's more to us than best friends. *That's* why I snuck out last night after you went to bed and put that Christmas scene together behind the shelter, because I wanted to show you that I wasn't just an asshole who kissed you and said it was a mistake. That I'm your best friend who knows that even if you don't like to do things for yourself, you deserve to have them done for you and that I see you, Sid. All of you."

Her brows knitted, and she crossed her arms.

He felt freer, like he'd shed a layer of skin that had fit too tight. "It's true, and I know I'm an idiot for walking around with blinders on, but I didn't even know I was doing it."

"You spent all day with Erika," she said quietly but firmly. "I saw you bring her here. That's not a guy who can't stop thinking about someone else."

"I didn't bring her here to fuck her. We went inside so she could take my picture with our dogs for *you*. I know that's fucked up, because you're into Zander and you want to move out, but I wanted you to have a picture of us at your new place. And I spent all day with her because we were going over angles and shots and shit for the calendar, but most of the time we were talking about *you*."

She lowered her eyes and flicked her chin, sending her hair tumbling in front of her face. "I'm not that interesting."

"That's where you're wrong, babe." He tucked her hair behind her ear, bringing her eyes to his again. "You're the most interesting person I know. You can talk about guns and war or animals and Tom Fucking Hardy." That earned a smile. "But that's not why Erika and I were talking about you. We were discussing the pictures I wanted her to take of you. I can't see your face in any of the pictures I have. You're always hiding behind your hair or your hand, and I was telling her that you'd do everything you could to hide your face today, and I wanted her to make you show it. And when you did, I couldn't get enough of seeing your beautiful smile and the eyes I can't stop dreaming about, so I had her take more pictures. I was going to tell you all of that after the shoot, but then you took off with Zander."

"Because that kiss messed with *me*, too," she said sharply. "I didn't want to be around when you took Erika up to your bedroom, and Zander asked me to go for a ride and grab dinner, so I went."

His thoughts stumbled. "Are you saying you're not *with* Zander? You guys didn't hook up?"

She shook her head. "I don't want Zander. We should talk about him."

Holy fuck. He was breathing so fast, his words flew from his lungs. "I don't care about him. If you don't want him, he doesn't matter. Just tell me what you *do* want, Sid."

"I want *you*, Gunny—"

He grabbed her face, and their mouths collided like thunder and lightning. He pushed his hands into her hair, kissing her deeper, *rougher*, leaving no space unclaimed. He wanted to possess her mouth with every part of his body. She grabbed his shirt, rising on her toes, meeting every stroke of his tongue with a hungry swipe of her own, like she couldn't get enough, either. Heat and desire surged through his veins. The feel of her in his arms breathed new life into his lungs, gathering all of his unsettled pieces and putting them back together. He wanted to touch her everywhere at once, to worship and cherish every inch of her. His hands slid down her back, one crushing her to him, the other claiming her ass. She moaned, and the sound seared through him, making his entire body ache for her. He needed to see her face, to leave nothing open to misunderstanding, and drew back.

"*Sid*" came out rough and hungry.

Her lustful eyes found his, narrowing in a challenge. "If you tell me this is a mistake, I'll castrate you in your sleep."

"We're not getting *any* sleep tonight, baby."

GUNNER SWEPT HER up and into his arms like she belonged there, reclaiming her mouth in a fiercely passionate kiss that sang through her. If not for the rampant beat of her heart, she'd think she was dreaming. Gunner took a step, and the dogs jumped up to follow.

"*Stay*," he growled, heightening her arousal as he carried her out of the living room.

She got even more nervous thinking about going up to his room like all the other girls had and said, "My room," just as he turned down the hall.

"I'm one step ahead of you, babe."

Relief took the edge off as he carried her into her bedroom, kissing her, and kicked the door closed behind them. He set her on her feet, standing so close, her entire body flooded with awareness. He took her face between his hands and brushed his lips over hers, whispering, "I'm so glad we're here. Tell me this is what you want."

"This is everything I want."

He couldn't know how much it meant to her that he was glad they were there, too, and she couldn't have told him if she'd tried as he sank down to one knee, running his hands down her legs. His piercing blue eyes held her captive as he pressed a kiss above one knee, sending titillating sensation scurrying up her thighs. "I love your legs, babe." He took off her boots and socks and rid himself of his own.

He pushed to his feet, the air pulsing as hot and frantic as her heart as he gazed deeply into her eyes. "You are the most beautiful thing I've ever seen." He ran his thumb along her lower lip as she tried to remember how to breathe. "Your sexy mouth is *mine* tonight."

"Only tonight?" She hated asking, but she needed to hear the answer.

His eyes narrowed. "How is that even a question after everything I just told you?"

She lifted her shoulder, hating the insecurity. "Just making sure."

"I'd never risk our friendship if I didn't think this was real." He ran his fingers down the sides of her neck and beneath the collar of her leather jacket, slowly pushing it to the floor, and trailed his hands down her arms. "By the end of the night, I promise you won't have any doubts."

He lifted her chin and kissed her, slowly and sensually and so perfectly, her knees weakened. His tongue slid over her lower lip, sending goose bumps chasing over her skin. His gaze remained trained on hers as he untied her shirt, speaking entrancingly low. "I have spent countless hours thinking about all the things I want to do to you."

Holy cow, we're really doing this. She was as nervous as she was excited.

He ran his index finger down the center of her chest and unhooked her bra. "You're breathing hard. Are you nervous or turned on?"

"Don't ask me that," she said shakily.

"I want to know." He pushed her bra to the sides and teased her nipples.

She closed her eyes as scintillating sensations skittered through her.

"Look at me, Sid."

She opened her eyes, and the desire staring back at her made her breathe even harder.

"If you're nervous, we'll take some time before we go too far." He palmed one breast, brushing his thumb over the taut peak, and her body ignited.

"*No*" came out so fast, they both laughed. "It's just a little weird being together after all these years."

"Want me to get the war paint?"

"Shut up." She couldn't stop smiling.

A wolfish grin curved his lips. "Don't worry. I'm about to give you something else to focus on." He reached over his back and tugged off his shirt, tossing it to the floor.

Her breath caught. She could *finally* touch him, taste him. "That's a good start. Keep going."

He grabbed her hips, pressing his erection against her belly.

"We're getting there," she said breathily.

He took hold of the zippers on the sides of her skirt, whipping them down fast. The leather slid down her legs and puddled at her feet. He stepped back, visually devouring her, and she froze. She was wearing her boy shorts underwear, which wasn't exactly sexy. "I wasn't expecting—"

"Shh." He grabbed her butt, pulling her close again. "You're so fucking sexy. You have no idea how hard it was to watch you prance around in this skimpy underwear when you first moved in." His brows knitted. "I forgot about that until just now. My right hand was named Sid for a few months."

She laughed. "I don't know if I should be honored or disgusted."

"Definitely honored." He kissed her again, so deep and slow, she came away light-headed. "I wanted you as badly then as I did when we first met. I hadn't realized how well I'd locked those feelings away until a few days ago."

She slipped her finger into the waistband of his jeans. "I'm glad you finally found the key." She opened his belt and unbuttoned his jeans. "These need to come off now."

He stripped off his jeans, revealing black boxer briefs straining over his thick arousal, the broad head poking out of the waistband. Her breath rushed from her lungs, and her eyes flicked up to his. Wickedness danced in those mesmerizing eyes as he peeled off her shirt and bra. His gaze trailed down her body, her nipples pebbling beneath their heat.

"You're way too hot to keep that underwear on."

He grabbed her by the waist and lifted her off her feet, tossing her onto the bed. She laughed as he came down over her, grinning like the beast he was, and lowered his mouth to hers, kissing her possessively. His fingers threaded into her hair and fisted, sending stings of pleasure through her core. She pressed her hands into his back, and he ground his arousal against her, his muscles flexing as she rocked her hips, earning a gruff and lustful moan that sent her heart into a sprint.

He kissed the edge of her mouth. "I want to taste *all* of you." He kissed her lips. "Make you feel so good, you can't remember your own name." He dusted kisses down her neck and over the swell of her breast, circling her nipple with his tongue, making her body tingle and burn. She ran her fingers through his hair, and he growled, "Yeah, baby, touch me."

The greediness in his voice spurred her on. When he lowered his tongue to her breast again, she held him there, arching beneath him as he sucked and teased, driving her out of her freaking mind. She writhed and rocked, his every taunt drawing a needy moan or a sharp gasp. One strong hand moved down her waist, holding her there, while the other snaked up to cup her face. She sucked his thumb into her mouth, swirling her tongue around it. He made a guttural noise, rising up and reclaiming her mouth in a punishingly passionate kiss, tongues thrusting, bodies grinding. Good *Lord*, she'd never been kissed so thoroughly. She felt it all the way down to her toes. When he tore his mouth away, her lips burned for more.

His hungry eyes drilled into her. "I look forward to doing very dirty things to your mouth."

Thrills darted through her, leaving no room for hesitation. His dirty talk emboldened her. "How about you get busy doing dirty things with *yours* right now?"

She pushed his shoulders, shoving him down her body, and he laughed, slowing to nip her breast. She gasped, and he grinned up at her.

"A little demanding, aren't you, MOS?" He slicked his tongue over her nipple, his eyes locked on hers. "I *like* your bossy side." He pressed kisses to the swell of her other breast. "But I'm not going to hurry through this with you. I'm going to enjoy every second of making you feel so good, you'll never want to leave this bed."

He wasn't kidding about taking his time. He licked and sucked, caressed and groped, moaning appreciatively as he tormented first one breast, then the other, squeezing her nipples and lavishing her sensitive skin with openmouthed kisses and tantalizing grazes of his teeth. Every slick of his tongue took her higher, and every touch of his hands made her moan and plead for more, until her entire body vibrated with need.

"*Gunner,*" she urged breathily.

He grabbed her underwear at her hips, dragged them slowly down. "Waxed bare. Perfect for an all-night buffet."

She laughed and covered her face.

"Don't hide from me, beautiful."

She lowered her hand, and Lord have mercy, the hunger in his eyes nearly did her in. He held her gaze as he continued moving slowly south, kissing and caressing every inch of her skin as it was revealed all the way down to her ankles. She closed her eyes, reveling in his tantalizingly warm lips and exquisitely addicting touch. He tossed her underwear aside and retraced that torturous path up her body with his mouth. Her skin was on fire, her thoughts whirling, as he wedged his broad body between her legs and kissed her inner thighs. He slid his tongue along the crease where her leg joined her hip and pressed a kiss to the apex of her sex.

"Watch me as I make you come."

Her pulse spiked as her eyes found his, and he slid his

tongue along the very heart of her, sending sparks skittering beneath her skin.

His eyes turned volcanic. "So fucking sweet."

God...

Lust twisted and burned inside her as he teased and taunted, every slick of his tongue taking her closer to the edge. "That's it, baby, give yourself to *me*." He brought his fingers into play, wreaking havoc with her most sensitive nerves, and her hips shot off the mattress. He pushed them down and sealed his mouth over her center, relentless with his tongue, teeth, and hands. The scratch of his scruff was electrifying, his appreciative noises and whispers adding to her pleasure. She couldn't think, could barely breathe, as an orgasm gathered force inside her like a wave barreling toward shore. She clenched her teeth and dug her heels into the mattress. He stroked over that magical spot inside her with deathly precision and took her clit between his teeth, flicking it with his tongue so exquisitely, violent gusts of pleasure crashed over her, sweeping and pounding, taking her up, up, *up* to the peak. She clawed at the mattress, sure her body would burst into flames as he continued his masterful ministrations. Her mind spun, her body racked with pleasure. He did something spectacular with his tongue, catapulting her to another crescendo, and then she was floating in a cloud of pleasure as he touched and licked and kissed her ever so lightly, until she sank into the mattress, breathless, her body riddled with aftershocks. But he didn't stop there. He teased her softly and slowly, his talented tongue taking her right up to the verge of madness and holding her there until she lost control again, and his name flew from her lips. *"Gunner!"*

When she collapsed to the mattress, boneless and winded, he wrapped his arms around her waist, pressing a kiss to her belly, and rested his cheek there, whispering her name. She ran her fingers through his hair, smiling, eyes closed, knowing she'd never forget the way he'd said it, full of wonder, appreciation, and more emotions than she could name. He kissed her belly again and continued tasting his way up her body. Every touch of his lips ignited sparks, and when those lips claimed hers with savage intensity, his hard length grinding against her center, she felt the rush of another orgasm. He kissed her with thrusts of his tongue, matching the rhythm of his hips, the friction sending her soaring again.

When he finally drew away and the world came back into focus, so did his handsome face—and that cocky grin she adored.

"Now, *that's* how it's done, sweetheart."

He was so full of himself she couldn't help but tease him and tried her hardest to keep a straight face as she said, "*Oh*, you thought that was…Okay, *yeah*. That was pretty good."

His brows slanted, his smile replaced with disbelief. "Are you fucking kidding me?"

"No, but I mean, we can practice and work on your technique so I don't have to fake it next time." The appalled look on his face shattered her resolve and she cracked up, rolling onto her side.

"You're gonna get it now, MOS." He bit her shoulder, and she squealed.

"You should've seen your face," bubbled out between laughs.

He rolled her onto her back, grinning just as arrogantly as he had before. "I'm taking that as a challenge."

"*Oh no.*" She giggled. "How will I survive?"

He lowered his lips to hers in a smoldering kiss, every swipe of his tongue lulling her deeper into his forceful domination. This was what she'd craved. What she'd always known they'd have, laughter and lust and everything in between. She was greedy, wanting their kisses to last forever, and at the same time, so eager for more, she pushed at his briefs. He broke their kiss long enough only to roll onto his side and kick them off. Desire rushed through her like a raging river as his heavy cock pressed against her thigh.

He skimmed his hand down her body, brushing his lips over hers, soft as a feather. "I could kiss you all night."

"Then do."

His smiling lips reclaimed hers, sweeter and slower this time, as if he were savoring every second just as she was. His hips pressed forward, and a low moan rumbled from his lungs. "Babe, do you have condoms?"

"*No.* Don't you?" She was on birth control, but she didn't know if he'd always been safe with other women, and she wasn't about to bring it up and kill the mood.

"*Fuck.* They're upstairs in my room." He ran his eyes down her body and slid his tongue over a nipple, sending electricity zinging through her. "Don't you dare get off this bed." He got up, his formidable erection bobbing enticingly as he reached for the doorknob. "Don't move, or I'll bend your hot little ass over my knee."

"Go ahead, but be aware that I spank back."

He flashed a wicked grin. "Where have you been all my life?"

She motioned around her, giving him a *right-here-Mr.-Oblivious* look.

"Right." He winked and stepped into the hall, closing the door behind him.

She heard him running up the stairs with the dogs chasing after him and his muffled shouts. "Get away from my ass. *Stop it.*" His footsteps raced across the ceiling, then back downstairs. She heard him yelling at the dogs again. He flew into the bedroom and closed the door, dropping a handful of condoms on the bedside table. "You're never going near them naked."

She laughed, and he came down over her. "You think it's funny to have three big dogs nosing my dick and my ass?"

"No, but imagining you running from them is. You were gone *way* too long." She wound her arms around him. "Get over here and kiss me."

His lips descended on hers with soul-searing intensity. The lingering taste of her arousal mixed with his own deliciousness magnified her desire. She wanted to memorize the weight of his body, the feel of his hard shaft pressing down on her. He tangled his fingers in her hair, deepening the kiss, and she moaned appreciatively. His hips rocked slowly and insistently, inciting a desperate pulse between her legs. He drew back on a series of tender kisses, *need* billowing off him. Neither one said a word as he grabbed a condom and rose onto his knees as he tore it open, giving her a glorious view. She was salivating to taste him, but that would have to wait. If he wasn't inside her soon, she might combust. His eyes bored into her as his hand fisted his cock, giving it a few tight strokes. Her sex clenched with anticipation.

"Hurry," she pleaded, earning a wicked grin.

He stroked himself again and dropped one hand between her legs, sliding his fingers along her wetness, then moving to that sensitive bundle of nerves that had her toes curling under, her hips bolting off the mattress as another orgasm took hold, and she shattered against his hand.

As she came down from the high, he ran his tongue along his glistening fingers. *"Mm-mm."*

Her cheeks burned as he rolled on the condom and came down over her. "I have a feeling I'm never going to get enough of you, Sidney Carver."

Hearing her full name wrapped up in all that heat brought a rush of emotions. He nudged her legs open wider, his eyes never leaving hers as the broad head of his erection pressed against her center. He took her in a ravenous kiss, pushing into her slowly. She'd known they'd be good together, but nothing could have prepared her for the blissfulness of feeling every blessed inch of him buried to the hilt, filling her so perfectly she saw stars. She clung to him, trying to get her brain to function, but the raw passion and overwhelming pleasure brimming in his eyes as he said, *"Jesus, Sid,"* did her in.

His mouth came eagerly down over hers, and they moved slowly at first, carefully, seeking the rhythm that would set them both free. As if their bodies had been made for each other, they quickly fell into sync, taking them from slow and careful to frantic and wild. Their kisses were a frenzied mix of feral and sensual, their hands everywhere at once, clawing, groping, clutching.

"You feel so good," he growled against her lips, reclaiming them with ruthless intensity.

Sidney felt like she'd been waiting her whole life for this very moment, and she was swept up in a world of overwhelming sensations. She bent her knees, opening wider so he could take her deeper, and he made a low, appreciative noise that lit her up from the inside out. She bowed off the mattress, but Gunner was too strong, his thrusts too powerful, and he drove her back down. He didn't miss a beat, guiding her legs around him and pushing his hands under her butt, lifting and angling so he could take her deeper, *harder*. His every thrust stole her breath. He held on to her so tight, he wasn't just claiming her; he was greedily possessing every inch of her, and she loved it.

He tore his mouth away with flames in his eyes, gritting out, "You're fucking unbelievable," and sealed his teeth over her neck, sending pain and pleasure whipping through her lightning fast and lava hot, bringing one earth-shattering explosion after another.

"Gunner—" flew out loud and untethered. He pushed his hands up her back, gripping her shoulders excruciatingly tight as he pounded into her and roared through his own powerful release, taking her right back up to the peak. They bucked and rocked even after they collapsed, breathless and panting, their bodies slick from their efforts.

Gunner held her like he never wanted to let her go, and she hoped he never would.

"HOLY SHIT," GUNNER panted out, kissing Sidney's sweet lips. Their hearts hammered to the same frantic beat as he tried to wrap his head around the intensity of their connection. That wasn't sex as he knew it. It was otherworldly, two souls coming together in ways he'd never imagined possible. Her pleasure had become his, slithering beneath his skin, unearthing more of the emotions he'd locked down for far too long, binding the two of them together in ways nothing ever had. He didn't want to move, didn't want to miss a second of being with her. She felt so unbelievably good and right, he knew it wasn't just the physical pleasure of her tight heat wrapped around his cock or her luscious body tangled up in his.

This was *Sidney*. The woman he trusted most. The person he'd spent years wanting to be with in every other way. How could this have been waiting for them for all that time?

"Did we just do that?" she asked breathlessly.

"Hell yeah, we did, and nobody's ever done it better."

She giggled, and it was the sweetest sound he'd ever heard. He rolled onto his side, needing to take care of the condom but hating the idea of leaving her. He loved seeing her this way, with her skin flushed, her body ripe, eyes glassy, like she was drunk on him. He kissed her softly, getting turned on again just looking at her. "I need to get cleaned up. I'll be right back."

"You're coming back?" she asked softly.

The disbelief in her eyes tugged at something deep in his chest. *Fuck.* Was he alone in not wanting to be apart? "You don't want me to?" *Please say you want me to stay.*

"No. I mean, *yes*, I want you to, but you don't..." She paused, her brows knitting. "Do you mean you'll come back for another round, then go up to your room? Or do you mean you're coming back and staying?"

She was so damn cute he could barely stand it. He drew her into his arms, gazing deeply into her eyes. "Let me make this perfectly clear. I'm going to come back and I'm going to fuck you six ways to Sunday, until we're both too tired to even think about getting out of this bed. Sound good?"

Her smile brightened her entire face, giving him her answer before she said, "Sounds like Christmas to me."

He laughed. "Babe, every day is going to be Christmas for us, so plan on being in this bed with me every night and waking up to my face every morning. Got it?"

"Got it." The relief in her voice was palpable. "But you never stay overnight with girls."

"You're right. I don't. But you're not just a girl, MOS." He grabbed her butt, kissing her hard. "You're my woman."

Nothing compared to the grin that earned. He kissed her again, then went to get cleaned up. When he returned, she was lying on her stomach, her arms tucked beneath a pillow, her cheek resting on it, eyes closed, a sheet covering her up to her waist. She looked peaceful and so damn sweet, part of him wanted to crawl beneath the sheet and hold her all night long.

But there was plenty of time for that.

He stripped the sheet away, and her eyes opened, a smile curving her lips. The tattooed lips on her ass drew his emotions to the surface again. He'd wanted to be with her so badly back then, he'd needed to take away her regrets over that tattoo. But now he realized he'd also wanted to be bound together by that ink. *Now* all he wanted was to take away any worries she had about him being with anyone else, because when he'd thought she'd been with Zander, he'd nearly lost his mind, and her mind was too beautiful to risk.

He ran his hands up her outer thighs, stopped to kiss those tattooed lips, then continued kissing his way up her body, caressing every beautiful inch as he rolled her onto her back and moved over her. "I'm done messing around, Sid. You don't have to worry about me and anyone else. I'd never hurt you like that."

She wound her arms around him, her gaze softening. "I know."

He lowered his lips to hers, and just like earlier, they quickly got carried away. He sheathed his length, and as their bodies came together, those overwhelming sensations stacked up inside him again, filling him up in places he hadn't known were empty. He held her tighter, kissing her more sensually, reveling in the sense of completeness overtaking him. He might have been blinded by their friendship for far too long, but now that he'd set his emotions free, he was never letting her go.

Chapter Thirteen

AWARENESS TIPTOED IN like a warm summer breeze, bringing the feel of Gunner's strong arms wrapped around her, his rigid cock hot and heavy against her belly, the hair on his legs tickling her skin. They were lying nose to nose. His hair was tousled, and his masculine scent warred with the boyish smile on his lips. That was a new, peaceful smile.

Her burly bestie really was a beast in the bedroom. Sidney was sore in places she didn't know she could be sore. But he definitely had a romantic side. They'd fallen asleep in this very position because he'd said he wanted to see her face as he drifted off. A little thrill accompanied the memory. He'd said so many sweet things throughout the night, like how he couldn't believe she was his, how they fit together like a hand and a glove, and how beautiful she was. She wanted to remember every word he'd said and everything about their first night together. He'd slept hard, but she'd woken up several times just to be sure she hadn't dreamed it all.

She couldn't believe how wrong she'd been yesterday. Once Gunner had explained that he and Erika were talking about her, she saw it all differently—the way they'd looked at her when whispering, the beautiful Christmas scene he'd arranged, and wanting her to take a picture of him and the dogs. How could she have been so wrong? She hadn't even thought he noticed when she'd left with Zander. What a surprise Zander had been, too. They'd gone for a ride and had ended up a few towns away, where they'd stopped for burgers and fries, and they'd ended up talking for hours. Zander had been a perfect gentleman and a supportive friend. The things he'd said about her and Gunner, like commenting on the rarity of their friendship and saying that sometimes guys couldn't see what was standing right in front of them had given her the sense that he'd known she was into Gunner. She felt a little guilty about using his name as her fictional crush, but she was glad she hadn't used *him*.

She looked at her hunk of burning love sleeping next to her with that goofy smile on his lips and felt so giddy, she wanted to shout, *Wake up! We're finally together! Can you believe it?* But she was almost thirty, not seventeen, so she slipped out from under his arm and went to pee, putting on his T-shirt along the way.

In the privacy of her bathroom, she did a little happy dance before emptying her bladder, washing up, and brushing her teeth. A quick glimpse in the mirror proved she also wore a goofy smile, but she'd proudly wear it all day long.

She quietly left the bathroom and put on a clean pair of underwear, slipping silently out of the bedroom. The dogs met her in the hallway, all curious noses and anxious whimpers.

"I know, I know." She petted them as they followed her to the front door. "I'm sorry we didn't let you in last night. It won't happen again." *Will it?* She thought about that as she put the dogs out. She couldn't imagine doing everything they'd done with the dogs in the room, and she couldn't wait to do it again! Her smile widened with the memory of Gunner running upstairs, snapping at the dogs. She'd thought he was crazy when he'd thrown a handful of condoms on the nightstand, but they'd used three. *Three!*

No wonder she was sore.

She went into the kitchen to make coffee. As it brewed, she looked at the pictures on the refrigerator. *You're always hiding behind your hair or your hand.* He was right. She had no idea why she always covered her face, but she loved knowing he'd not only noticed but had gone to great lengths to get pictures where she wasn't hiding behind her hair.

Snowflake wound around her feet, and she picked her up, cuddling against her fur. "Hi, sweetie. Are you hungry?"

She fed the cats and began making pancakes, feeling like she was walking on air.

A few minutes later, Gunner's arms circled her from behind, and he nuzzled against her neck. "*Mm-mm.* You've always looked good in the mornings, but you look fucking incredible now that you're *mine.*"

Oh, how she loved that! She transferred the pancakes to plates and turned in his arms. "I guess that means you have no regrets."

"The only thing I regret is not tying you to the bed so you couldn't sneak out this morning."

Her body flamed at the thought of being tied up for his taking. He pressed his lips to hers, tasting minty fresh.

"We don't have to be at the Hog until eleven to hide eggs and help decorate."

Her thoughts came to a screeching halt. "It's *Easter.*"

"All day long, babe." His hands slid down her back, and he trailed kisses up her neck.

"I forgot." She leaned her head back, giving him better access, every touch of his lips stealing a little more of her thoughts. "Is that going to be weird?"

"What?" He slid his tongue around the shell of her ear, making it even harder to concentrate.

"Us, together, around everyone?"

"No." He nipped her earlobe, sending a spear of heat through her core. "Why would it?"

"Because we *just* got together last night, and..." He continued kissing and nipping, and her thoughts kept flitting away. "I don't want to have to answer a bunch of questions or take attention away from the kids and the event."

"Mm-hm." He backed her up against the counter, wedging himself between her legs, and lifted his shirt that she was wearing over her head and dropped it as he lowered his mouth to her breast.

"Oh *God*." She closed her eyes, pushing her hands into his hair. "Maybe we should just play it cool."

"Fine," he whispered against her skin. "We'll play it cool." He brushed his lips over hers, grinding his hard length against her. "But right now I'm not playing. I'm coming in *hot*."

He crushed his mouth to hers, urgent and demanding. Desire pounded through her, their bodies rocking and gyrating. His hands dove into her hair and his tongue delved deeper into her mouth. She moaned at his delicious possession. She was wet and so damn ready her legs were shaking, and he was hard as stone. She ached to be one with him, only now it was *her* turn to satiate the other needs she had. But the thought of being tied to the bed was also taunting her. How was it possible to want him so much? She felt like a nymphomaniac, but she didn't care, and pushed a hand into his briefs, palming his erection.

A guttural, appreciative sound rumbled up his throat as she stroked him. "Fuck yeah, baby," he said between passionate kisses. "I *need* your hands on me."

"How about my mouth?" She could hardly believe she'd said it, but she needed more of him. He drew back with fire in his eyes, fueling her inferno. "Have you ever...ridden bareback?" she asked nervously.

"Never," he growled. "We wouldn't have had sex if it wasn't safe, even with protection. I'd never put your health at risk."

Relief swept through her. She turned them so his back was to the counter and yanked down his briefs, sinking to her knees as he stepped out of them. He lowered himself to the perfect height, holding her gaze as she fisted his cock. She dragged her tongue from base to tip, earning another raw, masculine sound. He pushed his fingers through her hair, holding it back, watching her licking and teasing the broad head of his cock as she stroked his shaft.

"*Jesus*, Sid. I could come just watching you jerk me off."

That made her want to pleasure him even more. She continued teasing him with her tongue, sliding along his length, over the crown, and stroking him. His thighs flexed, his teeth clenched, and his hands fisted in her hair. She knew he wanted to take control, and she loved feeling his restraint as he let her lead. When she finally lowered her mouth over his shaft, his chin fell to his chest, and he uttered a curse as she began working him with her hand and mouth. She slowed to tease the tip, squeezing tight as she followed her mouth with her hand, earning one hungry moan after another. Those erotic sounds echoed in her head, making her entire body pulse with need. She quickened her efforts, sucking harder, stroking faster. His cock swelled in her hand.

"Fuck, baby," he gritted out. "You feel so good, I'm not gonna last."

She grinned around his cock, meeting his hungry gaze as she pulled him out of her mouth and dragged her tongue along the crown. His jaw was clenched so tight it had to hurt. "Based on last night, I'm pretty sure you'll recover fast enough so we'll still have time to do that thing you regretted not doing before we have to leave."

His eyes blazed so hot, she was surprised the kitchen didn't go up in flames. She took him to the back of her throat, working him fast and tight, until he was moaning, thrusting, *cursing*. She was so turned on, she was on the verge of losing it, too. She squeezed her knees together to stave off her needs and cradled his balls. His entire body flexed, his fingers tugging her hair. Pleasure and pain coalesced into something hot, bright, and magnificent as his hips shot forward and *"Sid—"* fell gruffly from his lips. She continued working him with her hand and mouth, taking everything he had to give, until his body stilled, save for a few rumbling aftershocks.

"Come here, beautiful." His voice was rough and gravelly as he lifted her to her feet. Breathing heavily, he cradled the back of her head with one hand, pushing the other into her underwear. His thick fingers slipped through her wetness a few times before expertly finding her clit.

Electricity shot through her, and she gasped.

Flames shimmered in his eyes, and he took her in a kiss so fierce and primal, it sent her into a frenzy. She pushed her underwear down, kicking it off as he feasted on her mouth, teasing her down below like he knew her body by heart. It didn't take long before she was crashing into ecstasy, her body bucking and clenching as her orgasm ravaged her. His name flew from her lips, but he held their mouths together in a torturously exquisite kiss, his roughness heightening her pleasure, until she went limp and breathless against him.

He gathered her in his arms, kissing her cheek and neck, holding her like she was precious. "I fucking *love* touching you."

"*More*" was all she could manage.

As he scooped her into his arms and carried her into the bedroom, she knew it didn't matter how many orgasms she had. She'd never get enough of being close to the man she'd loved forever.

THE GROUNDS OF the Salty Hog were littered with colorful plastic eggs tucked between tufts of grass and half-hidden under leaves and trees as far as the eye could see. Pastel streamers brightened the old rustic restaurant, and the din of children laughing and shouting filled the air as adults mingled and watched over them. Gunner's family had been hosting the Easter egg hunt since he was just a boy, and it never got old. The same families were still attending, only now the adult children of those families brought their own children to hunt for eggs.

Gunner held Rosie's hand as she pulled him past his parents, who looked like they were having the time of their lives playing with a group of children. The little bundle of energy was dressed in a frilly pink dress and white tights and had been dragging him from one side of the lawn to the other for the past half hour.

"Come on, Uncle Gunny, *faster!*" Rosie tugged him toward another group of children gathering eggs down by the water. Tank and Blaine stood between the kids and the water's edge.

Their ever-watchful guardians.

"I'll give you *faster*."

Holding her basket of eggs in one hand, he scooped her up in the other, holding her under his arm like a football. She squealed, spreading her arms out to the sides as he ran across the lawn. He looked around for Junie and saw her and Zeke walking toward the woods on the other side of the parking lot. She was wearing the explorer backpack Zeke had given her last year and holding Zeke's hand. Those two turned everything into an adventure.

"Look, Papa Tank! I'm flyin'!" Rosie yelled, giggling as Gunner swooped her through the air and plunked her down to her feet. He handed her the basket as a group of children ran over, waving their arms and calling out for turns.

Justice's four-year-old daughter, Patience, dropped her basket and jumped up and down. "Do me! Please!" Patience was a ballet fanatic, and she wore a black sweater and tights with a pink tutu and matching ballet shoes. Her mass of short, dark twisted curls was pulled away from her face with a big pink ribbon.

"I wanna fly!" Starr's toddler, Gracie, hollered, her blond hair bouncing around her adorable face.

"You're next, Gracie girl." Gunner lifted Patience over his head, and she giggled and squealed as he zoomed her through the air. He caught sight of Sidney watching him from halfway across the yard, where she was talking with Steph and Madigan. Damn, she was beautiful. He could still hear her laughter ringing in his ears from when he'd chased her around the bedroom pawing at her as she'd gotten dressed.

She smiled the secret smile he'd come to know last night. The one that said she was his and he was hers, and *man*, he loved that. It was hell trying to play it cool when he wanted to tell everyone there what that smile meant. But he wanted to talk to her father first, anyway. Colonel was supposed to be there an hour ago, but he must have changed his plans.

"Okay, princess. It's Gracie's turn." As he set Patience down, Justice nodded appreciatively.

"You'll be here all day doing that," Justin said as he and Chloe walked by.

"And we'll be chasing Grandpa Mike all day. Come on. I just saw him put another plastic egg in his pocket." Chloe pulled Justin toward their grandfather, who was looking around as he picked up another egg from the ground and not-so-nonchalantly slipped it into his shirt pocket.

Gunner chuckled as Justin and Chloe walked away. He'd always been happy for them, but he'd never quite understood how Justin had gone from wanting to hang out with the guys to wanting to be home with Chloe. Now he understood.

The kids weren't the only ones flying high today. He felt lighter and happier than he could ever remember feeling. He'd smiled the whole damn morning as he and Sidney had worked through their chores at the shelter, like a teenager rather than a man who had been through war. He found himself paying closer attention to the little things he'd always liked about Sidney but hadn't thought too much about, like the way she hummed as she fed the cats and had a full-blown conversation with Chewy when she was feeding him and Gunner was cleaning out the goat house, just like he did. She'd worked with Chappy, and they'd both spent extra time with Liberty. Even that had felt different. *Better.* And he swore Liberty had felt it, too.

When he set Gracie down, a gaggle of kids ran over, tugging

at his jeans and shirt. His gaze found Sidney again, still watching him, laughing at the kids vying for a ride. He swore her eyes had become brighter and her smile more radiant in the last twenty-four hours. He could see them years from now, chasing their own kids around as they hunted for eggs.

The thought hit him out of nowhere, and he chewed on it for a minute. He was getting way ahead of himself. He'd never even *thought* about settling down, but as he lifted a giggling boy and raced around with him, he couldn't shake the idea.

Several airplane rides later, he spotted Zeke and Junie coming back from the woods. Zeke had one hand protectively on her back. Junie had both arms wrapped around a bucket, and she was staring into it with a big grin. The roar of a motorcycle caught Gunner's attention as Sidney's father pulled into the parking lot.

"Zeke!" Gunner waved his cousin over as a handful of kids begged for turns.

"Uncle Gunny, we found a fwog!" Junie's eyes glittered with excitement as she showed him a little green frog at the bottom of her bucket.

"That's great, Junebug." He tousled her hair and exchanged knowing glances with Zeke. River had told the girls stories about frogs, and now they associated them with their late father.

"I'm gonna show Wosie!"

As Junie scampered off, Zeke looked at the kids' eager faces and said, "What are you, the Pied Piper today?"

"Something like that. Would you mind taking over airplane rides? I want to talk to Sid's dad."

"Go ahead." Zeke turned to the kids and clapped his hands. "Okay, kids, Pilot Zeke is ready for takeoff. The line forms here."

As the kids fell into line, Gunner headed for Sidney's father.

Zander intercepted him. "Hey, can I talk to you for a minute?"

"Yeah, let me just catch up with Colonel first. Give me five minutes." Gunner's nerves strung tight as he jogged over to Sid's father. He didn't know what had gone down between him and Sidney the other morning at breakfast, and he knew his reputation gave him more than three strikes, but Gunner was a man of honor, and he'd do whatever it took to win her father's approval.

"Hey, Colonel. Got a minute?"

"Sure. What's up?"

"I want to talk to you about Sid. You know she means the world to me, and we've been through a lot of shit together. But things have changed between us, and I wanted you to be the first to know."

Her father's eyes narrowed. "Changed how?"

Gunner glanced at Sidney, and his heart thundered. "We're together, as a couple."

"A *couple*." His jaw clenched. "You and my Sidekick?"

Gunner's gut tightened. "Yes, sir. I know you probably have reservations because of my history with women, but it's not like that with Sid. I'm all in with her, and I'll do whatever it takes to prove that to you and to her."

He lifted his chin. "You think you can just shut off that side of yourself?"

"That's just it, sir. I don't think it's a matter of shutting anything off. I think I needed to *open* something up and let my true feelings for her come out. She's everything to me, Colonel. She's my best friend. The person I look forward to seeing every morning and every night. I didn't think I could have this with her without jeopardizing our friendship, or I would've been with her right after we'd met. But I didn't want to risk losing our connection, so I found other ways to keep that part of myself away from her. This is too much information for you, but you should know. I never had a single woman spend the night because I didn't want anyone to steal our mornings from us." He hadn't even realized that until the words left his mouth, but they were truer than anything he'd ever known. "I'm not proud of the way I've gone through women, but on the upside, I'm not a kid, Colonel. I know what I want, and she's standing right over there looking at us like I'm spilling all of our secrets."

Her father finally cracked a smile. "Which you *are*."

"Yes, but only because I don't want this to be a secret. I want the whole damn world to know, but I won't let that happen until I have your blessing. No matter how long it takes, I will show you that I am worthy of being your daughter's man."

Her father looked at Sidney for a long moment before turning serious eyes on Gunner. "Son, she's all I've got in this world."

"I'm well aware of that." He swallowed hard.

"If I didn't trust you, she never would have moved into your house."

Gunner felt like he'd won the lottery. "Thank you for your trust."

"Gunner, you showed me what she meant to you and what you were made of when you changed your life to give her the only life outside of the military that she'd ever talked about. A life she'd spoken of having with *you* even back then. I will be forever grateful for that. But if you want to thank me for trusting you, don't give me a reason to regret it." He held out his hand, and when Gunner shook it, he tugged him closer with a death grip on his hand. "Because if you hurt her and *she* doesn't put you six feet under, I will."

There was no humor in his voice, and Gunner respected that. "I'd pull that trigger myself before I'd hurt her."

They talked for another minute, and then Gunner made a beeline for Sidney, feeling on top of the world.

Zander jogged over, falling into step beside him. "Dude, can we talk?"

"Shit, sorry, Zan. I forgot. What's going on?"

"Listen, you know I don't like to get caught up in other people's business, but I think you're making a big mistake with Sidney."

Gunner stopped in his tracks. "What the fuck does that mean?" *And how do you know about us?*

"It means you've got the greatest girl under your roof every night, and after talking with her for *hours* last night, I think she's into you. But you're out there fucking around with women you don't give two shits about, and now she's moving out. If you have half a brain in that head of yours, you'll do everything you can to change that."

Relief flooded him. "You know what?" He couldn't stop his grin from breaking free as he clapped Zander on the shoulder. "Thanks for clearing that up for me. You're absolutely right."

He turned on his heel and went to get his girl.

"UH-OH. SOMEONE LOOKS like his briefs are in a bunch," Madigan said.

Sidney followed her gaze to Gunner stalking toward them, eyes locked on *her*, and her pulse ricocheted.

"*Ladies*," he said playfully, draping an arm across Sidney's shoulders and pulling her close enough to speak directly into her ear. "I've seen you in those jeans more times than I can count, but they hit differently knowing you have on the GET BUSY underwear beneath them."

Her cheeks flamed. "Gun—"

He silenced her with a hard press of his lips, and he didn't stop there, deepening the kiss.

"*What* is *this*?" Madigan said loudly.

"The hottest kiss *I've* ever seen," Steph exclaimed.

Sidney tried to break away, but Gunner held her tighter, kissing her longer as cheers and whistles rang out around them. She came away breathless and dizzy, grinning like a fool again. Their family and friends were looking at them with approving smiles and curious expressions.

"About damn time," Baz called out.

"What happened to playing it *cool*?" Sidney whispered loudly from behind her unstoppable grin.

"What can I say, MOS? You make me too hot to play it cool." He pressed his lips to hers again, inciting more cheers.

"I guess I'm not getting a new roommate," Madigan said, making them all laugh.

"Sorry," Sidney said, although she couldn't be happier.

"Don't be. This is way better than you moving in with me," Madigan said cheerily. "This is what I've wanted all along."

Me too.

"Damn, bro. You wasted no time at all," Zander said.

Gunner kissed her temple. "I'm no fool."

"How long has this been going on?" Steph asked.

I've loved him forever.

As if Gunner had read her mind, he said, "Sid's always been my girl, but *this*"—he kissed her again—"this is new."

"Well, *okay*, then! I love Sid, so don't screw it up," Steph said, causing a rumble of laughter.

"Another one bites the dust," Blaine shouted.

Ginger reached for Conroy's hand and said, "I think you mean another one found his ride or die."

Tank hollered, "Double wedding!" and everyone cheered.

"Ohmygosh." Sidney hid her face in his shirt, laughing.

Gunner lifted her chin, grinning down at her. "You're going to need to get over that embarrassment, sweetheart, because I'm going to make sure everyone knows you're mine."

As he lowered his lips to hers, she realized she wouldn't want it any other way.

Chapter Fourteen

PREACHER AND REBA'S house was packed with family and friends for Easter dinner. Sidney was glad it was buffet style because, after a whirlwind afternoon of answering questions and being congratulated, she was so happy she felt like she might burst. There was no way she could sit still. She was having a hard enough time standing still as she chatted with some of the girls about Leah's wedding, and Gunner wasn't making it any easier. She could feel his eyes on her, just as they'd been throughout the day. Watching, winking, keeping her in a heightened state of awareness, which made her even more jittery. They'd gone home after the Easter egg hunt to check on the animals and hadn't been able to keep their hands off each other.

She stole a glance at him, talking with Baz and Blaine by the patio doors. The wolfish grin Gunner had been sporting since he'd outed them sent her body into a frenzy. Was it normal to want to run into his arms after being together for only one night? To want to spill her guts about how happy she was to anyone who would listen? Was *that* why she'd never felt comfortable with girl talk? Because she hadn't ever felt like *this* before?

"How about you, Sid?" Madigan nudged her. *"Hello."*

Shoot. "What? Sorry. I was—"

"Drooling over Gunner again," Steph said in a singsong voice as Junie tugged Ginger past them toward the dining room. Ginger flashed an approving smile at Sidney.

Sidney winced, and they all laughed. "Sorry. I'm really not one of *those* girls."

"I was never one of those girls, either, until Justin got his hooks in me." Chloe looked across the living room at Justin, talking with his parents.

"All Tank has to do is look at me and I get all fluttery inside," Leah said.

"That's probably your little Tankette flexing its muscles," Steph joked.

"Well, I've never zoned out like I have today," Sidney said. "What did you want to know, Mads?"

"I asked if you wanted to go shopping with us next weekend for dresses to wear to Leah and Tank's wedding. You'll probably want to get something to match Gunner, right?" Gunner and Baz were going to be Tank's best men at the wedding, and Junie and Rosie were Leah's *girls of honor.*

"We're supposed to match? Really? Is that a thing?" Sidney asked. "I've never had a date for a wedding."

"Hey, I was your date for Chloe and Justin's wedding," Madigan reminded her.

"I know, but this is different. I've never thought about that type of thing. It's hard enough finding a dress I feel comfortable in." She looked down at her jeans and pink Converse, and her gaze moved over the other girls' outfits. Leah wore a pretty floral dress, and Chloe had on slacks and heeled ankle boots with a dressy blouse. Madigan and Steph were wearing jeans, but they had on cute sweaters and dressy boots. "Should I have dressed up tonight? I always wear jeans, but now that I'm with Gunner, do I need to think about that?"

"*No*," Madigan insisted. "And you don't have to match with him at the wedding, either. I just thought you might want to."

"Do you think *he'll* want me to?" Why was she so nervous over a dress? She glanced at Gunner holding Rosie by the dining room table, and the answer came to her. Because that beautiful man was finally hers, and she would do anything to make him happy and proud to be with her.

"The only reason Gunner would care about matching is because he wants everyone to know you're his," Madigan said.

Sidney smiled. "That's reason enough for me to try to find a dress to match."

"You know you don't have to change for him, right?" Steph asked.

"I know he likes me as I am. But now that I'm thinking about it, I guess there's a teeny-tiny part of me that wonders if I should dress up for him sometimes."

"Dress up in the bedroom—that'll be enough," Chloe said.

They all laughed.

Steph's gaze turned serious. "I've known Gunner my whole life, and he's never done anything like what he did with you today. That was huge, Sid. He's crazy about you. It wouldn't matter if you wore designer clothes or rags."

"Remember what Ginger said?" Leah asked. "*When a wild one settles down, you know they're all in, heart and soul, because they found their special person more excitin', more groundin', and more everything than anyone else who has crossed their path. They've found their ride or die.* You're Gunner's ride or die, Sid."

"Plus, he's been staring at you like he can't wait to get his hands on you since you guys got here," Madigan added.

Sidney's cheeks burned. "I didn't think anyone else noticed."

"Do you really think anyone could miss the sparks flying across the room?" Steph teased. "I'm waiting for the curtains to go up in flames."

Sidney grinned. "Well, I *hoped* nobody noticed."

"We'll pretend we didn't," Chloe said. "But don't worry, we'll find you a great dress that you feel comfortable in. Leah, did you and Tank decide what the guys are wearing?"

"*I* didn't, but the girls did." Leah smiled sweetly. "Thanks to them, I get to see him in a bow tie after all! They're wearing dark slacks, white dress shirts, and pink bow ties with blue polka dots on them, for the baby."

Sidney tried to imagine Gunner in a bow tie. The guys had worn suits and ties to Justin and Chloe's wedding, and Sidney hadn't been able to take her eyes off Gunner the whole night.

"Your girls are the sweetest," Madigan said. "I can't wait to see Tanky in a bow tie."

"Me either," Leah said dreamily. "Did I tell you about the dresses we got for the girls?"

Leah's eyes brightened as she told them about the dresses and shared more details about the wedding. Sidney was happy for them, but she was also happy for the rest of the Wickeds. She knew how much everyone else had worried about Tank ever letting his walls down after Ashley had died since he'd been the one to find her. She glanced at Gunner again and wondered if their family had ever worried about him like that, since he and Ashley were so close. But she didn't have time to ponder that for long, because Steph touched her hand and motioned to her father coming out of the kitchen, heading in their direction.

"Don't hate me," Steph said quietly. "But I'm having defi-nite age-gap fantasies about your dad."

"Me too," Madigan whispered.

Sidney laughed. Her father hadn't said much after he'd found out about her and Gunner. But he was a thinker, and she had a feeling he'd been processing the information this whole time.

"You girls look like you're up to no good," her father said.

Sidney and the others shared an amused glance.

"Would you ladies mind if I borrow my daughter for a few minutes?"

"Of course not," Leah said. "Fathers and daughters should spend as much time together as they can."

Her father looked empathetically at Leah. "Thanks, sweet-heart." As he led Sidney away from the others, he said, "How're you holding up?"

"Fine. Why?"

"Well, this is your first time with Gunner's family as his girlfriend." His brow knitted. "Do kids still call it that? His girlfriend? His girl? His old lady? You're too young to be an old lady."

"Dad." She laughed. "I'm hardly a kid."

"You're my kid, Sidekick. This is new for me, too. I just want to say and do the right things. How do you feel?"

"Like I'm in a dream that I never want to wake up from."

"That's good, baby. Are you nervous?"

She shrugged one shoulder. "I wouldn't be human if I wasn't. Know what's funny? I've never been nervous with Gunner before I started really liking him."

"Emotions are tricky. They have a mind of their own, and they can play with your insecurities. I'm going to go out on a limb and assume he was the good friend you thought you'd screwed something up with."

She nodded. "Yeah. He was. I'm sorry I lied to you, but I didn't want to put you in the middle."

"Is that what you're nervous about?"

"No. I'm not really nervous about anything in particular. I know how he feels about me, and I know it's real. I just hope being together doesn't change me or what we have."

"You're the most consistent person I've ever known. You're the same strong-willed tough cookie you were at four years old. But you're both going to grow from this relationship, and with growth comes change. That's a good thing, Sid, but with all good things there are difficult moments, and you should expect a few."

"Wow, way to pop my bubble. Can't you just tell me it's going to be rainbows and puppies forever?"

He chuckled. "I've never cushioned the blows of life, and I'm not about to start."

"But what if I change in a way he doesn't like?"

Her father's brows slanted, and he studied her face. "You mean like I changed before your mom left?"

She nodded. She hadn't even known she was worried about that until just now.

"Nobody can predict the future. But you see that man over there?" He nodded toward Gunner, who was lifting Rosie into the air and making her giggle. "Right after you were injured, he called me and told me not to worry, that he'd make sure you had everything you needed to be happy in life outside the military regardless of how your recovery went. That is not a man who will abandon you for anything."

Sidney got choked up. "You never told me he called you or

said those things."

"Because those were promises made by a young man who had told me for several years that he planned on being a career marine and it would take an act of God to get him out. I wasn't sure he'd follow through, and when he did, there was no need to tell you, because you were living his promise."

She looked at Gunner, remembering what he'd said about how he'd locked away his feelings for her, and still he'd created this amazing life for her—for *them*. "Thank you for telling me now."

"I just have one question."

"What's that?"

"What the hell took you two so long? Con and I were sure you'd be all over each other after you moved in together."

"Dad!" She laughed.

"Hey, I'm just being honest." He hugged her and kissed her cheek. "I know the answer anyway."

"Oh, *really*? What is it?"

"Sometimes you have to live a little before you can see what's really in your heart. In the military you're told what to do and when to do it. You're taught to ignore your emotions because thinking too much can get you killed, and nobody prepares you for how to be a civilian. How to find your place in this world and be the person directing your life, making the tough decisions, and feeling the very things you were taught to disregard."

She thought about the texts Gunner had sent to her during her months of recovery—*You've got this, MOS. Nobody can make your recovery happen but you. Don't worry about tomorrow. Let me do that. Focus on today. Fight for yourself, MOS. I believe in you. Rosco's fighting for you—you fight for him, too. It's okay to be pissed off or sad. Put those emotions into recovering. No matter what happens, you've always got me*—and she realized she'd had someone teaching her all along.

"YOU KEEP LOOKING at Sid like that, and the smoke detectors are going to go off," Tank said as he sidled up to Gunner.

"Do you ever wish you had a window into Leah's thoughts?"

"All the time." Tank took a drink of his beer. "Your girl looks happy."

"She looked like she was going to cry a few minutes ago. What could her father have said to cause that?"

"She's a chick. They can get teary over just about anything."

"Not Sid. She almost never tears up."

"Dude, you're thinking too much. He's her old man, and you just told the world you're sleeping with her. He's saying dad stuff."

"Yeah, I guess you're right." He watched Sidney's father hug her. She glanced over her father's shoulder at Gunner, and their eyes connected with an electric charge. He blew her a kiss, but Justin, Reba, and his grandfather walked into his line of sight, blocking his view of Sidney. He returned his attention to Tank as their father joined them. "Man, the right girl can really mess with your head."

Tank laughed. "You think?"

"Sounds like I got here just in time," their father said.

"It's crazy. I've seen her every day for what feels like forever, and suddenly I can't get enough of her. I just want to be with her, you know? I don't even care what we're doing. When she was talking with the girls, I wanted to be right beside her, and I know that's messed up, so don't give me shit."

"That's not messed up, son," his father said. "That's how you know it's real. You've seen her as your friend. You've protected her and shared your life with her, and now you're finally allowing yourself to accept what I think most, if not all, of us have suspected all along. That she's your everything." He glanced at their mother sitting on the couch with Junie on her lap. "Your mother and I have been married for so many years it's hard to remember my life before her, and I *still* want to be with her every minute. But women need space, and so do we. At least that's what she tells me. She says she *needs* her girl time."

"Yeah? Well, I need *my* girl time, too. With *Sid*."

Tank chuckled. "The way you kissed her today tells me you're not lacking in that department."

"That was quite a coming-out party," their father said. "For a minute there, I thought Sid was as shocked as we were."

"She was." Gunner smirked. "We were supposed to be playing it cool." But he'd played it cool for years, and he was done with that shit.

Tank scoffed. "That ain't possible when you find your sweetheart."

Gunner caught a glimpse of Sidney across the room, and he felt that magnetic pull once again. "Truer words have never been spoken."

Chapter Fifteen

SIDNEY HUMMED AS she finished feeding the cats dinner at the rescue, thinking about the ways in which her life had changed in the week since Easter. Work was as busy as ever. She'd spent a lot of time with Liberty, who was doing well, and working with Chappy. Not much had changed there, except that she and Gunner couldn't keep their hands off each other. But that was true from the moment she woke up with his big body wrapped around her and the dogs and cats strewn across their bed, through breakfast, which now included steamy kisses between bites, all the way until nighttime, when they left a trail of clothing from the living room into her bedroom and fell asleep tangled up as one.

Life was beautiful, and Gunner made *her* feel that way, too. She'd had a great time shopping with the girls yesterday. They'd helped her find a gorgeous sky-blue dress she felt more than comfortable wearing and matched the blue polka dots on Gunner's bow tie for the wedding. She also discovered that she was actually pretty good at talking about her personal life now that she had one. She'd gushed about how surprisingly romantic Gunner was and had told them about the sweet and naughty notes he'd left by the coffeemaker over the last week and his to-do list he'd written on the kitchen calendar with things he'd like to do to *her*. She'd kept the dirty details to herself, but she'd also told them about the to-do list he'd made for *her* and had left on her pillow, which had his name written all the way down the page. But one of her favorite things he'd done was setting aside three nights to binge a series featuring Tom Hardy. He'd made popcorn, stocked up on Kit Kats, and had given her a sweatshirt with TAKEN BY GUNNER & THE CREW in a red heart over a picture of him and the dogs.

The girls had been as smitten as she was.

She pulled the food cart into the stockroom. Gunner slipped in behind her—and locked the door. Her pulse quickened at the seductive look in his eyes.

"Fancy meeting you here." He stalked toward her like a lion closing in on his prey.

"Gunner." It was a half-hearted warning, which fell silent as he ran his hands down her hips and growled like a bear, sending all sorts of thrilling vibes through her.

"Yes, *Sidney?*" He dipped his head, nipping at her neck as he unbuttoned her jeans and pushed his hand into her underwear. She closed her eyes as he sealed his mouth over her neck, his fingers sliding over that magical spot and through her wetness in a mesmerizing rhythm.

"God." She grabbed his waist to combat her weakening legs.

"Mm," he murmured into her ear, backing her up against the wall and pushing his other hand beneath her shirt. "I have a surprise for you. *After* you come."

He was the most giving lover, always chasing her pleasure before his own. He unhooked the front clasp of her bra, taking her nipple between his finger and thumb and squeezing just hard enough to send shocks of heat between her legs. She gasped, rising up on her toes. He quickened his efforts, obliterating her ability to speak. Desire pounded through her, drawing out a stream of needy noises. He captured her mouth in slow, drugging kisses, imprisoning her in a web of arousal so thick and pleasurous, she wanted to live in it.

A knock sounded at the door, and her eyes flew open.

"Gunner? Sid? Are you in there?" It was Tori. She'd already caught them making out twice this week!

"Yeah." Gunner didn't relent, his hungry eyes drilling into Sidney as he continued stroking over that spot that had her gritting her teeth against her mounting climax.

"I thought you were leaving?" Tori said.

"We're *coming*." A sly grin followed his double entendre. "Give us a minute."

Tori said something about getting a room, and Sidney tried to scowl, but Gunner knew just how to touch her to make it impossible for her to do anything more than hold on for dear life as he sent her soaring. Thankfully, his mouth covered hers, because the pleasure was so intense, she couldn't silence the gratified sounds escaping.

When she finally came down from the clouds, his arms circled her, his heart beating quick and sure against her cheek as he kissed the top of her head. She loved those moments after they fooled around, when he just held her like he'd gotten everything he'd wanted. He tipped her face up and kissed her.

"As much as I love everything we do, Tori's going to quit if you keep this up at work," she warned.

He rocked his hips forward, his arousal pressing into her belly. "I'm keeping it up, so we'll just have to give her a raise."

She laughed. "You are so bad."

"I think you mean so *good*." He kissed her again, so passionately, she wanted to rip off his clothes and climb him like a mountain. He drew back, grinning like he knew it. "Come on, babe. We're getting out of here." He reclasped her bra as she closed her jeans.

"Where are we going?"

"You'll see."

They went home, and he sent her to get a sweatshirt. When she returned, he'd put all four dogs in the double-cab truck and had Sidney climb in beside him. He'd kept her by his side every time they'd gone anywhere this week, and she loved it.

The dogs looked as excited as she was as he drove out of the gates. Gunner wouldn't tell her where they were going, but it didn't take long for her to figure it out as he headed toward the bay and veered down the dirt road that led to Wicked Carver Beach. They hadn't been there in several weeks.

"I'm so glad we're here. I missed it."

He helped her out of the truck. "Between rehabbing Chappy, nurturing Liberty, getting ready for the photo shoot, and then being outed for sleeping with Cape Cod's hottest bachelor, I figured you could use a break."

"That last one was the doozy," she teased as the big dogs jumped out of the truck, sniffing the ground excitedly.

Gunner set Opha Mae down with the others and grabbed blankets from behind the seat. He handed them to her, slung the backpack of dog toys over his shoulder, and pulled a cooler out. He set the cooler down and went around to the bed of the truck, retrieving his leather log carrier and the backpack with the tools they used for bonfires. He hoisted the second backpack over his shoulder.

"Wow. You thought of everything." She reached for the cooler, but he snagged it first.

"It's our first real date. I've got to earn some nookie points."

He leaned in for a kiss as she reveled in his thoughtfulness.

The dogs led them down the narrow sandy path toward the beach. Gunner stopped by their wooden sign sticking up in the tall dune grass at the crest of the dune, standing sentinel over the bay. Their names were burned into the wood with a fancy tool he'd borrowed from Preacher. The first time he'd taken her there, they'd watched the sunset and stayed for hours, until they'd seen a shooting star. She remembered feeling a sense of peace that she'd never felt in her whole life, as if she'd found the place she was always meant to be.

"We need a picture by our sign." Gunner whistled for the dogs to come back. "This is our first time coming to our beach as a couple."

She got all fluttery inside as he settled the dogs by their sign and wondered if she'd ever stop getting butterflies over the little things he did. He crouched beside Granger, Belleau, and Rosco, and had Sidney sit in front of him with Opha Mae on her lap. They squeezed in tight, as he tried to fit them all into a selfie. It took about twenty tries to finally get a good picture. But even the bloopers were keepers. He'd caught them in various stages of laughter with the dogs climbing over them or licking their faces.

Sidney added those moments to the long list of things she'd never forget.

They took the dogs for a walk along the shore and played Frisbee and fetch. Granger dropped the Frisbee, and Sidney lunged for it, snagging it seconds before Gunner could, and he chased her around the sand and tackled her, smothering her laughter with kisses. The dogs barked and ran over, and they ended up rolling around with them, too.

Sidney set out blankets in the sand, and Gunner built a fire as the sun went down over the bay, spreading vibrant ribbons of orange and yellow along the horizon. They placed the standing metal grate over the fire and cooked enough hamburgers for them and the dogs. Gunner withdrew two plastic containers from the cooler. "Homemade potato salad and cut-up fruit."

"Did you have your mom make us her famous potato salad?" She loved his mother's potato salad.

"No. I had her show me how, and we made it together."

"You *did?*" She'd never smiled as much as she had the last week.

"Yup, and *not* for nookie points. I did it to see that smile." He kissed her. "I'd do anything to see your smile."

Tank's romantic efforts had nothing on Gunner. Everything he did and said seemed romantic to her.

They talked as they enjoyed their dinner, basking in the gentle breeze and being serenaded by the crackling fire and the sounds of the sea and their dogs. Afterward, with the dogs lying on their own blankets, Sidney and Gunner lay nose to nose, warmed by the fire, kissing and talking.

"I hadn't realized how much I needed this."

"That's okay. I knew, and I've got you, babe. You can count on me."

"I thought I liked you before, but then you do something like this and say things like that, and I fall even harder for you."

"I like where this is going."

She smiled. "Thank you for a perfect evening."

"You're my girl. There's nothing I won't do for you."

She'd waited so long to hear that, she took a moment to enjoy it.

"What are you thinking about?"

"How lucky I am. I'm glad you never had a real girlfriend

before me."

"Why is that?" He tucked her hair behind her ear, searching her face.

That was another thing she was getting used to. Gunner liked to see her face, and she was still learning to fight the urge to shake her hair back into her eyes.

"Because I get to be your first with nights like this, and you get to be mine. That makes it even more special."

"Our beach is sacred. I've never brought another woman here."

"I know that, but I meant it in a bigger way. I've never done anything like this, lying together talking, cooking on the beach with someone special. I've never shared my heart with anyone."

He put his arm around her, pulling her closer. "You know I haven't, either. How could I, when it'd been locked away with my feelings for all these years?" He kissed her as she tried to slow her runaway heart. "Do you remember the first night we were here?"

"When we saw the shooting star?"

"Yeah." He lay on his back, pulling her over so her head rested on his arm. "Maybe we'll see one tonight."

"It's a little cloudy. It might be hard to see them."

"In that case"—he went up on one elbow, gazing at her with those sexy eyes—"we'll just have to make our own."

Chapter Sixteen

WHOEVER SAID TIME flies when you're having fun knew what they were talking about. It had been almost a month since Gunner and Sidney had become a couple, and life had just gotten better. Chappy had been adopted, and when Sidney had taken him up to the trees on the hill to say her goodbyes, Gunner had snapped a few photos of them. It was strange how he wanted to capture every little thing she did in pictures. But if losing his sister had taught him anything, it was to seize every moment, and they'd definitely been doing that.

They'd gone out with everyone to the Salty Hog only a couple of times in the last few weeks, and he'd never been happier. He *wanted* alone time with Sidney, to learn all the little things he wasn't able to when they were only friends. Like how incredible it felt to lie with her as they watched movies and how even her laughter sounded different as her lover. They didn't even have to be doing anything. Some nights they sat outside on the porch with the dogs, with Sidney tucked against his side, talking or not, and even *that* was amazing. Then there were the things that made him realize how much he'd been holding back, like when he tickled her and gave in to his feelings, and they'd end up naked and tangled up in each other, and when they went for motorcycle rides with his girl wrapped around him and he didn't have to ignore the way she made him feel. That was fucking awesome. They'd gotten into the habit of sleeping in Sidney's room, and that suited him just fine. He didn't mind giving up his king-size bed or the extra space. With four dogs, two cats, and two adults in her queen-size bed, she couldn't wiggle too far away. Not that she tried. She was as insatiable for him as he was for her.

He'd thought their lives had always been in sync, but as he looked at her in the gym mirror while he set the dumbbells on the rack, there were no words to describe how great it felt to be falling for his best friend.

Sidney was wearing her baseball cap, threadbare sweatshirt, and shorts, and she was still the most beautiful woman he'd ever seen. The gym was a tough place for him these days. Where he'd once taken guys checking her out more or less in stride, now it twisted him up inside.

"Lookin' good, MOS." He walked behind her as she struggled through her last set of biceps curls. "Come on, babe. You've got this."

"Maybe if someone hadn't woken me up at four this morning, I'd have more energy." She sounded exasperated, but she was smiling.

He dipped his head beside hers, speaking directly into her ear. "I didn't hear you complaining as you came for the third time."

"Shh!" She blushed a red streak, her gaze darting around them.

He chuckled and pressed his body against her back, loving the hitch in her breathing. "Finish the set hard, and I'll rejuvenate you." He lowered his voice again. "With my *mouth.*"

Her eyes widened, but she pumped out the last few reps almost as hard as she blushed. She put the weights on the rack and fanned her face. "I need some water." He followed her to the water fountain, and she tried to shoo him away. "Stay back with your dirty talk and tempting body," she whispered. "I need space to cool off."

She was so damn cute when she was flustered. He couldn't resist stepping closer. "And *why* would I do that when it's so much fun to get you hot and bothered?"

"Gunner." She narrowed her eyes.

"Is that a warning or a challenge?"

"Does it matter? You turn warnings *into* challenges."

He gathered her in his arms. "Damn right I do."

Earlier that morning, when she'd lain spent and sated, he'd gone in for another round, and she'd said, *I can't take any more.* A minute later she was begging him *not* to stop.

"Don't tell anyone this, but I like that about you." She went up on her toes, meeting him with a tender kiss that quickly turned passionate. "Your lips need a warning label."

She breathed deeply, and they headed for the pull-up bars to finish their workout. "Is it hot in here?" Her eyes filled with mischief as she took off her hat and shook out her hair, catching the attention of the guys around them.

A sliver of jealousy clawed at him.

Wickedness glimmered in her eyes as she took off her sweatshirt, looking sexy as sin in a skimpy workout bra and shorts, catching even more attention.

Those claws dug deeper. *"Sid.* Put that back on."

She smirked. "Why would I do that when it's so much fun to get you jealous?"

He gritted his teeth as she climbed onto the stool and began doing pull-ups. *Two can play at this game, baby.* He went to the bar and jumped up behind her, placing his hands outside hers, and wrapped his legs around hers as he pulled them both up.

"What are you *doing*?" she asked frantically.

"Enjoying my payback."

As their bodies moved up and down in perfect sync, he saw the other guys watching them in the mirror. *Eat your heart out, fellas. She's all mine.* Sidney was watching him in the mirror, too. She licked her lips, muscles straining as they did one pull-up after another, and she pushed her ass against him, and *fuuck,* that felt good.

Too good.

He released her legs and dropped to the floor, turning toward the wall to adjust himself.

She dropped from the bar, too, laughing. "Guess you enjoyed your payback a little too much."

She grabbed her sweatshirt and hat, and he smacked her butt, earning a scowl. So he did it again, then hooked an arm around her shoulders, kissing her temple. "I plan to enjoy it even more in the shower when we get home."

"Oh, poor me," she teased.

They left the gym, kissing as they walked across the parking lot, and ran into Kent on his way in. They'd made regular follow-up calls to see how Cheddar was doing after the adoption was finalized, but they hadn't seen him at the gym since.

"Hey, man. How's it going?" Gunner asked. "We haven't seen you around lately."

"Everything's great. I've been walking Cheddar in the mornings instead of coming here, making sure we get some time together before work." Kent looked curiously between them.

"I bet he loves that," Sidney said. "How's he doing?"

"Amazing. You were right, Sid. He's just what I needed." Kent whipped out his phone and showed them pictures of him and Cheddar hiking at Great Island, playing fetch on a beach, and lounging on a couch together.

"He looks happy," Sidney gushed. "And you do, too, Kent. I'm so glad it worked out."

Kent put his phone in his pocket. "Me too. I hadn't realized how much I needed the company. You can't get lonely with a dog around."

"That's why we have four." Gunner put his arm around Sidney again, pulling her closer.

"Four, wow." Kent's brows knitted. "I didn't realize you two were a couple."

Gunner and Sidney shared an amused glance as they said, "Neither did we."

LATER THAT AFTERNOON, Sidney was getting Liberty ready to see how she did with other dogs. She'd gained weight, strength, and confidence over the past few weeks, and had proven to be affectionate, playful, and good-natured. But before they could place her in a home, they needed to take a pulse on her socialization skills with other animals. Some dogs needed to be the only pet in a home, but others could be worked with to overcome their issues. Sidney and Gunner believed every animal was lovable and deserved a good home. Some were too severely abused or neglected to fully recover, but that didn't mean they needed to be put down. They simply needed to be placed with a special person or people who understood their limitations.

They'd been observing Liberty when they walked other dogs by her kennel and out in the yard when she and the other dogs were in separate fenced areas. Liberty was curious, and since she'd settled in, her fearfulness had gone away, too.

She petted Liberty's head. "Are you ready to meet Rosco?" They introduced rescue dogs to Belleau or Rosco as test introductions because they knew they could trust their dogs' every move. "He went through a rough time, too, but like you, he bounced back. I think you'll like him. Gunner and I will be right there with you in case you get nervous."

She led Liberty out of the shelter and ran into Steph on her way in. "Hi. Volunteering today?"

"Yeah. I had a slow morning."

Liberty's tail wagged, and she tugged on the leash to get to Steph. "Someone is happy to see you."

"I'm happy to see her, too." Steph knelt to pet Liberty. "Today's your big day, Lib. You're a lucky girl. You get to meet Rosco. Everyone loves him, and I know you will, too."

"We're just on our way up to the field."

"I'll walk with you." Steph looked curiously at Sidney as they walked across the grass. "And how are *you* doing? Gunner must be keeping you extra *busy* at night, since you guys haven't come out with us lately." She waggled her brows.

Sidney knew her unstoppable smile gave her away. They did have a lot of sex—at night, in the morning, in the shower, in the kitchen—but that wasn't all they did. "Let's just say we're enjoying our time together."

"I *knew* you were screwing like bunnies!" Steph lowered her voice. "I bet he's amazing in bed, isn't he?"

"*Steph!* I'm not answering that, and we don't *just* have sex. We do other things."

"I bet you do. Things with *your* mouth and *his*…"

Sidney's jaw dropped. "I meant like playing with the dogs and going running."

"Running to the *bedroom*." Steph laughed, which made Sidney laugh, too.

"Shut up. We hang out, and we watch movies." It didn't matter that the movies were only half-watched most of the time or that they rarely got through their runs without Gunner smacking her ass or stealing kisses. She loved every second of their life together. It didn't matter what they were doing. Being with Gunner was so much better than she'd ever imagined.

"I'm just teasing. Besides, everyone knows you can't be with a man like Gunner and not have sex all the time. I mean, just look at him." Steph motioned to Gunner heading down from the farmhouse with Rosco.

His eyes were locked on Sidney, and his lips tipped up in the hungry smile that made her pulse quicken. But this was not their play time. She looked at Liberty, glad her tail was wagging as she watched them approach.

Steph leaned closer. "I mean, I've never liked Gunner like that because he really *is* like a brother to me. But I get it. He's the whole package: a good, loyal guy who's funny and easy on the eyes. If not for the whole burping-the-alphabet thing, he might be worth cloning."

They both laughed.

"But I have to ask," Steph said. "Did you like him for a while, or did this really sneak up on you guys, like he said?"

"It snuck up on us." That wasn't a total lie. It had snuck up on Sidney, even if it was months ago. She wished she could tell Steph the whole story, but she hadn't even told Gunner the truth about Zander yet. Every time she tried, he'd say he didn't want to talk about Zander or that whatever happened before they came together didn't matter. She had a feeling he wanted to avoid talking about their past personal lives because of his history with women, but she still *wanted* to tell him the truth. She just needed to find the right time.

"You two look like you're up to no good." Gunner winked at Sidney, then nodded toward Liberty as they neared. "She looks good."

"Yeah, she's ready." Sidney walked Liberty over to Rosco, and the dogs began sniffing each other. Liberty didn't exhibit any nervous or uncomfortable behavior. At one point she lay down, letting Rosco take the lead.

Sidney and Gunner praised the dogs, and Steph said, "Liberty's doing so well."

"What'd you expect? She's been in my girl's expert hands." Gunner smirked. "And *man* does she have good hands."

Steph rolled her eyes. "When is your honeymoon period going to lighten up so you can go out with us again? I miss you guys."

"If you mean when are we going to require less time alone, that would be *never*." Gunner leaned in and kissed Sidney. "But we don't want to deprive you of our company, do we, Sid?"

"Can you believe that cockiness is *all* mine?" Sidney teased.

"Better you than me," Steph said. "Why don't we hit Undercover Saturday night?"

"What do you think, babe?" Gunner asked.

"Sounds good to me."

"Yes!" Steph took out her phone. "I'll let everyone know."

After a few minutes, they took the dogs into the pen and removed their leashes so they could play.

"I love watching you guys with the animals. I can't wait to

see you with kids. You'll be great parents," Steph said.

"*Kids?*" Sidney said with shock. "We just got together."

"So what?" Steph said.

"We're not talking babies yet, that's what," Gunner said.

"But they'd be so cute with your blue eyes and Sid's dark hair," Steph gushed.

"Oh my gosh. Would you *stop?*" Sidney laughed.

Gunner shooed Steph away. "Get outta here, troublemaker."

Steph giggled as she headed back toward the shelter, calling over her shoulder, "You know I'm right!"

Relieved that he'd put an end to the conversation, Sidney focused on the dogs, who were playing well together.

"Freaking Steph, huh?" Gunner said as he came to her side.

She rolled her eyes.

They watched the dogs play, discussing how well Liberty was doing and their next steps toward getting her adopted. Then Gunner reminded her he had church tonight.

"What do you want to do after you get back?" Sidney asked. "Or are you going out with the guys?"

"The only thing I want to do after church"—he gathered her in his arms—"is you."

"Good answer."

He kissed her and held her a little tighter as they observed the dogs for a while. "What do you think about what Steph said?"

"Going to Undercover? It'll be fun. We haven't gone out for a while."

"Yeah, it will be. But I meant the other thing." His expression turned serious. "*So*, do you?"

A nervous flutter rose in her chest. "Do I what?"

"Want kids?"

"I haven't thought about it," she said honestly.

"Neither had I, until Easter." His smile reached his eyes. "Why don't we think about it together?"

"Gunner...?" You thought about it at Easter? "Are you sure you want to talk about this?"

"Babe, I'm crazy about you, and I want this to work, so why not talk about it?"

"I don't know," she said nervously, watching the dogs play happily in the grass. "Because you could change your mind and then it won't matter anyway."

"Look at me, MOS."

She looked up, and his piercing stare nearly stopped her heart.

"I know thinking about kids and parenthood is a little scary for you, because it brings up your mom leaving and everything that goes along with it. But I'm not your mother. I'm not going anywhere, and neither are you, because I'm not giving you up."

It had been so many years since they'd talked about her mother, she struggled to keep her emotions at bay. She wanted to say she loved him, and she'd never leave him, either. That she'd waited for what felt like her whole life to have what they had now, but her emotions were too raw to get a word out, and she couldn't say those three words until she told him the truth about Zander.

"I'm not asking you to marry me and have kids, Sid. I'm saying that I feel lucky every morning when I wake up with you in my arms. And yeah, we might be kind of new as a couple, but we've got years of trust and friendship under our belts, which is a better foundation than most couples. We've seen each other at our worst. Hell, we've wiped each other's puke off the floor when we were sick. It doesn't get more real than that. And if you really think about it, we've had needy four-legged kids since we first started living together."

He was right about everything, but even more important, he made her feel safe enough to want the things she hadn't let herself think about. "How do you always know just what to say to take my worries away?"

"Because I know *you*, MOS. You like to know what's waiting for you up ahead, and now that we're together, I'll always be three steps ahead of that."

"You know me better than I know myself. Do *you* want kids?"

"Yeah, I do. I look at Junie and Rosie and see the love between them and Tank, and I want that one day. But I'd like to know what *you* want, and it's okay if you don't want kids. There's no pressure from me."

"I do want a family one day, but I'm not in a rush. I want to be *us* for a while and to make sure we can get through whatever comes our way as a couple before bringing kids into the picture."

"Don't worry, babe. I'm in no hurry to go from our endless sexcapades to sneaking into the pantry just to cop a feel, either."

She laughed. "The *pantry*?"

"That's what Tank said. Now shut up and kiss me."

She glanced at the dogs. "In front of the *children*?"

"You're gonna get it." He silenced her laughter with a sweet, enticing kiss.

Chapter Seventeen

EARLY SATURDAY EVENING, Gunner and Sidney sat on the couch looking through the proofs from Erika on his laptop for the hundredth time since they'd received them yesterday.

"See how Muffin's face looks a little more serious in this one?" Sidney pointed to a picture. "I think he looks more like he's following every word Zeke is reading. Don't you?"

"If you say so, babe." She was meticulously studying every picture, pointing out things Gunner was sure nobody else would notice. He loved that she noticed the differences, but they'd spent hours going through them last night, and he could only stare at the same pictures for so long.

She looked at him incredulously. "You seriously don't see it?"

Granger was sitting beside him, his boxy head tilting toward Gunner, as if he were waiting for an answer, too.

"You've shown me fifteen pictures of Zeke and Muffin in the last five minutes. They're all great. It doesn't matter what I see. Just *pick* the one you like so we can get ready to go." They were meeting everyone at Undercover soon.

"Fine." She moved the photo of Zeke and Muffin from the Proofs folder to the Approved folder and studied the other pictures they'd chosen.

He tried to keep a straight face as her beautiful eyes landed on a photo of Zander wearing a cupid thong, holding mistletoe above his crotch, and Blaine wearing boxer briefs that had WORLD'S GREATEST boldly written above a picture of a rooster on his crotch. They were both sporting arrogant grins.

"What the...? *Gunner!*"

Sidney turned the cutest scowl on him, and he cracked up, sending the dogs leaping off the couch. They knocked the laptop off his legs, and he and Sidney lunged for it, banging their heads together. She shrieked, the dogs barking and running around, and they both lost it, laughing hysterically as he caught the laptop inches from the floor. Sidney was doubled over with laughter. He put the laptop on the coffee table as he sat up, and the back of his head smacked her cheek. She *yelped*, laughing so hard she snorted, causing them both to howl with more laughter. The dogs jumped onto the couch, and Sidney covered her face, snorting as Gunner hauled her into his arms, the two of them laughing so hard they had tears in their eyes.

"Stop!" *Snort. Laugh.* "Ohmygod!" *Snort. Laugh.* She pressed her lips together in an effort to quell her laughter, and another snort broke free. Her eyes bloomed wide, and he crushed his lips to hers, silencing her adorable snorts. In the space of a second, her happy eyes narrowed, and she poked him in the chest. "That is *not* going in the calendar."

God, he loved her sass. "We'll see about that."

"We *can't* print that. People with children buy the calendars."

"How about we *negotiate* in the shower." He pushed to his feet and reached for her hand.

"I'm totally up for that, but just let me get through *one*

more month." She reached for the laptop.

"Come *on*, babe. You've been staring at other guys long enough."

"But our final choices are due Monday, and if we miss the deadline, we won't have calendars to sell at the fundraiser."

"Okay." He took off his shirt and stripped off his jeans.

Her gaze trailed down his body to his boxer briefs. She bit her lower lip, lust pooling in her gorgeous eyes. Damn, he loved that.

He ran his hand down the front of his boxer briefs, cupping his package. "Guess it's just you and me in the shower, big guy." He headed down the hall.

"Wait!" She ran after him.

Their mouths came together as hungry and wild as ever as they stumbled through the bedroom, peeling off her clothes and his briefs on the way to the bathroom.

"You don't play fair." She pushed off her underwear as he turned on the shower.

"That's because I'm not playin', sweetheart."

He swept an arm around her waist, dragging her into the shower, earning more intoxicating laughter. They stood beneath the warm water, kissing, their hands moving swiftly over each other's slick bodies. They'd been showering together for weeks, but he knew he'd never get enough of her. She was just as eager, groping his body like she owned it, which she did. She stroked his cock as he feasted on her mouth, teasing her between her legs. He covered her clit with his thumb, working that sensitive bundle of nerves until she went up on her toes, her head tipping back with a sigh. She looked so fucking hot with the water streaming down her breasts. Her hand stilled on his shaft, and he lifted his thumb.

"Don't stop," she pleaded.

"Stroke me, baby."

She made a mewling sound as her fingers tightened around him and slid along his length. He moved his thumb over the spot that had her breathing harder.

"Oh yeah, that's it. *Tighter.*"

She squeezed as she stroked, sending fire through his veins, and he quickened his efforts, earning more sexy sounds.

"Damn, MOS, you always feel so good." He gritted his teeth against the pressure building inside him and reclaimed her mouth, fierce and demanding. He pushed her back against the wall and nudged her legs open wider with his foot. She grabbed his ass as he aligned their bodies, still working that magical spot with his thumb. He knew just how to drive her out of her mind and took great pleasure in the lustful sounds streaming from her lips.

"*Gunner,*" she pleaded.

"Come for me. Then I'll give you what you really want." He added pressure with his thumb, palmed her breast with his other hand, and squeezed her nipple. She cried out as her nails dug into his flesh, severing his restraint. His hips shot forward, burying himself in one hard thrust, gritting out, "*Fuuck.*" He kissed her roughly and greedily, teeth gnashing, tongues thrusting, her body clenching like a vise around his cock, sending unrelenting pleasure searing through him as he followed her into oblivion.

As they finally came down from their high, he gathered her trembling body in his arms, kissing her cheek and shoulder. "I have no willpower with you."

"That makes two of us." Her eyes glittered with happiness.

He kissed her as they moved under the warm shower spray.

"I'm looking forward to showing you off tonight." That earned the sweetest embarrassed smile, and like everything else she did, it drew him deeper into her. He wanted to love and protect her, to nurture that sweetness and her toughness. Not a day passed that he didn't kick himself for burying his feelings for so many years when this had been waiting for them all along.

She dipped her head so her wet hair fell in front of her face and reached for the bodywash. He took the bottle out of her hands, bringing her gorgeous eyes to his again and his lips to hers.

THERE WAS STANDING room only at Undercover. Colorful lights illuminated the dance floor, where people were swaying and grinding to the music. Sidney moved to the beat in her chair beside Gunner, trying to keep up with the conversations going on around her. When they'd first arrived at the bar, the bubble of happiness they'd lived in had popped and reality had brought a rush of insecurities. This was Gunner's old stomping ground, the place he'd picked up women, and she'd worried about everything. Would he see someone he'd hooked up with and regret being tied down? Would he look at the gorgeous women around them and wonder why he'd settled for her? They were awful, unfair insecurities, especially since everything he did and said made her feel confident and adored. But she was only human.

Except she was more than just human. She was *his*, and she reminded herself of the way his eyes had smoldered when she'd come out of the bedroom dressed and ready to go. She'd wanted to dress up for him tonight and had put on the sexy black dress Dixie had sent. But it was so far out of her comfort zone, she just couldn't do it. She'd ended up wearing a sexy black V-neck blouse and jeans, and the second he'd set his eyes on her, he'd tried to back her right into the bedroom again.

That memory had squashed those insecurities, and he had been so attentive to her, putting his arm around her, whispering sexiness or secrets, he left no room for worry.

"Hey, Zeke, did you ever connect with that woman you were supposed to go out with the night we rescued Liberty?" Baz asked.

Evie leaned forward so she could see Zeke around the others. "You had a date?"

"The night just got a little more interesting," Steph added. "Who is she?"

"Her name is Raven, and we've gone out a few times," Zeke answered.

Evie's eyes lit up. "I *love* her name. Do you like her?"

"If he liked her, we'd have met her already," Baz said.

"Not unless we went to his place. Blow-up dolls don't go over well in bars," Zander teased, and everyone laughed.

Zeke shook his head and took a drink of water. He was Madigan's designated driver tonight. But Zander, being the limits pusher he was, tossed out another barb, and Zeke said, "Let's talk about how many third and fourth dates you've had?"

Zander smirked. "What can I say? I like variety."

"Or you're such a disappointment, women never want more." Zeke gave Zander a don't-fuck-with-me look.

"Damn, bro," Maverick said. "Zeke has your number."

"Zeke doesn't have shit. It would be selfish keeping all of *this* for one girl." Zander motioned toward his body.

As the others joked around, Gunner pulled Sidney closer. "You saved me from being an asshole forever." He kissed her cheek. "How about we disappear into a dark corner and I'll thank you properly?"

Thrills darted through her. Thankfully, she'd never had to watch Gunner doing *that* with other women, which made the idea of sneaking off with him even more enticing. She loved that he made her want to do things she'd never even considered doing with anyone else. But she didn't know if she could actually do it without worrying about being caught, so she said, "I'm pretty sure that's where Blaine and Marly went. They said they were going up to get drinks twenty minutes ago."

"That means a precedent has been set." His eyes turned hungrier. "Is that your way of giving me permission?"

She wanted to say yes, but he kissed her before she could get the word out.

"I swear it's like you've always been together," Chloe said.

"It feels that way." Gunner hugged Sidney against his side. "Doesn't it, babe?"

"We have. Just not like this." Sidney grabbed Gunner's face and kissed him, earning cheers from their friends.

Blaine and Marly came through the crowd, and Blaine put a tray of shots on the table. "Guess who got these free?"

"Way to go, Marly," Gunner said.

Marly set down another tray with more shots, lime wedges, and salt and parked a hand on her miniskirt-clad hip. "*Nope.* It was him, and I don't get it. I mean, I look good tonight, right?"

"Hell yeah, you do." Zander winked.

"Thanks." Marly sat beside Steph. "So can someone please tell me why that hot dark-haired bartender made me pay for shots while Colton gave Blaine freebies?"

"Because Colton will do anything to get in Blaine's pants," Steph answered. "He hits on him every time we come in." Colton Garner owned the bar. He knew Blaine was straight, but he hadn't known it the first time he'd hit on him, and he'd been doing it ever since.

Blaine smacked his own ass. "With an ass like this, who can blame him?" He sat beside Marly.

"I know *why* Colton gave you drinks, but I flirted hard with the other guy and he didn't bite." Marly's eyes widened. "Maybe he's gay, too."

"Or maybe he has a girlfriend, or he's into blondes, or he's just not into hooking up," Zeke suggested. "There could be any number of other reasons."

Marly reached for a shot. "I'm going with the girlfriend thing, because most guys who are into blondes aren't that discretionary, and I've never met a guy who wasn't into hooking up. Not that I was looking for a hookup. I'm more of a long-term girl."

Blaine coughed to cover a laugh. "If you say so."

Marly swatted his arm.

Blaine laughed. "Are we doing these shots, or did I shake my booty for nothing?"

As they all grabbed shot glasses and lime wedges, Gunner said, "I want to make a toast to my girl."

"*Aw,* so sweet," Chloe said.

"*Gunner.*" Sidney leaned against him, feeling all warm and tingly inside.

He held up his glass. "Here's to gettin' *jiggy* with my best friend."

Everyone laughed, and he kissed her *hard.*

"You're ridiculous." She was so happy, she could barely

contain it.

"If I am, it's your fault. Here's to us."

As she lifted her hand to lick the area between her finger and thumb, he pushed her hand down to her lap, shaking his head. His seductive stare sent sparks through her core as he held up his hand and said, "*Lick.*"

Her pulse sprinted. She felt everyone watching them, but her gaze was riveted to his, and she couldn't look away as she slid her tongue along the rough skin between his index finger and thumb, loving the flames igniting in his eyes and in her belly. Neither one said a word, sexual tension pulsing in the space between them.

"Holy shit," Blaine said under his breath.

Gunner sprinkled salt on his hand, his gaze never leaving hers, a challenge rising to greet the desire in his eyes. "Go for it, MOS."

She could barely breathe past her hammering heart, and she couldn't believe she was doing this in front of everyone. She didn't just lick the salt off his hand. She bit that salty area, sliding her tongue over and along his skin. His leg pressed against hers under the table, heightening her lustful state. She tossed back the shot. The liquid burned on the way down, and she grabbed the lime. The second she bit into it, Gunner pushed her hand and the lime away, hauling her into a deep, passionate kiss that seared through her, obliterating the cheers and comments ringing out around them.

She came away light-headed, but he kept her close, their eyes locked, want and need thrumming between them as he said, "My turn."

"I don't know if I can handle another." Marly fanned her face.

"No shit," Baz said.

Madigan picked up Zeke's beer and held the glass to her cheek. "I think I need a cold shower."

Sidney buried her face in Gunner's shoulder, and everyone laughed. Gunner lifted her chin and kissed her. "Don't leave me hanging, baby."

She didn't recognize the bold, feminine being she was becoming with him, but she loved every second of it and loved him even more for making her feel safe enough to discover that side of herself. "I never will."

Gunner acted like nobody else was in the room, holding her gaze as he licked her hand so sensually, she had to squeeze her thighs together to quell the ache he caused. A knowing smile curved his lips as he put salt on the wet spot. He sucked the salt off so salaciously, Zander told them to get a room—and she wished they could. Gunner downed the shot, and didn't miss a beat as he dragged the lime over *her* lips and kissed her so deeply she was sure she'd combust, earning another round of whoops and cheers. If ever she had a reason to be embarrassed it was now, but when she met Gunner's gaze, gone was the challenge, replaced with a sea of emotions so vast she wanted to drown in them, and she leaned in for another kiss, giving their friends something more to cheer about.

"Okay, that's it," Marly said exasperatedly. "I need to find a guy to do shots with."

"Didn't we have this conversation? Guys want what they can't have. You need a wingman to get a guy's attention," Madigan exclaimed.

Gunner hugged Sidney against his side, speaking for her ears only. "I bet you're the only girl who got her wingman's attention instead."

Guilt swamped her. He was so open and loving, and she still hadn't told him the truth about the ruse.

"I'll be your wingman, Mar." Zander walked around the table and stood behind Marly, massaging her shoulders. "And you can be my wingwoman. If we play this right, maybe we can parlay this into a threesome."

"Get your hands off her." Blaine shoved him away from Marly, glowering.

"Zan, you know Blaine's her bodyguard. You're toying with your life," Evie said sharply.

"I could take him down if I wanted to." Zander headed back to his seat.

"He's not my bodyguard. He just thinks he is." Marly pushed to her feet. "Come on, girls, let's go dance. I can't sit here for another second thinking about what I don't have."

"Yay! Let's go." Madigan said, and all the girls stood except Sidney. "Come on, Sid."

"I think I'll sit this one out." She was too sidetracked, needing to figure out how to tell Gunner the truth about Zander.

"Come on, Sid. You two lovebirds can go five minutes without each other," Steph said.

Madigan pulled Sidney up to her feet. "Sorry, Gunner, but it's girl time."

"Go get 'em, beautiful." Gunner blew Sidney a kiss as the girls dragged her onto the dance floor.

He'd said that to her every time she'd danced with the girls, but tonight his words hit like a spear to her heart. He'd supported what he'd thought she'd wanted with Zander even though he'd clearly disagreed with it, and the whole thing had been a sham. She *had* to tell him.

She tried not to think about it as she danced with the girls, but when the third song came on, she was still feeling sick to her stomach over it. She glanced in Gunner's direction, shifting and bobbing her head to see him beyond the dancing crowd, but she could only catch glimpses and saw him talking with a blonde. Sidney's stomach knotted, her insecurities rising to the surface. Had he ever slept with that woman? Did she make him miss that side of himself? *Ugh.* She *hated* the jealousy and questions bombarding her. She had the ridiculous thought that she should have worn that damn dress, but she knew that wouldn't fix the problem. Gunner had never given her a reason not to trust him. She was the one with the guilty conscience.

Steph touched her arm. "Are you okay?"

No. "Yeah, just tired. I think I'll get some water." As she weaved through the crowd, she vowed that when they got home, she'd tell him the truth about that stupid mission. He'd understand, wouldn't he?

Oh God. What if he doesn't?

As she neared the table, Gunner came into view, sitting in his chair talking with the leggy blonde, who was leaning her hip against the table beside him. Two other women were talking with Baz and Zander. How many times had she seen this play out and watched Gunner leave with a woman?

Sidney stopped walking and turned away, pushing her hands into the front pockets of her jeans. Anger and jealousy twisted together like barbed wire. What was wrong with her? She *trusted* Gunner, and he was with her, not that girl. Her anger turned inward for letting jealousy make her question herself. She'd gone to war and had never once questioned her abilities. She needed to assess her *battlefield,* and forced herself to look at them again. Gunner's sexy smile cut straight to her heart. *That's* the man she fell in love with. The guy who could talk to anyone, and *yes*, he could probably charm the panties off a nun, but that didn't mean he wanted to. The blonde definitely looked like she was already six steps ahead, wondering if she could turn one night into more. *Sorry, blondie, but he chose me. I'm his ride or die, not you.*

She gave herself a pep talk, telling herself to walk over there and claim him. To let every woman in there know he was hers and that nothing could come between them.

Oh God. I hope that's true.

She headed for the table. *I can do this. I can do this.* The blonde's gaze flicked her way, and Gunner turned in his chair. Sidney froze, her confidence dwindling. She slid one hand into the front pocket of her jeans.

"Excuse me, but there's my girl." Gunner stood up and reached for Sidney's hand as the blonde gave her a stink-eyed once-over and sauntered around the table to the brunette talking with Zander. "You okay, babe? You look a little funny."

Relief swept through her. "Yeah, I'm okay."

He led her to the dance floor and drew her into his arms, slow dancing despite the fast beat. The girls were dancing a few feet away, and Steph gave them a thumbs-up.

Gunner held her tighter, his brows knitting with concern. "If you're worried about that girl, don't be. I was just being nice. You're the only woman I want."

Her throat thickened. The only man she'd ever loved was gazing into her eyes like she was the only girl in the room. She should be over the moon, but instead, she wished she'd never made up that mission so she wouldn't have to tell him it was all a lie.

"I know."

"Do you?" He kissed her softly. "Do you know that you

could put me and fifty gorgeous women on an island where nobody would ever know if I touched them, and I promise you I never would?"

"I know you'd never hurt me like that" barely made it past the emotions clogging her throat.

"You're right, but do you know why?" He didn't wait for an answer. "Because you're a part of me. Being with you is all that matters, and hurting you would devastate me. I'm not just crazy about you, MOS. I'm in love with you."

Tears sprang to her eyes. *Ohgodohgodohgod.*

"I know it's big, and I didn't plan to say it here, like this, but I don't ever want you to worry about anyone else. I'm yours, MOS. Only yours for as long as you can stand me."

She swallowed hard, willing the tears not to fall. "I'm yours, too, and I love you, Gunny. But..." She swallowed hard.

"There's a *but?*" The serious lilt in his voice amped up her nervousness.

"Can we go someplace and talk?"

"Yeah, absolutely." He put his arm around her just as Madigan danced over to them.

Madigan took one look at her face, and her smile faded. "Sid, are you okay?"

She nodded. "I think the tequila got to me."

"We're going outside for a minute." Thankfully, he didn't give Madigan time to question them.

Sidney got more nervous with every step as they made their way through the crowd and out the front door. She sucked in a lungful of the brisk night air, and Gunner held her tighter against his side, walking away from the entrance.

"I didn't mean to overwhelm you, babe."

"You didn't." They went to a grassy area beside the parking

lot, which overlooked the bay. She stepped out from beneath his arm, trying to find the words to tell the most honest man she knew that she'd lied to him. She wrapped her arms around herself to ward off the cold air sweeping up the bluff, but her trembling had nothing to do with the temperature.

"Sid, what's going on?"

"I have to tell you something, but I'm afraid to."

He put his arms around her, his honest eyes making it even harder. "How can you be afraid to tell me anything after what I've just told you?"

"Because we never lie to each other, but I *did*, and I'm so sorry." She was breathing so hard, she feared she might pass out.

His jaw tightened, eyes narrowing as he took a step back. "You lied to me?"

She nodded, tears threatening again.

"About what?"

"Zander." Her voice cracked.

His nostrils flared, his hands curling into fists. She went to him, but he backed up. "What the fuck, Sid?"

"It's not what you think," she said anxiously. "I've never been with him, and I never wanted to. I wanted *you* the whole time, but I was afraid to tell you."

Confusion riddled his brow. "What…?"

"The *mission*. It was all a ruse to get your attention."

His jaw clenched. "So you said you wanted my *cousin*? What the hell kind of sense does that make?"

"It wasn't supposed to be Zander! I was going to make up a name to make you jealous, but the girls were talking about how to get a guy to notice you, and I came up with that stupid plan to ask you to help me get a guy's attention. A *fake* guy, not Zander." Her words flew like unstoppable bullets. "I was about to forget the whole thing when you said Zander's name, and I was so nervous, I just went for it."

"You let me believe you wanted to be with my cousin because you thought it would make me *notice* you? What kind of fucked-up plan is that?"

Something inside her snapped, and anger flew out. "A good one, obviously, because you finally *did*."

"What do you mean, *finally*? I've always noticed you. I changed the direction of my entire career—my entire *life*—for you."

"Yes, but not in the way I wanted you to! The rescue is another reason it was so hard to tell you! When you opened it, I thought you felt the same way about me and that we'd get together, but we didn't, and our friendship and the rescue was—*is*—everything to me. I was afraid if I told you how I felt, it would screw us up and I would lose everything."

"So you didn't trust *me* to figure out my own feelings? That's just *great*, Sid." His voice escalated.

"I trust you with my life, but I wasn't going to risk the only friendship that meant anything to me just because *I* wanted more. You *told* me you locked away any feelings you had for me, so don't you *dare* try to pretend that if I had told you, you'd have seen me as you do now. We both know that in your eyes, I didn't measure up to the girls you were with." Tears streaked her cheeks. "You saw me as a really cute *dude*, remember? Do you have any idea how much that hurt?"

He grabbed the sides of his head, pacing. *"Fuuck."*

"*Fuck* is right, because even then I loved you. *All* of you. The good *and* the bad." She was shaking, crying tears of anger and sadness, and there was no stopping either from coming out. "I loved you so much it hurt. I couldn't pretend my feelings didn't exist anymore or listen to one more girl leave your bedroom without losing my freaking mind." She swiped at her tears. "And the only other option was to move out and start over somewhere else where I didn't have to see you every day." A rush of tears stole her voice, but she was so angry at herself for lying and angry at him for not understanding, she forced the words to come. "I had to do *something*!"

"And your answer was to *lie* to me?"

His words cut like a knife, but it was the hurt and betrayal in his voice that slayed her.

"*Dwayne!*"

They both spun around at the sound of Steph's voice. She was running toward them, her face a mask of worry.

"What's wrong?" Gunner snapped.

"Bethany's in the hospital," Steph said frantically.

He gritted out, "*Shit.* Is she okay?"

"I don't know," Steph said anxiously. "I have to go—"

"I'll take you." He gritted his teeth, turning a pained glower on Sidney, driving that knife even deeper.

Steph looked between the two of them, concern rising in her eyes. "Are you sure? I can get—"

"*Go.* I'll get a ride home." Sidney held Gunner's gaze for what felt like an eternity but in reality was probably three seconds before he grabbed Steph's arm and headed for the truck. It took everything she had to remain standing as she watched her world drive away.

Chapter Eighteen

GUNNER HAD CALLED his father and Tank on the way to the hospital so they could spread the word about Bethany, and nearly all the Dark Knights and many of their wives had shown up. Steph was talking with her parents, and they looked like they were barely holding themselves together. His mother and aunt looked just as bad. Bethany had been like a daughter to them, and he hoped to hell she pulled through, because a person could take only so much, and many of the people in that room had already suffered a lifetime of loss.

Including himself.

He felt Sidney's absence like a missing limb. Zeke had given her a ride home, and when he'd arrived at the hospital, he'd let Gunner know she was safe but that she'd looked like hell. Gunner was sure he did, too, but Steph had asked him to be the go-between and answer any questions people had, and he didn't want to let her down.

He tried to push those feelings aside and focus on the here and now as he addressed the group. "We truly appreciate everyone coming out to support the Lockwoods. Here's what we know so far. They found Bethany on Hutchinson Beach. She was beaten pretty badly and stabbed twice, once in the back and once in the chest. She's in surgery now." Gunner felt like he'd been stabbed in the back and the chest, too, but at the same time, Sidney's hurt and desperation had cut him to his core. The attack on Bethany added fuel to his fire and a mountain of worry to his shoulders, and the suckiest part of it all was that the only person he wanted to talk with about any of it was the one who had betrayed him.

"What was she doing out in Osterville?" one of the wives asked.

"They're pretty sure it was a drug deal gone bad," Gunner answered. "Cuffs spoke to the Osterville police, but nobody on the street is talking."

"We'll get to the bottom of this," his father reassured everyone, sharing a determined nod with Preacher.

"We're putting together a team tonight," Preacher said. "If you've got time to give, come talk to me. We sure could use it."

Preacher and the other members headed across the room, but Gunner was rooted in place, watching the women hugging and talking among themselves and the guys planning how to find Bethany's attacker. Sidney's father was in the thick of it, strategizing with Preacher. The support in that room could carry the burdens of a thousand people. But they were Sidney's support system, too. Who was there for her tonight?

His chest constricted as his father sidled up to him.

"Mads said Sid isn't feeling well. You look a little green around the gills yourself. You okay?" his father asked.

Not even close. "As good as I can be. You?"

"No, son, I'm not. I have this image in my mind of Bethany as a little girl playing in the yard with Ash. It makes me sick to think someone did those horrible things to her. Hopefully she'll pull through and she and her family will move past their differences."

"They see her drug use as a betrayal, like she did it to them. It's crazy."

"It's not crazy. That's pain and grief speaking. You know how that can skew the way a person sees the world."

Did he ever.

"Bethany was just a kid when Ash died, and she blamed herself. She needed a way out from under all of that, and she just took the wrong path and got lost," his father said. "I wish her parents wouldn't hold it against her. I wish they'd do whatever it took to get her back home safe and sound, without placing blame, and hold on to her so tight, she'll never get lost again." Grief shone dark and painful in his eyes. "Then, when she knows she's safe and loved, they can help her see her way clear to a different, better path."

Gunner got choked up, knowing exactly what he was thinking. "We all would have done that for Ash, Dad. But"—*She didn't keep her side of the bargain*—"we never had the chance." Sidney hadn't kept her side of their bargain, either, but the thought of losing her crushed him.

His father cleared his throat. "Anyway, I hope they come back together as a family, and you can be damn sure we'll find out who did this and justice *will* be served."

"I know." He saw Steph hurry out of the waiting room holding her temples. "I gotta check on Steph." He went after her, and when he caught up, her face was pinched tight. "Hey, babe. What can I do?"

"Smack some sense into my parents." She turned angry, teary eyes to him. "They don't get it. Addiction isn't something she can control."

"Your parents are scared, and they don't know what to do

with that fear. I'll talk with them."

"No, I can do it. It's just frustrating and I'm terrified of losing my sister, and I can't..." She huffed out a breath and wiped her tears.

He pulled her into his arms. "I'm sorry. What can I do?"

"Stop talking about it." She pushed out of his arms. "It's overwhelming and talking about it isn't going to make a difference. Just distract me. Tell me the truth about what was going on with you and Sid, because I know I interrupted something."

"It's nothing."

"Now *you're* going to be an idiot, too? Come on, Gunner. I saw tears in her eyes, and you look like someone ran over your dog."

"You know me too damn well."

"Yeah, well, you know me, too, and you know I'm not going to let this go. So spill it."

He gritted his teeth. "She lied to me."

"About what?"

"It doesn't fucking matter. I'd *never* lie to her."

Steph rolled her eyes. "Of course it matters. Cheating on you is a big, hurtful lie, but *Oh yes, it feels so good* is a lie all women tell."

"Not *Sid.* She's got me." He smirked despite the battle raging inside him.

"Ohmygod. Seriously? All women do it, but that doesn't matter. You don't have to tell me what she lied about, but we all know she adores your annoying ass. I can't imagine her lying about anything big."

"Well, she *did.*" Hurt and anger brought the truth. "Before we got together, she asked me to be her wingman and help her get another guy's attention, but it was all a lie she'd made up to get *my* attention."

Steph half laughed, half scoffed. "*That's* what you guys were fighting about? Oh, *boo-hoo*, the player got played, and now you've got an amazing woman willing to put up with your crap. Sorry, but I can't muster any pity for you."

"Damn it, Steph. I *trusted* her, and now I feel like our whole relationship is built on a lie, and that pisses me off. What the hell am I supposed to do with that?"

"You are as frustrating as my parents. Open your fucking eyes, Dwayne. Do you *really* feel like that? Because I think that's bullshit and you know it. Your relationship is built on years of friendship and trust, and the way you used to talk to her, I bet if you were more introspective, you might realize you were crazy about her back when you were in the military."

"I know I was. I'm not an idiot."

"That's up for debate. But that's not the point. The point is, maybe you lied, too, even if only to yourself. We *all* lie, and maybe they're not big lies, but can you blame her for being so into you she'd do anything to get your attention? I don't think you're pissed at her. I think you're hurt, and I think it hurts so bad that you don't know how to handle it because you've never been in a real intimate and meaningful relationship with a woman. Well, guess what? This is the real world, where sisters do drugs and Sid had to lie to get your attention. People *aren't* perfect, Dwayne. We both know you've said and done shit that you regret, too."

Sidney's tear-streaked face appeared in his mind. *You saw me as a really cute dude, remember? Do you have any idea how much that hurt?*

"Yeah, I have." *And she still risked everything to try to get my attention.*

"Here's the thing about relationships with women that you need to learn," Steph said compassionately. "When something like this happens, you either get through it together, or it's the beginning of the end."

"It's not the fucking *end*. I just hate the way it feels." And he knew his tough, sensitive girl felt even worse. Did Sidney think it was the end? *Damn it.* He had to get to her. "Steph, I've gotta—"

"Go, before you lose the best thing that ever happened to you."

GUNNER SPED HOME and flew through the door, tripping over the dogs. "Sid!" The house was dark, but there was light spilling into the hall from her bedroom. He hurried down the hall with the dogs on his heels, and his heart nearly stopped at the sight of Sidney packing a bag. She looked up with red-rimmed eyes, breaking his heart anew. Her nose was pink, and there were crumpled tissues on the bed. "What are you doing?"

Tears welled in her eyes. "I thought I'd stay at my dad's and give you some space."

"Like hell you will." He picked up the duffel and dumped out the clothes.

"Gunner." She grabbed the duffel.

"You went through all of that to get me, and now you're just giving up on us, MOS?"

"I'm not giving up," she said sharply. "I know how you feel about lies. I hate them, too." Tears spilled from her eyes. "I'm so sorry that I broke your trust, but I'm going to figure out a way to earn it back."

"Then you'd better get a bigger duffel." He grabbed a handful of his shirts from the stack of clean clothes on the dresser and pushed them in the bag.

"What are you *doing*?"

He snagged his jeans from another pile and put them in the bag. "We promised never to abandon each other. If you go, I go, and so do our four-legged kids. So your father better start buying more groceries."

"*Gunner*," she said with a small smile. "That defeats the purpose."

"What purpose is that? Giving me *space*? I had enough space tonight to realize what an idiot I am." He didn't mean to raise his voice, but the fear of losing her sent his emotions into overdrive. "I lied to myself for years about you, and I lied to you when I said you were like a cool dude. I had to do something to keep from pushing you up against a wall and kissing the living hell out of you. This is *our* home, Sid. I bought it for *us*, and you're not going *anywhere*." He threw the duffel bag across the room, sending the dogs scurrying into the hall, and hauled Sidney into his arms. "I don't give a shit about the lie, MOS. I hid from my feelings because I was afraid of losing you, but you believed in us. You fought for us. You risked everything because you were determined to win, and *yes*, the lie hurt, but not more than the hurt I've caused you or the pain of losing you."

Tears flooded her cheeks.

He framed her beautiful face with his hands, brushing her tears away with his thumbs. "I'm sorry for being an asshole with blinders on for so long and for making you feel like you couldn't come to me and tell me that you wanted to get me naked and make me yours."

She laughed softly.

"*God*, I love your laugh, baby."

"Just don't make me snort."

He laughed and kissed her tenderly.

"I'm so sorry, Gunny."

"It's okay. We're going to screw up, babe, or at least I will. But we can't run away when we do. Let's make a new pact to always figure things out together, okay? To support each other whether we're scared, assholes, or idiots."

"Okay." She put her arms around him.

"I love you, MOS. You're the only one I want buying my little blue pills when we're ninety and reaping the benefits every single night."

Her eyes widened. "Every night? At ninety?"

"Hell yeah. Are you afraid of the challenge?"

She shook her head. "I'm looking forward to it."

As he lowered his lips toward hers, the dogs pushed their noses between them. "Don't worry, guys, Mama's not going anywhere. She's stuck with us."

"And *she* couldn't be happier about it and will be honest about her feelings from now on."

She went up on her toes to kiss him, but he remembered what Steph had said and *had* to know the answer. "Do you fake it in bed?"

"What?" She laughed. "I don't have to. I've got *you*."

"I knew it. Could you tell Steph that?"

She laughed again. "Shut up and kiss me."

"But—"

She glowered, and he lowered his lips to hers, sealing their promises with a soul-soothing kiss and thanking his lucky stars for the girl who had risked it all to make him hers.

Chapter Nineteen

THE LATE-AFTERNOON SUN streamed in through the master-bedroom windows as Sidney slipped her feet into the high heels she'd bought to match the simple sky-blue dress she was wearing to Tank and Leah's wedding. Gunner had spent the morning with the men in his family decorating Tank and Leah's backyard, but they hadn't let any of the women see it. They wanted to surprise them all. Gunner had been talking about how beautiful it was all afternoon, and Sidney was probably as excited as Leah was to see what they'd done.

It had been a whirlwind month since she and Gunner had first said those three special words, and they'd become even closer, which she hadn't thought possible. They'd gone back to the hospital after they'd made up and had been there when Bethany had come out of surgery. Gunner and his family had seen Bethany several times before she'd entered rehab to make sure she knew they didn't blame her for Ashley's death and knew they would support her in any way they could. The Dark Knights caught Bethany's attacker, and she pressed charges, which provided some proof to her parents that she was serious about getting clean, and helped Steph convince her parents to give therapy a try to figure out how to deal with their feelings.

Their family seemed to be making progress. Sidney and Steph had also gotten closer. Now when Steph needed someone to talk to, she sought out Sidney and Gunner, which was nice, like having a real sister.

Sidney felt blessed in so many ways. She'd gotten closer to all the girls. It was funny how opening up with Gunner had helped her open up in other aspects of her life. Leah's bridal shower had gone off without a hitch and had been loads of fun. The fundraiser had been a huge success, and riding on the back of Gunner's motorcycle during the fundraising ride had felt as monumental as their love. Summer had brought tourists to the Cape, which meant busier days at the rescue as they hosted more adoption events. But she didn't mind the long summer days spent working side by side with Gunner because not only did she love their stolen kisses and stockroom make-out sessions, but it meant Liberty and several other animals had found their forever homes, and those long days led to scorching-hot nights spent wrapped up in each other's arms.

She stepped around Belleau and Opha Mae, curled up on a dog bed by the windows. Rosco and Granger were sacked out on Sidney and Gunner's bed, and Twinkles, who they'd adopted three weeks ago, was sitting in front of the closet waiting for Gunner, her favorite human, to find his dress shirt. Twinkles looked adorable in her tiny diaper, but she was like Houdini, and more often than not she managed to make it disappear.

Sidney looked in the mirror, loving the short, sleek dress even more than she had when she'd bought it. So many things had changed in the last few weeks, and embracing her feminini-ty was just one of them. The way Gunner worshipped her body made her feel sexy in ways she never had, and she loved seeing his response when she wore sexier lingerie or a short skirt when they went out. Moving into the large master bedroom was another welcome change. Just like Gunner had said he would be, he was always three steps ahead of her. He'd surprised her when she'd spent the afternoon with her father last weekend, and he and his brothers had gotten rid of his bed, painted the master bedroom, and had moved her things upstairs for their *fresh start*. Neither of them was in a rush to get a king-size bed.

She'd been floored when she'd discovered the picture of her he'd had on his dresser. She'd never seen it before. It was taken a couple of years ago during a suicide-awareness rally. They were surrounded by dozens of people, but they were looking at each other like they were the only two beings on earth. That picture was proof that even when he'd suppressed his feelings for her, they'd still been too strong not to shine through. It was no wonder she'd known in her heart that they could be so much more than friends.

She turned to see the open back and crisscross spaghetti straps of her dress as Gunner came out of the closet buttoning his dress shirt, eyeing her lasciviously. He was always gorgeous, but in that crisp white shirt and dark slacks, he literally took her breath away.

"Damn, baby." He swept her into his arms, his hips moving enticingly against her as he kissed her neck. "Think anyone will mind if we're late to the wedding?"

She didn't have a chance to answer as he took her in a mind-numbingly slow and salaciously deep kiss, making her want to say *no*, his brother wouldn't mind. But they were already short on time, and Tank would surely notice if one of his best men was missing. She reluctantly drew back, earning a growl as he tugged her close again.

"I'm not done with you."

She giggled, loving his playfulness. "We really can't be late."

"Then you shouldn't dress like that." He nipped at her lower lip. "I'm going to be thinking about taking this sexy dress off you all night."

"And now I'll be thinking about *that*, too. But we have to go."

"Do I really have to let other guys see you in this dress? Can't you throw a sweatshirt on over it or something?"

"No." She laughed, and he kissed her again. "I'll meet you downstairs."

Rosco and Granger leapt off the bed and followed her down to the kitchen. As she walked past the new rescue calendar hanging on the wall, she did a double take. It was on December again. As if the nearly two dozen pictures of her he'd gotten from Erika and hung on the refrigerator and in his office at the rescue weren't enough, he changed the calendar back to her month every single day. She changed it back to June, reveling in his devotion.

She got a drink of water and looked over those pictures on the fridge as she drank it. Her attention was drawn to the picture of Gunner and his dogs that he'd had Erika take for her when he'd thought she was moving out. Granger, Belleau, and Opha Mae wore signs around their necks that read WE'LL ALWAYS BE. Gunner was crouched beside them wearing a YOURS sign. It didn't matter how many times she looked at that picture; she still got choked up that he'd thought like that even when she'd been set on moving out. Her gaze shifted to one of the many candid shots of the two of them that Erika had surprised them with after they'd chosen their final calendar pictures. She'd caught the moment when Sidney had first seen the Christmas tree Gunner had set up for the photo shoot. Sidney radiated happiness, but the way Gunner was looking at her outshone even that. She had no idea how she'd missed that loving look and misread all that he'd done. What a roller coaster of a day that had been.

She turned at the *click, click, click* of Twinkles's nails on the hardwood floor as the tiny pup trotted into the kitchen. "Hey, sweet pea. Did you wiggle out of your diaper again?" As she scooped her up, she heard Gunner and the other dogs making their way downstairs.

"Come on, guys, let's go outsi—*Damn it, TW!*"

Sidney winced, whispering, "Did you pee on the floor again?"

Gunner strode into the kitchen, walking on the toes of his right foot, brows slanted as he took Twinkles from her and lifted the wide-eyed pooch to eye level. "Where's your diaper?"

Twinkles tilted her head.

"We had a deal. You wear a diaper, and you can sleep in our bed." Gunner's tone was dead serious. "You took off your diaper, so you'll sleep in the dog bed tonight."

Twinkles whined and licked Gunner's chin.

Sidney grabbed paper towels and tried not to laugh, because every day Twinkles got out of her diaper and peed on the floor, and every day Gunner threatened to make her sleep alone. But night after night, when Gunner and Sidney were spent and sated from their lovemaking, Twinkles climbed the steps by the bed that Gunner had built for her and slept curled up on Gunner's pillow.

Gunner cuddled Twinkles against his chest, his burly arms making her look even smaller. "I love you, peanut." He kissed her head. "But you've got to keep your diaper on."

Sidney melted a little every time he loved on the dogs. Most of the time she couldn't believe that incredible, loving man was hers and this wonderful, chaotic, animal-filled life was theirs. But then he'd look at her like he was now as he pulled her close, and he would kiss her like he'd waited his whole life to do it, and she knew this life they were building was as real and as true as the ocean was blue, and nothing could ever take it away.

A SHORT WHILE later Sidney was in Leah's living room with Ginger and the other girls, all of whom looked beautiful in their fancy dresses. The drapes were drawn, because Leah didn't want to see the backyard or Tank before the wedding began, but Sidney had seen the breathtaking decorations before coming inside. The trees and decks were draped in miles of white silk, and dozens of white chairs with pink ribbons on the backs flanked the grassy aisle, which was lined with more roses. Twinkling lights were wound around the deck railings, tree trunks, and branches, which would look spectacular when the sun went down. Preacher had built a beautiful arched altar, and they'd decorated it with lush greenery and a stunning array of flowers. Several long tables covered with white tablecloths, pink runners, and gorgeous floral centerpieces formed a U around a makeshift dance floor.

"Watch, Grandma Gingy!" Rosie yelled.

Junie and Rosie were twirling in their white sleeveless dresses. The pink sashes with blue polka dots tied around their waists matched the men's bow ties, and their curls bounced wild and free around their giggling faces.

"Be careful," Ginger warned. She was gorgeous in a flowy, gunmetal-blue, knee-length, chiffon halter dress with a silk band around her waist.

Leah put her hand on her belly. "I swear this baby is as nervous as I am. It's been kickin' all day." She looked like she'd walked out of a fairy tale with her thick curls billowing around her face, wearing her gorgeous wedding gown. The finely threaded and laced bodice accentuated her petiteness, and the softly gathered tulle skirt hung beautifully over her baby bump, falling to the tops of her heels, so she had no chance of tripping down the aisle. The back of the dress was equally stunning, with an open V that laced together with threads of silk. The pièces de résistance were the ethereal shoulder accents and transparent tulle that draped down her back, giving her an angelic aura.

"There's nothing to be nervous about, sweetheart," Reba said. "All you have to do is walk down that aisle with Grandpa Mike and take my big, burly nephew as your husband."

"There's nothing I want more in this world than to marry Tank. I don't know why I'm so nervous." Leah sighed. "I have somethin' old. Ginger gave me this beautiful bracelet that belonged to her great-grandmother." She showed it to the girls, and they *ooh*ed and *aah*ed. "My dress is new, and Grandpa Mike lent me these pearls that had belonged to Tank's grandma, just like he did for Chloe, and for Ginger and Reba when they got married. And this is blue." She lifted her dress, showing them a white garter with a blue ribbon sewn into it. "So why do I feel like I'm goin' in for my biggest test unprepared?"

"Because you're a bride," Chloe said. "You're supposed to be nervous. This is your big day."

"I guess you're right," Leah said softly. "I wish my daddy and River were here to see our weddin'."

Ginger took her hand. "Honey, they are here. They're with you every minute of every day, watching you do a magnificent job of raising the girls."

Leah teared up, just as she had been on and off for the past hour. "I know they are. I can feel 'em."

"Hopefully not when you're in the bedroom," Evie said. "Because that would be creepy."

They all laughed.

Leah gasped and touched her stomach. "My goodness. That was a *big* kick. I think this baby wants to climb out of my body and run down the aisle to its daddy."

Rosie stopped twirling and said, "Babies don't run, Mama! Papa Tank said it'll just lie there, eatin' from your boob, sleepin', and poopin'. But it won't eat from Papa Tank's boob 'cause he has *booby wings*."

Everyone cracked up.

"*Wosie*," Junie exclaimed. "They're piercings, not booby wings."

"I see Tank's been educating his future tattooist," Madigan said.

"Gotta start them young," Steph added.

"I can call them booby wings if I want to!" Rosie began twirling again, chanting, "Booby wings! Booby wings! Papa Tank can't feed the baby 'cause he has booby wings!"

"Mama told you that Papa Tank can't make *milk*!" Junie hollered. "He's a *boy*, and he has a penis!"

"*Junie!*" Leah chided as everyone burst into hysterics.

"Booby wings! Booby wings!" Rosie chanted.

Sidney could see Leah getting anxious, and she scooped Rosie up. "How about we peek out the patio curtains and see who's out there?"

"I wanna peek!" Junie ran after them.

"Thank you, Sid," Leah said. "I'm sorry about what Junie said. She had *so* many questions, I figured it was better to answer correctly than to mislead her."

"Of course it was, honey," Reba said. "The girls are too smart for nonsense. Junie is so much like my Zeke was at her age, she'd know if you weren't telling her the truth."

"Rosie is just as rascally as Gunny was," Ginger said as she joined Sidney and the girls by the patio doors.

"Was?" Sidney teased, looking out at Gunner walking with Baz, Conroy, and Grandpa Mike toward the patio. They were all so handsome in their black leather vests and polka-dotted bow ties.

"There's Papa Tank!" Junie pointed to Tank and Preacher heading up to the altar. She and Rosie banged on the window, causing the men to look over.

The girls waved, calling for the men, and Conroy hollered to Tank, who turned around. The love that rose in his eyes was as real as the love in Gunner's as his eyes locked on Sidney, sending those butterflies in her belly swarming as he strode slowly toward the doors.

Ginger whispered, "*That* is the look of love, baby girl."

Yes, it is.

Conroy gave them a thumbs-up, mouthing, *We're ready to start!* and the girls cheered and jumped up and down.

They all wished Leah luck and hugged her, telling her how beautiful she looked and how happy they were for her, and then Sidney and the other girls who weren't in the bridal party went to find their seats.

Gunner reached for Sidney as she stepped onto the patio, wrapping his strong arms around her and grinning harder than she'd ever seen.

"Why are you looking at me like that?"

"Because you're mine and I can." He pressed his lips to hers. "And because I love you more than anything in this world."

"Okay, Romeo," Steph teased. "We need to sit down before Leah loses her mind."

He gave Sidney another quick kiss and smacked her butt as she walked away. She tried to glower at him over her shoulder, but failed miserably, smiling like a goon and earning a hearty laugh from him.

Sidney sat between Madigan and Steph and said, "Tank looks like he's ready to burst."

"I've never seen him this nervous," Madigan said.

"That's not nerves," Steph said. "That's *hurry the hell up and make her my wife already.*"

The music started, and everyone turned to watch the procession. Conroy and Ginger walked down the aisle first, smiling proudly. They were such a handsome couple, with his silver hair and deep dimples and Ginger's gorgeous strawberry-blond waves cascading over her shoulders. Baz and Junie followed them down. Junie was carrying a pretty basket and tossing rose petals out as they walked. Baz winked at Evie, and Evie whispered to the girls, "He's so full of himself."

The music changed to a faster beat as Gunner and Rosie came down the aisle twirling and dancing, both of them tossing rose petals from a basket Gunner carried.

Rosie hollered, "Papa Tank! Look at me! We gettin' maw-wied!" and everyone laughed. When they got to the row where Sidney was sitting, Gunner blew her a kiss, and Rosie yelled, "Siddy! Uncle Gunny loves you!" causing another round of laughter.

Happiness bubbled up inside Sidney, and as she watched them dancing down the aisle, she knew Steph was right. Gunner was going to be an amazing father one day, and she hoped to be right there by his side.

Rosie ran straight to Tank, who was already holding Junie's hand, and Gunner took his place beside Baz as the music stopped. The din of the crowd quieted, and then River's voice rang out of the speakers, singing "Put Your Records On" and drawing everyone's attention to Leah and Grandpa Mike at the top of the aisle. River had made videos playing the guitar and singing that song, which he used to sing to Leah. Leave it to Tank to find a way to have Leah's brother at their wedding. Tank must have arranged for it without her knowing, because the surprise and gratitude in her eyes were unmistakable. Leah covered her mouth with a shaky hand as her tears broke free.

"It's Wiver! Wiver's with us!" Rosie yelled, jumping up and down as Leah and Grandpa Mike made their way down the aisle.

Sidney wiped tears from her eyes, and she wasn't the only one. All the girls were crying, and Madigan was passing tissues down the row. It only got worse as Leah stepped up to the altar, and Tank wiped tears from *his* eyes.

"It's okay, Papa Tank!" Rosie exclaimed. "We gettin' maw-wied!"

Tank put one arm around Rosie and one around Junie, holding them against his legs as Preacher began the ceremony. Gunner's gaze found Sidney again, where it remained as Tank and Leah said their vows.

Steph whispered, "That'll be you and Gunner one day."

As Tank and Leah were introduced as man and wife and applause exploded around them, Gunner's loving eyes remained trained on Sidney, and she thought, *I sure hope so.*

THERE HADN'T BEEN a dry eye in the backyard when Tank and Leah had said their vows, and when Zander played his guitar and sang "Imagine" by Ben Platt for their first dance, even Gunner had teared up. The reception was as beautiful as the ceremony, and the evening passed in a blur of dancing, delicious food, and falling deeper in love with his girl. As Gunner danced with his mother, he looked at Tank dancing with Junie and Rosie in his arms and filled with happiness for his brother and his very special girls. He wanted that with Sidney, and longed to get her in his arms again. He glanced across the dance floor to watch her dancing with her father.

"She's pretty special, isn't she?" his mother said.

"You have no idea how special."

"Oh, I think I do."

The sparkle in her eyes told him she had more to say. "Go on."

"I'm just happy for both of you, sweetheart. You've had Sid by your side for your entire adult life. She knows and loves the real you, the person who I'm not even sure your father and I know as well as she does. From the first time we met her, we knew you were two of a kind. You may not realize how rare it is to find someone who you can truly be yourself with, but it's a one-in-a-million connection."

"I know how rare it is, Mom, and how lucky I am that she didn't give up on me years ago."

"That's the thing about love. You can try to ignore it or

push it away, but like the air we breathe, once it's found us, we can never get enough. It's nice to see you giving in to who you really are."

"I bet you thought I'd never settle down."

"Oh, I always knew you would." She smiled. "You have too much love to give not to share it with one special person. You tried to change that after we lost Ash, and that's understandable. You and your brothers were each her special person in different ways. You were her secret keeper. Even when you were little, you could get her to tell you things she wouldn't tell anyone else. I think that's why you've kept everyone at arm's length since she died, to keep from feeling that special connection and the pain that can come from it. But you and Sid already had it, whether you knew it at the time or not."

He glanced at Sidney again.

"There it is," his mother said dreamily, drawing his attention.

"What?"

"The look that reminds me so much of how your father looks at me. You look like you want to carry her off into the sunset."

"That's not a bad idea. I love you, Mom, but would you mind if I swapped places with her father?"

"I think I can handle dancing with that handsome man so you can get your girl."

They danced over to Sidney and her father. "Mind if I cut in, Colonel?"

He looked at Sidney. "What do you think, Sidekick? You want to dance with this guy?"

She looked at Gunner like she wanted him to carry her off, too. "More than you can imagine."

"Thanks, Colonel." As Gunner drew Sidney into his arms, the song changed to "Anyone" by Justin Bieber.

Sidney's eyes narrowed. "Do *not* ruin this song for me."

She was so damn cute, warning him like she'd do something about it. He held her tighter, swaying to the music as he sang about dancing under diamonds, not wanting to lose her, and how she was the only one he'd ever love.

Surprise rose in her eyes. "You know the words?"

"You love the guy's songs—of course I know the words." He twirled her around, then held her close as he sang the last line. He kissed her slowly and sweetly, and she went soft in his arms. There was no better feeling than that. "What do you say we get out of here and go make our own music?"

"Yes, please."

They congratulated Tank and Leah and ran to his truck, kissing and laughing along the way. Sidney sat beside him, tucked beneath his arm where she belonged. They kissed at stoplights and made up silly lyrics to the songs on the radio. When they got home, the dogs greeted them excitedly, with the exception of Twinkles, who was in her crate so she didn't pee on the furniture while they were out.

"I'll let Twinkles out," Gunner said. "Why don't you grab us a glass of water and I'll meet you in the bedroom?"

SIDNEY HUMMED "ANYONE" on her way into the kitchen, and her heart skipped a beat at the sight of a wrapped gift on the counter with her name scrawled across it.

You sneaky thing.

She tore it open, revealing a photo book with FALLING FOR MOS above the picture of her wearing her military garb from helmet to boots, carrying Rosco over her shoulders. Her heart swelled with love. She opened the cover, finding the very first picture they'd ever taken together. It was taken after a morning run on the military base. Their clothes were sweaty, and Gunner had his arm around her. They were making silly faces, and she was holding a peace sign up in front of her face. The picture was captioned HOW IT BEGAN. She turned the page and was met with AT FIRST IT WAS PHYSICAL above a collage of pictures of her. There was one taken from behind of her in her workout shorts and another with her hand in front of her face, her eyes visible between her fingers. There was a third picture of her wearing a sweaty tank top that clung to her breasts, her hair hiding all but half her smile. Beside the collage, Gunner had handwritten I MEAN, THAT ASS, THAT SMILE...

She laughed as she turned the page, revealing the picture of her and Rosco taken from behind at sunset with BUT THEN I GOT TO KNOW THE SWEET, STUBBORN WOMAN BEHIND THAT SMILE. Her throat thickened as she turned page after page, finding pictures of her and of the two of them taken throughout the years. There were pictures of them armed and dangerous in the military, laughing and giving each other bunny ears when they were off duty, scowling at who-knew-what, and a handful of other pictures in which her face was mostly covered, leading all the way up to the calendar photo shoot and the picture of her lying on her stomach with Twinkles standing in front of her, their noses touching, beneath which Gunner had written I FELL IN LOVE WITH EVERYTHING ABOUT YOU, AND I KNEW I COULDN'T LET YOU GO. She took a deep breath, trying to keep her tears at bay as she turned the page and found a picture of her sleeping on her side in their bed between Rosco and Granger. Belleau was lying by her feet, and Twinkles was cuddled against her belly. On the bottom of the page he'd written, THE QUESTION IS...

She turned the page, but the next one was blank. "Gunny—" She turned around, and found him standing beside the four dogs, holding Twinkles. They each had a sign hanging around their neck. As her gaze moved over them—Rosco's read WILL, Opha Mae's read YOU, Belleau's read MARRY, and Gunner and Twinkles wore signs that said US?—her tears sprang free. With her heart threatening to steal her voice, she said, "You want to *marry* me?"

"More than anything in this world. It's always been you, baby. I want a lifetime of making up our own lyrics and eating food off your plate." His eyes darkened. "Among other things."

"Me too," slipped out in a whisper.

"I want to raise our four-legged kids together and adopt a thousand more. And I want to have kids of our own—smart-mouthed boys and sweet, stubborn girls who put them in their places. We'll teach them to do more for others than they do for themselves, and when they become pain-in-the-ass teenagers, we'll love them so hard, they can't help but turn out as good as we did."

More tears spilled down her cheeks.

"But most of all, I want to spend the rest of our lives side by side, doing what we love during the day and doing each other at night."

Laughter bubbled out.

"You know you want that, too, MOS, so say yes before I lose my mind."

"Yes, Gunny! Yes!" She ran to him, getting caught in the dogs

as they jumped and barked excitedly. Gunner swept one arm around her, still holding Twinkles in the other, and lifted her off her feet, kissing her hard.

"I love you," he said against her lips, and kissed her again.

She felt her chest getting wet, and he must have felt it too, because they both looked down, quickly realizing Twinkles had peed. "I think she's excited for us."

"That makes two of us." He eyed Twinkles. "Nice move, TW. Now I can get your mama naked."

Sidney grinned. "I think that was a given."

"Does that mean you're up for some crazy Wicked love?"

"Only every night for the rest of my life. Think you can handle that?"

"Hell yeah, baby. Every morning, every night, and every other time your sexy little heart desires."

Ready for More Wickeds?

Grab Madigan Wicked's book below, and then continue reading for information on more of my sexy love stories. Remember, you can jump into any series any time. They can all be read as standalone novels.

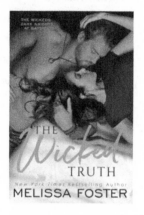

When a mysterious stranger crosses paths with Madigan Wicked, their connection is undeniable, yet neither is open to love. He's on a road to redemption, and she's been hurt before. But love has been known to bully its way into even the most resisting hearts. When the wicked truth of his dark past is revealed, will it be too much for them to overcome?

The Bradens & Montgomerys
What happens when you find your soul mate but she belongs to someone else?

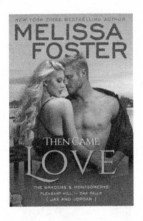

Famed wedding gown designer Jax Braden faces his toughest competitor yet—his heart. Passion ignites between Jax and soon-to-be bride Jordan Lawler. But honesty is everything to both of them, and neither will cross those lines. Loyalties are tested and hearts are frayed as Jax and Jordan are drawn into a love too strong to deny. (No cheating involved)

**Fall in love with Dare Whiskey in book one of
The Whiskeys: Dark Knights at Redemption Ranch series**

She's the only woman he's ever loved, and the one he could
never have...

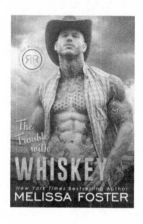

Years after losing one of their best friends to a dare gone wrong,
Devlin "Dare" Whiskey continues to live up to his name,
endlessly testing fate, while Billie Mancini buries the best parts
of herself. Billie is beautiful, tough, and determined not to go
back to the adrenaline-driven lifestyle she once craved like a
drug and now fears like the devil. But Dare is done watching
her pretend to be something she's not and takes on his most
important challenge yet—showing the woman he loves that
some dares are worth the risk.

Read the series where Chloe, Steph, and the Wickeds first appeared

Start Bayside Summers today!

Desiree Cleary is tricked into spending the summer with her badass half sister and a misbehaving dog. What could go wrong? Did I mention the sparks flying every time she sees her hunky, pushy neighbor, Rick Savage? Yeah, there's that…

Love Melissa's Writing?

Discover more of the magic behind *New York Times* bestselling and award-winning author Melissa Foster. The Wickeds are just one of the many family series in the Love in Bloom big-family romance collection, featuring fiercely loyal heroes, sassy, sexy heroines, and stories that go above and beyond your expectations! See the collection here:

www.MelissaFoster.com/love-bloom-series

Free first-in-series ebooks, downloadable series checklists, reading orders, and more can be found on Melissa's Reader Goodies page:

www.MelissaFoster.com/Reader-Goodies

More Books By Melissa Foster

LOVE IN BLOOM SERIES

SNOW SISTERS
Sisters in Love
Sisters in Bloom
Sisters in White

THE BRADENS at Weston
Lovers at Heart, Reimagined
Destined for Love
Friendship on Fire
Sea of Love
Bursting with Love
Hearts at Play

THE BRADENS at Trusty
Taken by Love
Fated for Love
Romancing My Love
Flirting with Love
Dreaming of Love
Crashing into Love

THE BRADENS at Peaceful Harbor
Healed by Love
Surrender My Love
River of Love
Crushing on Love
Whisper of Love
Thrill of Love

THE BRADENS & MONTGOMERYS at Pleasant Hill – Oak Falls
Embracing Her Heart
Anything for Love
Trails of Love
Wild, Crazy Hearts

Making You Mine
Searching for Love
Hot for Love
Sweet, Sexy Heart
Then Came Love

THE BRADEN NOVELLAS
Promise My Love
Our New Love
Daring Her Love
Story of Love
Love at Last
A Very Braden Christmas

THE REMINGTONS
Game of Love
Stroke of Love
Flames of Love
Slope of Love
Read, Write, Love
Touched by Love

SEASIDE SUMMERS
Seaside Dreams
Seaside Hearts
Seaside Sunsets
Seaside Secrets
Seaside Nights
Seaside Embrace
Seaside Lovers
Seaside Whispers
Seaside Serenade

BAYSIDE SUMMERS
Bayside Desires
Bayside Passions
Bayside Heat
Bayside Escape
Bayside Romance
Bayside Fantasies

THE STEELES AT SILVER ISLAND
Tempted by Love
My True Love
Caught by Love
Always Her Love

THE RYDERS
Seized by Love
Claimed by Love
Chased by Love
Rescued by Love
Swept Into Love

THE WHISKEYS: DARK KNIGHTS AT PEACEFUL HARBOR
Tru Blue
Truly, Madly, Whiskey
Driving Whiskey Wild
Wicked Whiskey Love
Mad About Moon
Taming My Whiskey
The Gritty Truth
In for a Penny
Running on Diesel

THE WHISKEYS: DARK KNIGHTS AT REDEMPTION RANCH
The Trouble with Whiskey

SUGAR LAKE
The Real Thing
Only for You
Love Like Ours
Finding My Girl

HARMONY POINTE
Call Her Mine
This is Love
She Loves Me

Acknowledgments

I hope you enjoyed Gunner and Sidney's story, and I look forward to writing happily ever afters for each of our Wicked world friends and family. If this was your first Wicked novel and you would like to read the books that came before it, start with Justin and Chloe's story, A LITTLE BIT WICKED. You might also enjoy reading the Bayside Summers series, the series in which we first meet Chloe, Steph, and the Wickeds. Start that series with BAYSIDE DESIRES.

Please note that the Wickeds is just one of the series in the Love in Bloom big-family romance collection. All of my books can be enjoyed as stand-alone novels, without cliffhangers or unresolved issues, and characters appear in other family series, so you never miss out on an engagement, wedding, or birth. You can find information about the Love in Bloom series here: www.MelissaFoster.com/melissas-books

I offer several free first-in-series ebooks, which you can find here:
www.MelissaFoster.com/LIBFree

If you'd like a peek into my writing world, I chat with fans often in my fan club on Facebook.
www.Facebook.com/groups/MelissaFosterFans

Follow my social pages for fun giveaways and updates of what's going on in our fictional boyfriends' worlds.
www.Facebook.com/MelissaFosterAuthor
Instagram: @MelissaFoster_Author
TikTok: @MelissaFoster_Author

If you prefer sweet romance, with no explicit scenes or graphic language, please try the Sweet with Heat series written under my pen name, Addison Cole. You'll find the same great love stories with toned-down heat levels.

Many thanks to my faithful assistants Sharon Martin and Lisa Filipe for somehow managing to deal with me and all of my crazies, talking me off ledges, keeping me on track every day of the year without fail, and for the million other things you do for me. Most importantly, thank you both for honoring me with your friendship. I have great appreciation for my incredible editorial team, Kristen Weber and Penina Lopez, my meticulous proofreaders, Elaini Caruso, Juliette Hill, Lynn Mullan, and Justinn Harrison, and my last set of eyes, Lee Fisher. My work would not shine without all of your help.

As always, heaps of gratitude go out to my family and friends for your endless support and patience.

Meet Melissa

www.MelissaFoster.com

Melissa Foster is a *New York Times*, *Wall Street Journal*, and *USA Today* bestselling and award-winning author. Her books have been recommended by *USA Today's* book blog, *Hagerstown* magazine, *The Patriot*, and several other print venues. Melissa has painted and donated several murals to the Hospital for Sick Children in Washington, DC.

Visit Melissa on her website or chat with her on social media. Melissa enjoys discussing her books with book clubs and reader groups and welcomes an invitation to your event. Melissa's books are available through most online retailers in paperback and digital formats.

Melissa also writes sweet romance under the pen name Addison Cole.

Free family trees and more:
www.MelissaFoster.com/Reader-Goodies